The Sweet Pea Secret

The Sweet Pea Secret

A LILY LIST MYSTERY

C.L. BAUER

For information contact:

www.clbauer.com

ISBN: 978-1-7363460-7-5

First Edition: May 2020
Second Edition: May 2021

10 9 8 7 6 5 4 3

The Lily List Mystery Series

Dedication

To our parents, who never met a stranger, always had a seat somewhere in the house, a plate of food for anyone who needed a meal, and a welcome to those who didn't need to spend a holiday alone. We didn't always understand but looking back they offered lessons of a lifetime. We learned that it is good to value faith, family, and forgiveness.

And to my nephew for this title!

Prologue

I survived my honeymoon. That didn't sound right, did it? But at one point, my life was in jeopardy. Heck, the entire world was in peril. But, in the end, the good guys sort of won. It all began perfectly. My wonderful husband planned the trip of my dreams to Paris. He planned this perfect romantic interlude after he coordinated a surprise wedding; so the man can plan. As a woman who appreciates post-it notes and an organized schedule, that just made me love him more.

The flight over was uneventful. The hotel was magnificent. My view was of the Eiffel Tower and the Tuileries Gardens. But my new husband, DEA agent Devlin Pierce, informed me we had been followed off the plane by a man he knew, a man he knew as a terrorist.

In the last two years of knowing the man I love; danger has stuck on my life like a doughnut on my hip. Our honeymoon was no exception. Suddenly, I was thrown in with a group of dangerous characters, and they were my husband's friends! Dr. Claude Barbin, a very French, very thin female friend of Dev's was already embroiled in some sort of plot involving diamonds, art, and drugs. She assigned an international agent to protect me. That man, Ari, was working with Dev's FBI brother, Jackson, to bait the terrorist, Khalid.

We had dinner with a drug trafficker whose son had attempted to murder me the year before. The conversation was light that night; indigestion was heightened. I watched as my husband and this man, Bernard Notte, bantered in their own unique cat-and-mouse conversational game.

We survived the night, but shots rang out on the sidewalk of the restaurant. Notte was shot by one of his partners in crime; I was protected by Ari. Dev and Claude pulled guns from somewhere on their bodies. Where does he hide that gun? Searching him for its hiding place would be a worthwhile adventure.

I had a night out as a princess, complete with a designer dress and jewels. We walked a red carpet to a gala within the Louvre. The scenery that night included princes and presidents, ambassadors and heiresses, and one old piece of pottery. The terrorist wanted the bowl for some sort of sentimental reason, and he was dying to get his hands on it. Actually, several people died in his successful attempt.

Lucky me, I found drugs within the event's decorations. That's when I met my brother-in-law, Jackson Pierce. He couldn't make it to our wedding, but he ended up on our honeymoon. I'm wondering about the family I've married into, but it's too late now. Eventually, the night ended with the terrorist's accomplice, an embassy official, holding us by gunpoint in Claude's office. Ari and Dev saved the day, and I found a new friend: the bookcase I hung onto for dear life. I named him Benny.

My dear husband took me back to the hotel that night, and we resumed our honeymoon in fine fashion. A little more romance, a flight back to his home in Virginia, and my new life was beginning. My Kansas City, Missouri business is now managed by my assistant, Abby. All is good there, but I'm having some difficulties in adjusting.

It all began when my jet lag didn't dissipate. I was lethargic and not eating very well. There were times I was ravenous. There were times when I couldn't keep anything down. I suspected what my symptoms meant, but I wasn't sure until I visited my father-in-law one afternoon.

He made me a hot cup of green peach tea and led me into the family den. After owning my flower shop and working almost seven days a week most of the year, doing absolutely nothing in the afternoon was an adjustment and a real treat. I plopped into one of his oversized leather chairs and placed my legs on the ottoman in front of me.

"The Army-Navy party was great," I commented. Dev and I had hosted the event for his small band of brothers. "That first one I came to last year was all Mexican food, but this year the guys came up with a down home cooking theme. Paul brought his wife's meatloaf and gravy, JT's cheesy mashed potatoes were amazing, Father Dan actually baked brownies that had some sort of cream cheese frosting, and your son made your wife's chicken and noodles recipe."

Jack Pierce smiled. "I remember that dish. I loved that one. We used to have it every Sunday afternoon until the boys were in high school. Were you the only woman again?"

I took a sip of the soothing tea. "Nope. They allowed Paul's wife, Jill, to come for the first time. Even though I enjoy the idiots, I wanted a little company."

My father-in-law nodded knowingly. The man's den was his very own mock psychiatrist's office. "You're feeling a little homesick, aren't you?"

Just lay me on the couch and charge me two hundred dollars. I couldn't lie to the man. "It has been," I sighed," an adjustment."

"And it hasn't helped that you've been ill since you came back from your honeymoon." My father-in-law smiled for some reason.

"I just don't understand what is going on. I thought it was the flu for a while, but I don't feel rotten all the time. I'm sure I just need a little time to get used to the water, my new life." Of course, I was now lying about my suspicions to the man I said I wouldn't lie to.

"Lily, I've seen your illness a couple of times before. I think I know what's wrong, and I bet you do too." He eyed me as though I had just told him the biggest whopper of a lie. He knew something.

"That I'm more tired than I knew?" If I used the old Pierce family trait of diversion, I might come out still holding all the cards close to my chest.

"Lily," Jack smiled, "my wife had the same symptoms. Pregnant you are."

I took a drink from my cup. I only allowed my eyes to show. I was hiding a smile. "Well, Doctor Yoda, are you sure?"

"That I am. If you didn't already know, and I suspect you do, I bet you'll be finding out officially pretty soon. My clueless son has no idea, does he?"

Jack Pierce did know his son very well. "Nope. I took

one of those home tests a week ago, and I have a doctor's appointment tomorrow."

"And you are going alone?"

"Well, actually, I was hoping you would go with me. You don't have to go into the office, but if you could drive me, I would really appreciate it."

"Of course. I don't want to get my hopes up, but I am thrilled just thinking about it."

I grimaced. I didn't mean to, but I did. We had just married in August. We had barely time to live together, and now we might be adding a baby into the mix. But at our ages, we had discussed that the sooner the better would be the option for us if we could be parents.

The doctor did confirm my suspicions and Jack's intuition. I waited until Christmas Eve night before I told my husband. We had just settled into bed, my head on his chest. Dev was talking about the church service we had just attended at Father Dan's parish.

"I want to give you your Christmas gift right now," I interrupted.

"I can wait, honey."

"But it is after midnight. It is Christmas."

Dev growled, his signature noise for somewhere in between mild nuisance and lack of understanding. "Fine. Let's go downstairs and open our gifts."

"No, we can stay right here, just like this." I moved up so I could see his face. "I have the best gift ever."

He smiled. "You are pretty confident about this."

"You have everything, but this." I kissed him softly and murmured, "Dev, we are going to have a baby."

"You aren't going to believe what I got you for Christmas," Dev interrupted.

I patted him on the chest. "Jewelry. You got me jewelry."

He shut his eyes in disappointment. "I guess I am a creature of habit."

I gently grabbed his chin. "Did you hear what I said? We are having a baby."

"Yes, I heard you. We are having a baby." He recited the sentence a couple of times before he smiled with understanding. "We **are** having a baby!"

What ensued was a series of smiles, kisses, a few profanities that sort of sounded like prayers, and declarations of disbelief. Isn't it funny how some people ask how it actually happened? The man knew exactly how it happened. I knew it happened in Paris, on our honeymoon. It was no surprise to me.

I knew at that moment that nothing would ever be the same for us again. My new life in Virginia with the man I loved would add a baby. We would become a family. When I changed my life, I really did it to the extreme.

1. Enjoy a Romantic Valentine's Day
2. Talk about new house
3. Splurge and have a decaf coffee
4. My ankles look like baby innertubes
5. I am so lucky--my husband cooks and cleans!

Chapter One

"You won't believe what came in the mail today." Lily Schmidt--now Pierce--sat on one of the tall chairs at the kitchen island as her husband made dinner. It took her two jumps before she reached her perch. She was only a few months pregnant, but it seemed as though the new life inside her adjusted her balance and just about every other bodily function.

Devlin Pierce continued to place the finishing touches on chicken parmesan. They had decided to stay in for this first Valentine's Day together. He still sent his wife, the former florist, a beautiful bouquet of hydrangeas, tulips, and her favorite lilacs. Their fragrance alone filled the living room. "A package? Your first bill with your married name on it?"

"Nope. I received a postcard from Ari. He sent it to me from Belgium. I guess they are still there?"

"I have no idea." Dev stopped and turned around to face her. "Wait a minute. A super-agent is sending my wife a postcard from Belgium? That's a little weird."

"I thought it was nice, not weird. Besides, Ari and I bonded over that whole drug fiasco in Paris, remember?" Lily coyly cocked her head and fluttered her eyelashes.

Dev growled. "I remember." He certainly did. A lovely

honeymoon in Paris with just a few hours of work had developed into an international fiasco complete with an art theft, drug smuggling, and one very dangerous terrorist. His own brother, an FBI agent specializing in art, had partnered with Mossad agent, Ari, in an attempt to take down the terrorist. Dev's past had arrived on his honeymoon and decided to stay awhile. "I just don't understand why he is sending a postcard. He's working."

"Maybe there's some sort of secret message in it or a really expensive stamp he's smuggling out of Europe?" Lily snorted at her own amusing tale. She looked over the card slowly, just in case. "Nope. It looks like an ordinary tourist postcard, complete with 'I wish you were here'. What a mensch."

Now it was Dev's turn to snort, stifling a laugh. *Mensch? Where did she pick that up? Probably from Ari.* He returned to his work at hand and plated their dinners. "I have the chicken, pasta, a side of green beans the way you like them, and the salads are on the table."

Lily was mesmerized by her husband. Who wouldn't love a man who cooked? There was just something amazingly sexy about a man with a towel over his shoulder, pulled up shirt sleeves, in dress pants, fixing dinner for his pregnant wife on Valentine's Day. He promised he'd clean up the kitchen too. *This marriage thing is pretty good.*

Dev carried the food to the table and helped his wife off her perch at the counter. "Mrs. Pierce," he said as he slid the chair out for her. As she sat, he kissed her neck. "Happy Valentine's Day, darling."

"And to you too. This looks amazing." Dev joined her at the table. "I hope you can keep it down. I also have dessert."

Lily hoped that too. She wasn't sick every day, but she never knew when it would happen. The other day at the grocery store, she'd been looking over the onions, and the aroma had made her immensely lightheaded. Then her stomach churned. She went running to the nearest restroom to lose that day's breakfast and lunch. *Note to self, Dev should buy the onions from now on.*

"So, what did Ari write?" Dev asked nonchalantly. Well, it was supposed to be in that tone. He didn't want to concern Lily just in case Ari did send a message in his postcard.

"Oh, the usual. He wished I was there. He said they had amazing chocolate. Oh, and he ran into an old friend of Dan's, someone named Brad. He said the man worked for an old friend of yours. Does that make sense?"

Dev looked up slowly from his food. "Brad and he worked for an old friend of mine?"

"This chicken is amazing. Yes, you can read the card yourself if you're worried."

"Later." He smiled at his wife. He was lying to her right now. His face showed no concern, but there was every reason to be concerned. Brad Keeting used to be a CIA operative. Dev thought he still was, but it sounded like he had jumped ship. He'd heard the rumors since Paris, but it was apparently all true. Keeting was working for one of the most dangerous men in the world. Khalid. *So that's why Ari sent Lily the postcard.*

"Everything tastes really great." Lily smiled. It did taste good. She'd barely eaten anything today. Instead, she'd been going over schedules and calling clients for Dev's aunt. Aunt Maggie had the most beautiful vineyard and resort just west of the craziness of Northern Virginia. The Pierce family nudged Lily into helping with some of the management of the venue, including wedding and event planning. *Note to self, call Abby tomorrow to make sure she survived her first Valentine's Day without me.*

Lily looked down at her hands. This was the first year in almost two decades that her nails were perfect, her fingers unscathed by rose thorns. But she'd discovered today she was missing the flower shop; she missed the people and the constant day-to-day schedule of running her own business.

"Honey?"

"What?"

Dev eyed her suspiciously. "Where were you just now?"

"Kansas City." She stopped and placed her fork onto her plate. "I was missing all the hours I used to work on Valentine's Day. I was missing that euphoria when this day was finally over."

Lily's honesty stunned him. He thought she was feeling unwell from the pregnancy, but he was suspecting she was more homesick than he had imagined. He thought he was enough to make her forget any doubts she might be having. "Do I need to start looking for positions in Kansas City?

Do you want to move back?"

Lily reached for her husband's hand and patted it softly. A tear escaped and trailed down her cheek. "Oh honey, no. I'll be okay. I'm just having some pangs of some kind. I thought I could just move my stuff here, have the business and my house settled with Abby in control, and just move on, but I'm feeling overwhelmed. Truthfully, I'm missing the shop, work, and my clients. But I have you and your dad, and my sister and brother and their families are just a few hours away."

Dev shook his head. "I understand that completely. The more I'm in the office, I miss being out in the field, but I know in a couple of years it will be impossible for me to be out there. You've given up a lot for me. Your entire world has been turned upside down since our wedding day in August. You haven't had much time to breathe."

Lily laughed. "I feel like I have too much time to breathe now. I felt a little better making those calls today for your aunt. It was comfortable talking to the brides and drinking coffee while I did it. Of course, now it is decaf, but it felt good to have a working day."

"So, should we talk about the house now or do you want to wait on that and just enjoy the evening?" The house in question was his aunt's, inherited along with the vineyard when her husband passed away. She had been the second wife. His grown children and she decided how his property was dispersed. Now that she lived at the vineyard, she had a six-bedroom beauty sitting empty.

Lily's face lit up. "Oh, I want to talk about it tonight.

Do you think we could do it? It's a big house, and you'd have a longer commute."

"The return on this townhouse will be good, very good. I bought low, and the housing prices have soared in Alexandria. My aunt sent a figure on her house today, and it was ridiculously low. We will be fine, and as far as that commute, I'll be working more from home in the next few years, if I stay with the DEA."

Lily's fork fell onto her plate. "If? You're thinking about leaving your job?" *Oh, come on, this is way too much change.*

Dev laughed out loud. "No, not right now, but you never know. I bet you never thought you'd be living here a few years ago."

He had a point. Lily nodded. "I get it. You just don't know what might happen."

"Right, so there's so many options, you just don't know. Are you ready for another move?"

Lily nodded quickly. "I would like all my clothes in the same closet. That would be a real dream come true." She still had boxes creating their own fortress in the other bedroom, and her summer clothes hung in that closet. She had purged so many things, but there were those photos and family mementoes that she just couldn't throw away. Part of her heart remained in Kansas City, but she'd brought as much of life there with her as she could.

"So, there's a three-car garage, two fireplaces, six bedrooms and five bathrooms."

Lily's eyes widened. "You'll have latrine duty."

Dev's eyes twinkled. Lily had agreed to move again. "It seems I've had that unique privilege since our wedding day when I had to help you with your dress so you could go to the bathroom."

"I really had to go." Her stomach was rumbling. The food had gone down in fine fashion, but now--

"And I have to really go right now." She held her hand over her mouth and ran.

The romantic night ended abruptly. Dev removed both plates and headed toward the kitchen. He grabbed a clean towel and ran cool water on it. He headed toward Lily who was kneeling in front of the toilet. Her husband joined her on the floor. He placed the cool towel on her forehead and swept a few curls away from her face.

"I picked up your favorite dessert."

Lily's tear-filled eyes finally looked at him. She attempted a smile. "Cherry?"

"Yep, and I have vanilla ice cream too."

"Give me an hour, and I'll be hungry again."

"Sorry about Valentine's Day," Dev murmured as he rubbed her back slowly.

"There's nothing to be sorry about." Lily leaned back against the bathroom wall. Her smile was weak but heartfelt. "This has been the best Valentine's Day I've ever had."

Dev shook his head. "Honey, I'm the luckiest man. My wife has the lowest bar ever for her husband on Valentine's Day." Suddenly, Lily was sick again. *Note to self, pasta sauce was banned from the house until the baby came. Oh, and call Aunt Maggie to accept her offer. My wife is moving again.*

Chapter Two

1. Talk to accountant about future trip
2. Make sure Abby is still alive
3. Convince Dev I'll be fine, again
4. Check in with doctor, again

"So, how did it go?" Lily smiled at the screen. Abby looked a little worse for wear, but she had survived her first Valentine's Day at the shop without her boss.

"Really well. I hired two contract workers from the junior college, and I had Amanda, you know, the girl I told you about. Everything went just great. Of course, I learned from the best." Just seeing Lily's face relieved some of the pain in her back and hands.

"You are too kind. I knew you could do it."

"Now, the next holiday is Mother's Day," Abby said slowly, "and I was wondering if you could possibly come back for that."

Lily froze. Maybe Abby would think that their connection was bad? "Um, well, Abs, I don't know. My sister and sister-in-law are planning a party, and I don't know the timing." She was grasping for excuses. The ladies were throwing her a small luncheon out at Maggie's instead of a large baby shower. But that wasn't the real reason.

"I understand. You have your life there, I mean, my own boyfriend has his life there too. It seems like everyone is moving to our nation's capital." Her disappointment was in every word she uttered. The two most important people in her life, Lily and Jeremy, had left her behind. *Well, there were days when it felt like they had deserted her.*

"Abby, I'll have to check. Of course, I would love to, but I need to check with--"

"Dev, I get it."

It was time to come clean. "No, my doctor."

Abby was in shock. "What's wrong?"

"I told Dev I was telling you today. Don't worry, I'm just pregnant."

Lily lost Abby's face on the screen. She thought maybe her assistant had passed out, but in seconds she could see Abby dancing around the room in celebration. "This is great!" Abby was dancing and screaming.

Lily drank some tea while she waited for Abby to come back to the screen. "I'm assuming you are happy about this?"

"Of course, you ninny. This is amazing. So, that's why you can't come in May?"

"Well, it may be. Since it's my first time pregnant, I don't know what to expect. I'm not sure the timing will work, but I was thinking about coming back to Kansas City next month."

"Oh, please, pretty please. You can stay in your house, and we can talk all night long, well maybe not all night long since you are pregnant. Don't pregnant women need more rest than regular women?"

Lily laughed at Abby's rambling. "So now I'm irregular?"

"I didn't mean that. I'm just so excited. I can pick you up at the airport, you can borrow the van or my car, heck I'll give you anything you need if you just come."

Lily could see that Abby was making every effort to make it easy on her. Her excitement proved she missed her old boss. She would need a car to run some of her errands, including a visit to the accountant. From now on she wouldn't be an employee at Lily's. Her stomach began to churn at that very thought. With all her new beginnings, it was frightening to let loose of the past.

"I'll send you my flight as soon as I book it. I have your schedule on the computer. Maybe I can go on a wedding with you?"

Abby clapped her hands enthusiastically. "Really? You want to still go on weddings?"

"Sure. I miss it a little when I'm lying around on a Saturday afternoon." Abby stuck her tongue out at her. Truthfully, Lily missed it quite a bit. She'd been thrilled to help Aunt Maggie with a New Year's Eve wedding and reception. Even though she didn't have her usual stamina, she was able to help with the decor and to make sure the client was happy. She had thought she could've done a better job on the flowers, but she wasn't a wedding florist right now.

"Abs, I really have missed you, and I can't wait to see you, and Mort. How is the dog?"

"Great. Here let me move the screen a little. She's sleeping right over here." Abby moved the computer to show the passed-out dog, well actually, the snoring dog.

"Gosh, I can hear her." Dev didn't snore, but that dog sure did. Dev did this funny little noise like a soft sigh. She always wondered what he was dreaming about. "I'll check on that flight, and I'll be there before you know it, Abs."

Abby was completely at peace, even her aches had vanished. It would be comforting to have Lily around again, even if it would be for a short time. She just needed to be reassured that she was managing the shop correctly, keeping the house up, heck just doing a good job at adulting. "I can't wait."

They ended the call, and Lily took a sip of her now tepid tea. Now all she had to do was check with the doctor and convince Dev she'd be fine traveling back home. No, she was headed back to Kansas City. Her home was here now. Her husband already voiced his opinion last night when she announced her idea; announced that she needed to physically meet with the accountant. He was less than positive about her idea. She accused him of being over-protective; he said he was concerned about her health. She was healthy except for her stomach issues and some swelling now and then in her ankles. But somehow, she had the suspicion he was not just worried about the pregnancy. Was she in some kind of danger again?

Chapter Three

"Damn it, I'm worried," Dev said as he slammed his fist on his desk. He looked straight ahead at his friend JT Humbolt. "I have to take the threat seriously, and Keeting has had it out for all of us ever since that time in Mosul."

JT shook his head and smiled. "I just thought he was still mad at Danny. Keeting didn't take Dan's prank with that tank very well."

"But now I think he's working for Khalid. That's a dangerous combination."

JT sat up straighter. With just the utterance of Khalid's name, the air turned to stink. He could see the fear in his friend's eyes; Dev was never this afraid. "What do you think they'll do? I mean, Brad Keeting is still listed as a CIA operative. Surely, he isn't actually working for Khalid."

"Ari seems to think so, and I had that feeling when we were in Paris that something wasn't quite right. I want you to check on Keeting, if you can."

JT hung his head down over his clenched hands. "Are we having our own little operation, Major?" His words were barely audible.

He looked up at his friend. Their eyes locked.

"Yes. I will do anything to protect Lily."

JT smiled. "Me too, anything. I don't have a wife or any kids that I know of so I don't mind going to the brig. You can count on me."

"I'll drop by Danny at the rectory, and I'd prefer if you tell Paul in person. His wife works at the children's hospital and could be an easy target. He has one girl in college and one in high school a few blocks from their house. He needs to have his own plan. Oh, and Lily wants to go to Kansas City in a few weeks. Do you have time to go with her?"

"Sure, boss. I have a few weeks off for rest and relaxation. I can do that anywhere, besides, Lily and I need our alone time. We're in love."

"Of course. Paris and she are in love too," Dev admitted blandly. JT looked at him like he had grown two heads. "Oh, and there's this little guy at the Louvre who thinks she's special, and Ari, and my brother, my father. The list is getting rather long."

JT laughed to relieve the tension. "She is pretty special. I have no idea what she sees in you."

Dev drummed his pen on his desk. "I'm beginning to wonder the same thing." He turned his chair to look out his window. He loosened his tie. This desk work created paranoia. He only hoped it was unjustified, but he was feeling uneasy, as though he was being watched. He knew, just knew, that someone was out there plotting something. His biggest fear was that someone's plot involved his pregnant wife.

"Hey Dev, what do I do with a pregnant woman? I traditionally avoid that sub-species of female."

Dev lowered his head. JT was an idiot sometimes, well a lot of times, but he would be the best protector of Lily. He turned his chair to face the former Navy SEAL. "She's not an alien, JT. She's just pregnant."

"So, no drinking at any bars and no smoking? That kind of stuff?"

Dev grabbed his head. Suddenly, he had a throbbing headache. He sighed. "Yes, JT, that kind of stuff. She'll need her rest. She's still throwing up at times, and her ankles swell. So, no bars, no cigars, no rock concerts, no late nights."

"What about the casinos? They have several there, right? When we were there for the wedding, I saw some ads for them. They have those buffets. She'd like that."

"No casinos. No buffets. Nothing." Dev's voice rose, almost to full on shouting.

"Geez, Dev, you don't need to yell. I get it. You must be really frustrated. I mean, you guys are still newlyweds. I feel for you, man."

"Get out. We're done, JT," he ordered, pointing toward the closed office door. As JT turned to leave, Dev chuckled. *JT, if you only knew how good my lovelife is, you'd be jealous!* Making love actually made Lily feel better, and Dev was more than willing to accommodate his suffering wife.

JT quickly removed himself from the office before Dev threw something at him. His old pal was so easy to irritate. He looked through the glass from the hallway and waved once he was protected from flying office equipment. His buddy glared.

"Gotcha, Dev." If need be, he would protect Lily with his life. He'd give his life for his friends and their families, but especially for Lily. She understood him. Even his family couldn't deal with his personality, his quirky behavior. But Lily could. She was his family now, and no one would hurt her on his watch.

1. Make sure accountant has everything he needs

2. Eat Mexican food, especially white queso

3. Must have white queso

4. Check Remaining boxes at the house

5. Find my green stuffed animal, the monkey

6. Go over shop accounts with Abs

7. Find somewhere for JT to sleep

Chapter Four

"Do not tell me you have to go to the restroom again," JT complained as he stood up from his seat so Lily could pass by. "I was just getting comfortable."

"Stop lying," Lily said as she slid out from her seat on the plane. "You are never comfortable in these seats. Your right shoulder is hitting me in the middle of my chest."

"By the way, is your chest getting bigger?"

Lily glared at her companion and slowly made her way through the airplane cabin. She didn't look back to see a smiling JT. He enjoyed pushing her buttons.

A few minutes later she was making her way down the narrow aisle. JT rose to allow her to slide in.

"If you had a relationship for more than five minutes, you might know that a woman's body changes when she's pregnant," she muttered as she picked up the magazine she had been reading.

"Ouch. That wasn't very nice."

"I'm not feeling very nice. My back hurts, my head hurts, and I have to pee every fifteen minutes. You wouldn't be nice either."

"You aren't going to throw up?" JT asked. He looked

down at her face, attempting to read her. Lily was an enigma. He wondered if Dev knew his wife's nuances, could read her emotions. He certainly couldn't do it.

"No. Right now my stomach feels pretty good. Oh, and my ankles are swelling like mini basketballs." Lily and JT looked down at her ever-increasing ankles.

"As soon as we land and we get the car, I want you to put your feet up in the back seat. I'll be your chauffeur. You'll just have to tell me where to go."

Lily didn't look up from the article she was pretending to read. "Oh, that won't be hard for me to do," she muttered.

JT smiled. This was going to be a wild week in Kansas City. "You know what you need?"

Lily looked up. "First class?"

"We're in business class. You'd only gain your own restroom up there."

Lily sighed. *My very own restroom?* "That, and about six more inches of legroom for you."

"Well, there is that, but I'm thinking we haven't given you a nickname yet. Everybody in the team has one except you."

Lily's mood softened. *I'm part of the team?* One tear escaped and slid down her cheek.

"It's nothing to cry about," JT whispered. "I know you're hormonal but stop that."

"Okay, so I've never heard about these nicknames before."

"We keep them secret, well not really, but we used them all the time over there, not here. You need one."

Lily eyed him suspiciously. "You aren't going to give me some weird one are you?"

"Nope. I have something in mind. Your husband's nickname is Boy Scout."

Lily nodded. *Of course, that's what Ari called him. Well, so did the terrorist. How did Dev get that moniker?*

"Danny is Ghost, and Paul is called Arrow. Danny could slide into any Taliban encampment without anyone hearing him, and Paul was a fantastic shot, but he was so much better with a bow and arrow. He still goes hunting with his dad every year in Pennsylvania. He always uses a bow, never a gun. Dev is a Boy Scout, he just is."

"And what is yours, JT?"

"Proudly, I will admit that mine is Popeye. I'm sure it was an homage to my Navy service."

Lily giggled. "Or these huge guns." She shoved his arm playfully, but his concrete body didn't budge. "I suppose you like spinach, your first girlfriend was named Olive, and you'd gladly pay me Tuesday for a hamburger today."

"So not only did you watch Jessica Fletcher mysteries, you watched old cartoons too?"

"Yes. I don't care what you name me, but please don't give me something stupid. That's all I ask."

"It'll have to be voted on, but I have it." JT appeared to have a lightbulb glowing over his head. "You will be Sweet Pea."

"Excuse me?"

"You know, Popeye had this little baby with him. I'm not sure if he was a baby he found or Olive Oyl's nephew. You'll be my Sweet Pea to my Popeye. It's perfect since you're pregnant. Yep, it's settled."

Lily didn't know whether to cry or smile. He was the sweetest Navy SEAL, CIA operative she had ever met. Heck, he was the only one she had ever met. She nodded, not saying a word. She did look like a baby when she stood next to him. She was Sweet Pea.

"Besides watching cartoons, what else did you do as a kid in Kansas City?" JT asked.

"I read a lot. We played Barbies."

"No G.I. Joe?"

"My little friend's brother had him, so yes, we played with him. He dated Barbie occasionally."

JT laughed. "Good for Joe. Did they get married? Did you do the wedding flowers?"

"No and no. We never played weddings. We did funerals."

JT was questioning the nickname now. "What? Funerals? Does Dev know about this dark side?"

"Um, I think I told him. My mom did so many weddings when I was little, I just couldn't bear to even think about them when I played. I would lay Barbie down on a small table, cover her with her little blanket, and lay a flower on her chest. We said some prayers. Ken cried. Joe cried and then we buried her under the weeping willow tree. It was a lovely service."

Lily's nonchalance didn't bother JT, in fact, his dark heart and quirky humor was discovering a kindred spirit. No wonder he liked her so much.

"We are going to have a great time, even if you are pregnant." He shoved softly. "You know, I volunteered for this duty."

As soon as the words left his mouth, he regretted them. "Dev made you come with me? He said you wanted to, and I only agreed to his overprotective idea because I thought you wanted to come." Lily's color had risen to a bright shade of red.

"It's not duty, really. He's just worried about you and what could happen to you if someone decided to do something to you." He hit his forehead. Why couldn't he lie to her? He had said way too much.

"JT, you tell me right now what is going on." Her tone was cold and actually frightening to the CIA operative.

"He will kill me if I tell you, but you scare me more. I'm beginning to think there's nothing scarier than a pregnant woman."

Lily glared. "You have no idea. These hormones make me insane. I eat jalapeno peppers out of the jar with strawberry jelly."

"Yikes and yuk." He saw fear and anger in her eyes. "Fine. It's like this. There is a real threat from a guy we used to know and his new boss. We think he's jumped ship and is working for a terrorist."

Lily nodded. "Ah, Brad Keeting is working for Khalid?"

JT pulled back in shock. "What the hell? Who are you?"

"I just listen, and I watch. Besides, I knew there was something more to the postcard that Ari sent me. A super-agent doesn't just send a postcard to some little woman from Missouri."

"Oh, Sweet Pea, you are so much more than just some little woman. I knew that the first time I met you. You listened to me. Possibly, you were the first person to listen to me in a very long time." He pointed his finger at her. "I'll be watching you. You're scary."

"I wish my husband was afraid of me." Lily's lamentation tugged at JT's heart. There were times he felt like the Grinch; his heart seldom felt anything lately.

"Don't underestimate yourself. You're always doing that. You scare him more than anything. Well, actually he's afraid of losing you." JT's dark brown eyes stole through Lily's soul.

"You're sweet, you know. That's very kind of you to

say." Lily needed to deflect. "Hey, JT, what did you want to be when you grew up?"

"We are resorting to small talk? Fine, I'll play. I wanted to be a cowboy."

Lily giggled. "You kind of are, aren't you?"

The flight attendant passed by and offered a smile. JT winked back. "I suppose. I am the wildcard of the bunch. I have less discipline than your Boy Scout, less faith than the priest, and way less devotion than Paul. I am a SEAL. I'm there for the team, less for myself. That's why my current occupation is perfect for me."

"And you never have to talk about what you are doing," Lily interjected. Dev had admitted to her that JT never talked about any mission, except to her.

"Yes, probably because it is in the past. You know I'm haunted by some things, but why relive them, or try to figure out what could've been? It'll make you nuts."

How did JT have more common sense than all of them put together? Lily shook her head. The answer to that and other things about JT would have to wait. They were making their final descent into Kansas City.

"What do you want the baby to be?"

"I want the baby to be happy and healthy. He or she can be whatever they want to be."

JT chuckled. "It would be funny if your child became a florist, or maybe even a Boy Scout. Yep, the kid could leave post-it notes everywhere, all over the house. The child would inherit Dev's growl and know how to make a fire out of two old shoes. I can't wait to meet this baby."

Lily gulped. She had so much to say, but her stomach was flipping. She could agree on one thing. She couldn't wait to meet this baby.

Chapter Five

1. Take JT and Abby out to dinner
2. Make sure everything is signed so I can do other accounting over the computer
3. Visit a few of my favorite places
4. Mexican food!
5. Find the monkey

"Are you sure you are well enough to help?" Abby was offering Lily a box to pack into the van.

"I'm pregnant, not dying." Lily was annoyed. If she was asked one more time if she was okay, she was going to throw a fit, or some item at Abby or JT. Just last night, JT had offered to carry her up three steps. *Holy Moly!*

"I've been looking forward to going on this wedding all week."

Hmm, I haven't even thrown up this morning.

"I just have to go over the order one more time." Lily watched Abby check over each item and each box. She was so proud of her right now. The little assistant was now the boss, and she was checking over her list. Lily thought she could see the occasional post-it note peeking out from the file folder. "We are good to go."

With that announcement came the arrival of their very large helper.

"Let's do this, girls," JT yelled as the three made their way into the van. "This should be fun. Maybe I can convince the groom to bolt."

Abby and Lily yelled 'no' in unison.

"Maybe I can tempt the bride to run away with me? You know my devilish good looks make women change their minds about other men."

Both women turned, looking at him and his impish smile. He winked at Abby.

"You didn't change my mind," Lily admitted and then turned around in her seat before he could see her smile.

JT mimicked her statement. "Well, that's because I didn't even try. I wanted Dev to be happy. That was my gift to him."

Lily rolled her eyes, and Abby laughed loudly.

"You are a saint, JT," Lily murmured, eventually smiling.

"If you had selected me, you would know that statement is completely untrue. Hey, Abs, you still dating the little nitwit?"

Abby stopped at a red light. She looked toward Lily. "Does everyone know about Jeremy being a nitwit?"

Before Lily could answer, the ever-interfering JT

answered. "We know everything. Besides, I met him at the wedding. He seemed like he was a nitwit, a nice one, but still a nitwit."

"Why is he with us at this wedding?"

Lily shook her head. "I didn't invite him. You did. You thought I was dying." Lily looked to the man in the backseat. "You, be quiet and do everything Abby tells you. No more comments. You are here for your brawn, not your declarations about the world as you think you know it. Got it?"

JT saluted. "Yes sir, ma'am. Mouth will be closed, opinions will not be shared, arms and legs will be ready for further orders."

Lily felt satisfied with herself, but Abby wasn't that confident.

"It's going to be a long day."

Lily turned back to the difficult child in the backseat one more time for a final threat just to assuage Abby's fears.

"JT, you cause any trouble at all, and I will call Gretchen Malloy."

JT gulped in feigned fear. "I'll be good. I promise. Please don't call Gretchen."

Lily smiled as she turned around in her seat slowly. Obviously, that's the only speed she had. "That should do it."

"But you know Gretchen is in Las Vegas at some wedding convention, right?"

"Yes, but JT doesn't need to know that. You won't have to worry about him now."

In less than three hours, the happy threesome was eating at one of Lily's favorite Mexican restaurants. Lily gazed longingly at Abby's margarita, featuring a lovely salting of the rim and the prettiest lime slice. Yes, it looked pretty to the pregnant woman, the woman who could not drink it. JT was throwing back a shot of tequila. That drink was less than attractive. He had a beer waiting for him. He also had a fist full of chips.

Lily didn't dare touch the salsa, a salsa she loved. Salsa was not her stomach's friend. She was beginning to realize the triggers that sent her running. But the salty chips soothed her hunger pangs. JT had nearly eaten the entire basket of the one food that didn't make her sick. She watched him gobble away.

The server came to take their orders. Lily stopped her before she left.

"Could you possibly bring me my own chips? Wait, could you bring three baskets of chips? Yes, three. That way we all have our own." She eyed JT in a threatening manner.

"What did I do?" His question was muffled by all of the chips stuffed in his mouth.

"You're eating like you're starving. Those chips," Lily pointed to the morsels, "are the only things that don't make me puke."

He shoved the basket toward her. *Never mess with a pregnant woman. Dev had warned him. He should've listened.* "Here. I don't want you sick. I'm starving. I worked hard for you women."

"You stood on a ladder and hung the flowers on that trellis," Abby added. "You can't be that hungry from just that."

"And yet, I am. That was a lot of work, I mean, what would you two have done if I hadn't been with you? That trellis was at least twelve feet tall."

"We would've done what we always do. Since Lily is pregnant, I would have climbed the ladder. She would've lifted the flowers to me, and she would've steadied the ladder. We would've been very careful and vowed to never do that again."

"Ah." JT took a drink of beer. "I never realized florists worked so hard, especially on a wedding. I've never thought that all those flowers had to be placed in such a precise manner."

Abby touched his arm in gratitude. "That was very kind of you to say. Thanks for noticing."

"Did you hear that the ring bearer went running with the rings?" JT began to laugh. "He was being chased by his grandmother, his mother, and a screaming bride. He kept running until he slammed into my legs. I held him captive until they could get there."

"You saved the day." Lily was amused at the softening JT.

"Don't you know I'm always the hero?"

Lily lowered her head. "And he's back."

"Oh, come on, Lily, you love me."

Abby was wide-eyed with amusement. Her boss's face was growing red. *Just exactly why was JT here with Lily?*

"JT, I do love you--like a brother." Lily placed a cheesy smile on her face.

"If you had met me first, Devlin Pierce would still be single."

Lily shook her head. At the very least this discussion was entertaining and kept her from thinking about her grumbling stomach. "And if I had met you first, I'd still be single."

"Burn," Abby said after spitting out part of her drink.

"You wouldn't have succumbed to my charms?"

"That's not it. You wouldn't have asked me to marry you. You aren't ready for a wife or a family. We are your family. I knew that from the second I met you. The guys are your family."

Abby waited for a funny retort, but there was no response. Instead, JT looked into his beer and sat silently across from Lily. He then looked up at her and smiled.

"Sadly, you are right. Those guys have been my family for a very long time, and now you are too. I'm a broken individual. No one needs to be around me."

Lily left the words lingering in the silence. Their food arrived and casual conversation took over. JT ordered two more beers, and Abby added another drink, plus tried a shot of tequila. Lily would be driving home.

"I had this meeting with a bride the other day. I wish you'd been there, JT." Abby dipped her chip into the salsa and crunched.

"Why did you need me?"

"I needed you to kick her out of the shop," Abby joked. "But seriously, the entire experience was miserable. She had an unrealistic budget, and her mother attempted to have her change her mind on a few items to save a little here and there. Then she picked a fight with her maid of honor who was there to offer support. I doubt she would've listened to anyone's opinion. Finally, she accused me of raising the prices on her because Lily had provided the flowers for her friend's wedding last year, and the total her friend had paid was half of what her flowers would probably cost."

"Sounds like a bridezilla," JT offered. Lily and Abby looked at him as though he had just grown horns on his head.

Lily laughed. "You know what a bridezilla is?"

"I am an enlightened man."

Raucous laughter followed his statement. Abby had tears in her eyes, and Lily was snorting with delight.

"Fine, you two need to stop it. I'm enlightened, and I try to avoid those kinds of women." His stern gaze had not stopped their merriment. "And, I watch reality television, okay? I love the gypsy weddings. And do not tell the guys."

"You've found your feminine side." Lily reached across the table and patted his hand softly. "I'm so proud of you. Also, by now, you should know there are no secrets between any of your friends, nor do I hold anything back from my husband, or the priest."

JT rolled his eyes. "The priest is the worst gossip. But Abby, did you raise the price on her?"

"No, of course not, but she had double the number of table arrangements, and she had four more bridesmaids than her friend. The best part was at the end of the appointment when I told her that if she didn't change some of the ideas and go to lower priced items on some of the tables, there was no way I could meet her budget. She yelled back at me that I couldn't tell her no."

Lily reached for another salty chip. "I do not miss that one bit."

"Abby, you shouldn't have told her no, you should have told her hell no, and get your butt out of my shop."

Lily rested her head in her hands. "Thank you, JT, for your advice. You can't do that. You have to be nice, but honest. You can't be abusive to the client or lie to them."

"I'd be out of business in a week," JT muttered.

Lily had heard him. "Probably, there just isn't the need for commando customer service."

"Yep," Abby added. "Abuse and lose a client business plans just aren't studied anymore. Those were the good old days."

The server arrived with their food, and JT was rescued. "That's the last time I share my feelings with you two. You ladies act like barbarians." He barely made the faux painful statement, when two napkins were thrown in his face. His smile was wide across his face; he hadn't had a good day like this in a long time. *Who knew weddings could be this much fun? It's the company I'm keeping.*

Hours later they arrived back at Lily's house. Abby and Mort had gone to sleep. After Lily talked to Dev briefly, she joined JT on the sofa. He was watching *Top Gun*.

Of course he is!

She shoved him with her hand as she sat closely near him. Slowly, he slid his arm around her. "You are not broken. You just aren't ready. Maybe you never will be. But you did get one thing right. We are your family. Don't you ever forget that, SEAL."

JT tightened his hold. He pressed his chin on the top of her head. "Lily Pierce you are like the little sister I never wanted."

"And you are the brother I never wanted. I already have a very nice one."

"Shh, he's going to say he has the need--"

"The need for speed." Lily finished his sentence and they shared a laugh and a high-five salute.

"You want to watch Jessica Fletcher?" JT held the channel selector ready to change to Lily's favorite.

"Of course. Unless they've changed it, try seventy-one."

Jessica popped up on the screen. Lily clapped her approval. "JT, is there anything else I need to know about this Brad guy and the terrorist?"

"Well, Sweet Pea, if Dev's suspicions are correct, this could get very messy. You'll need to be careful, and you'll need to listen and do everything Dev says. When we get back, I'll check in with some of my contacts."

"You'll keep me in the loop, right?"

JT looked down at his friend. Her eyes were looking up at him, searching his face for answers. "Yes, Lily. Dev might kill me, but I'll keep you in the loop. You are part of the team now. We are stronger with you."

"That was so nice. Thank you."

After a brief silence, JT talked to the screen. "Geez, she's such a meddling old biddy."

"Don't say that about Jessica."

He looked down at the very sleepy Lily. He thought this would be a good time to ask one more question. "I was wondering, just how big will your boobs get?"

Lily was awake now. She shoved hard against him and moved off the sofa. "I'm going to bed now, you jerk. And I have one thing to say to you." She briefly stopped as she headed down the hallway, her head peeking around the corner. "Go Army, beat Navy, Popeye."

He waved back at her and smiled. Before he found comfort sleeping on the sofa, JT rechecked the locks on the front and back doors and made a thorough security check of the windows. He knew Dev had that feeling that made you watch over your shoulder. Now he had that same awful feeling. He swore he could feel that Khalid was on America's shore. Khalid was close, out there somewhere. As he thought that, the hairs on the back of his neck itched.

Dev would yell at him when he found out that he promised he'd keep Lily in the loop of information. Dev always liked to keep everything close to the vest. He wouldn't appreciate JT's promise one bit. But he wouldn't lie to Lily, not to Sweet Pea. Besides, Lily might be able to help them. She'd proved herself in Paris when she'd found those drugs and discovered that fake artifact. Even Dev had admitted the woman had skills.

He settled on the sofa as well as he could, pounding the pillow into submission. He shut his eyes and fell asleep with a thin smile on his face.

He dreamed about spinach for some reason. He didn't even like spinach. He was more of a hamburger man, and Olive Oyl was way too thin.

Chapter Six

1. Pack overnight bag
2. Need more post-Its
3. Check with wholesaler on delivery
4. Check in with the bride and her mother

Strangely, Lily was euphoric as she stood surrounded by buckets of flowers in the back storage room of Aunt Maggie's Virginia vineyard. She could do this. Yes, she was getting further along in her pregnancy. But it was all coming back to her, and she liked how she was feeling. Just a few weeks ago in Kansas City, Lily had realized she really did miss the weddings and the world of flowers. Besides, the work kept her mind off her growing belly, swollen ankles, and her constant need for chips of any kind and chocolate, preferably eaten together. It was also good to be away from a fawning husband. The other night he wouldn't even allow her to take her own plate to the kitchen.

She wouldn't deny that she was tired. It wasn't just the changes to her body but moving into the new house was posing another challenge. Dev's townhome sold within two days. Now it was a rush to make the new house a home before she gave birth at the end of the summer.

Crud, it was going to be hot in a few weeks. I'll have sweat where I've never had sweat before.

It was good for her to be busy; it was even better for Dev to be busy. He'd already painted, with his father and Dan's help, every room she wanted freshened. He'd set up their bedroom, the living room and the dining area so they could move in immediately. There were still boxes in every other room, and there were a lot of rooms. She'd have to get used to that after all the years she'd lived in a smaller home. Of course, Dev was setting up a security system that could protect a queen. JT had revealed the threat, Dev provided the precaution. She didn't complain.

She knew her husband was worried about her. Just the other day he had come home to a weeping wife, sitting on the couch, feet propped up on pillows, a chocolate bar in one hand, and the other hand in a bag of chips.

Dev had thrown his briefcase down on the floor and sat next to her providing a secure arm around her shoulders. "Honey, what's wrong? Are you feeling fine? How about the baby? What did the doctor say today?"

Lily sniffed. She removed her hand from the bag and wiped her nose on the edge of her sleeve. "He said I was geriatric."

Dev didn't think he heard her correctly. "Say again."

"Geriatric. Old. He said I have a geriatric pregnancy. I'm older. I'm old." Lily wailed loudly. "I'm old. If we have another baby, they'll probably call it an ancient pregnancy."

Dev would rather be among the Taliban right now.

He had no clue what should be said or done. *But we are older. Anything I may say could be the wrong thing. This is a landmine field.*

"What do we need to do? More vitamins or certain foods?" He gently removed the chocolate bar from her hand and laid it on the coffee table in front of them.

"No, everything is good. My labs were all good. They need to monitor me more than the regular pregnant woman because I'm old." Lily looked to Dev for some answer. Of course, she didn't know what the question was.

"Lily, honey, we were surprised when we became pregnant as fast as we did, remember?"

Lily moved her legs off the pillows and sat up straight. "**We** did not become pregnant, I did. Oh, I know. I know we weren't even sure if we could have a baby. I also know we are very blessed. I'm healthy. The baby is healthy. I just hated that word. It made it sound like I had an old egg or something."

Dev was relieved she'd stopped crying. It seemed as though the pity party had suddenly come to an end. "I can assure you, there's nothing old about you or your reproductive system. We wanted a family. We've been blessed with one very quickly. I call that efficiency."

"As I recall, it was also frequency."

Dev lowered his long lashes that Lily loved so much. "Well, there was that." He kissed her softly on the cheek.

Lily examined his handsome face. He didn't look old

to her. When she looked in the mirror, she didn't see some old hag. She saw a puffy face, especially in the morning. The face puffed in the morning, and in perfect balance, the ankles did it in the afternoon. Every oil in her skin had seemed to evaporate. She'd turned to Dev to layer on moisturizer on her back almost every night. Oh, and then there was her hair. It was growing like crazy and curlier than ever. It wasn't even summer yet. *I'm going to look like Shirley Temple after she's stuck her finger into an electrical socket!*

Lily sat in silence for a moment. Dev's face was just too perfect. She eased up off the couch and stood in front of him. She extended her hand out to him. "Come on."

"Where are we going?" Lily was calm, and Dev was alarmed at the change in the emotions. But she was doing a lot of that lately, alarming him. *She's like a crazy roller coaster.*

"Upstairs. I've been reading about how the new dad can be involved in the pregnancy. I bought this stuff to prevent stretch marks, and I need you to rub it on my belly."

Dev's eyes widened. "Right now? Before dinner?"

Lily pulled on his hand. "Yes, right now. Besides, I'm not very hungry."

Of course not, she's been eating chocolate and chips all afternoon. "Fine, honey. Let's go."

He followed her up the stairs into the bedroom. Dev sighed as he looked at the full boxes in the closet and three others in the corner of the room. He'd get to them this weekend. He'd promised Lily this move, and all this chaos would be under control before the baby came.

Lily had stretched her body on the bed with the lotion in her hand. "Dev?"

"Honey, let me get these work clothes off."

Lily smiled one of those smiles that could be genuine or fake. "That's a good idea, just take them off."

Dev stopped in his tracks. His tie and shirt were removed. There was something in her voice. He turned to face her again, and she smiled sweetly. Her finger was crooked, beckoning him to the bed.

"I thought you wanted me to help you with that lotion," he murmured as he walked slowly to the edge of the bed.

"That too. I may be old and pregnant, but I'm not dead yet."

"And I'm not hungry."

They called out for pizza later that night. Lily smiled thinking about that day. It had gone from one of the worst days to one of the best. After they'd made love, the baby kicked several times, and the lotion was finally layered on her belly.

It was time to stop daydreaming and get some work done. She just had a couple more touches to do, and she'd be ready to call it a night. "Crud," she yelled out loud. The baby kicked, and she dropped a blush rose onto the floor. She leaned down slowly to pick it up but fell short of her goal. She stretched as much as she could, every fiber in every finger, but no. She missed the mark.

Lily moved a chair nearer the flower. She sat down and leaned awkwardly to hover over the target. "Nope." She sat up slowly. She was a little light-headed.

"What are you doing?" Dev stood in the door frame, larger than life, leaning with his arms crossed over his chest.

"I bet you think you are special because you can probably pick this flower up, right?" *He has a flat belly and can actually lean over, darn him.*

Dev walked the few steps toward the target, picked up the lovely pink rose, and handed it to his seated wife. "For you, my lady."

"You don't have to be charming."

"But I am." Dev kissed the top of her forehead. He jumped up on the counter to take a seat above her.

Lily moved the chair away and stood up. "No, you are exasperating. You can see your feet. You are showing off, jumping on that counter like that. And I still have a summer to live through. Why are you here so early?"

"I'm not, in fact, my aunt says you should be done."

Lily added the rose to the vase. "I just have two more things to do, and I'm finished with everything. Your aunt has a team for tomorrow's placement of all the flowers. I'll just oversee it." She headed over to the other two arrangements that needed a few more blooms. She checked every post-it note and every instruction near the flowers. Stepping back to look at all her work, she announced that every bouquet and arrangement was finished. "I could use some food and to get off of these elephant feet."

Dev jumped down from his perch and took her by the hand. "Aunt Maggie made chicken and dumplings. They were always my favorite." He looked down at her feet and frowned. "I wouldn't say they were elephant feet, but those ankles look like you have done way too much, and you need water."

Lily smiled. "Actually, it felt so good to work again. I needed this." She stood on tippy toes and gave him a quick kiss on the cheek. "Please don't be overly concerned. Please."

Dev let it go. Her pleas touched his heart. He knew she was missing the shop, her work, probably even her home and Kansas City. JT had given him a full report upon their return to Virginia. He said she cried a few times, well more than a few times. Lily had cried when she saw her house and the shop, but she also cried when they left the airport, put gas into the van, bought groceries, and especially when she had to leave Abby and Mort. When they left, she cried all the way back to KCI. Lily had given up so much for him, and now he had uprooted her again with the move to the larger house. He was about to say something charming when he was distracted by the three goldfish in the bowl across from them. He pointed toward the fish. "What's that?"

Lily giggled. "Rescued table decorations."

"Huh?"

Lily led him out of the work area, turning off the lights as she closed the door. "Your aunt had a client's anniversary party last week, and the customers thought bowls of goldfish would be the ideal centerpiece. It was perfect until a few of the guests had a few too many drinks and the fish became appetizers. They had a contest to see who could eat the most in the least time. Your aunt rescued Larry, Moe and Curly Joe."

Dev nodded. Somehow, it made sense. "It figures my aunt named the fish."

"I named them after the Stooges. She was going to name them Thing One, Thing Two, and Cat. That's just silly. Does your aunt put those little carrots in her chicken and dumplings? I wonder if she made biscuits. I could go for a buttery, soft biscuit…"

Dev followed behind the rambling woman who was headed to the food. *And Larry, Moe and Curly Joe aren't silly? Memo to self, discover her ideas for the baby's name, soon; very soon.*

Chapter Seven

$\mathcal{D}$ev and Lily missed the newspaper story on page two of *The Post* in the Sunday edition. They were still at the vineyard assisting with the wedding. But Paul Pellino yelled an obscenity as he slammed his fist on the table. His wife Jill had decided brunch at the club would be a nice distraction for both of them after a long week of work. Her coffee cup shook, the cutlery jumped off the plate. The club's attendants were gawking.

"Paul, honey, what is going on?" She whispered, but Paul's outburst had created a din of noise. The manager was actually on his way over to their table.

"Sir, is there anything I may do for you?" He hovered over Paul in an attempt at some sort of intimidation. He had no idea who he was trying to control.

"What? Yes, but no. I'm so sorry for the interruption and the language. It was something in the newspaper." Paul was stammering. He placed a thin smile on his face and grabbed his wife's outstretched hand. "Please forgive me, everyone," he said a little louder as he attempted a casual smile.

The manager nodded. "Many are outraged by what they read in the paper these days. I just needed to make sure there would not be another situation."

Paul smirked. "No more situations here. Thank you. I'm sure you have something else to do."

The manager realized he had been dismissed unceremoniously and walked away.

"What was all that about?" Jill could see beads of sweat on her husband's forehead. Paul always said the team thought Dev was Mr. Cool, but she knew her husband had him beat. The man's pulse never quickened, nor did he lose his temper, even when their oldest daughter totaled the new car.

Paul leaned in and lowered his voice. He folded the newspaper and placed it to the side of him on the table. "There's a war story in the paper, a story that lists special operatives' names. Our names are in there."

"That's not right, is it?"

"Of course not, but some new congressman requested the information. He said one of his constituents had a concern. That doesn't sound plausible, but the request went out and some nut released it. The congressman gave the story to the newspaper, imagine that."

Jill could hear disgust and worry in his tone. Now she was worried.

"Is it only your team?"

"No. They have a whole list of operatives, SEALS, Rangers, Green Berets. I also saw a few members of Delta Force and some Marines we all knew. Geez, what were they thinking?"

"Honey, what am I missing? Are you all in trouble, or danger?" Jill saw more sweat above Paul's creased brow.

"No trouble, but they just gave the terrorists a hit list. We are all in their crosshairs. I need to call Danny. He still has some contacts in the Pentagon. His parish might look at him differently, and what about my co-workers? Geez, JT could have some mission compromised, and then Dev could be in the same situation."

"And Lily is pregnant," Jill added.

"Damn," he whispered. This was a mess. They needed to neutralize this threat, but how could you do that once their names were out there? Someone needed to talk to the reporter, the congressman, and the constituent. *Who the hell had a concern?*

Later that night, a dark figure knocked on the hotel door in downtown Washington, D.C. He waited. He knew someone was in the room. An eye appeared in the peephole. "Come on, open the door."

Slowly the door opened. The man on the other side looked as though he had just exited the shower, wet and only a towel around his waist. "I was taking a shower. I thought you were supposed to have patience. Isn't that in your job description?"

The man pushed his way in and shut the door behind. "I'm a priest, not God. As I recall, you were never the patient one."

Ari smiled. Dan knew him very well. The priest looked good, maybe a few pounds heavier and a few grey hairs peppering his hair, but he was still his friend, Dan Parsons. "Make yourself a drink while I put some clothes on."

"Jackson isn't here? His dad said he was staying with you."

"He went out for dinner. He'll be back. He knew you were coming. Dev doesn't know we are here in town, does he?" Ari called out from one of the bedrooms in the suite. When he was in Washington, D.C., he always stayed at this hotel. They had the best security in the town and a tremendous view of the historic city.

"No, not yet. Jack won't tell him, yet, but JT tells me he already had a feeling that something was off." The priest looked around the extravagant suite. The view was spectacular from the wall of windows. The kitchen was modern; the bar was full. The living area was in the center with what seemed like doors to bedrooms surrounding it. *Jackson and Ari staying here together?* Dan shook his head. Strange things do happen every day.

Dan heard the key card slide into the lock, and the door opened. Jackson Pierce entered, two large sacks in his arms. "Hey, Dan. I have Chinese, enough for you too."

"Thanks. It's been a long Sunday."

Jackson laughed. "Those masses will take it all out of you. How is the priest business?" He headed over to the kitchen and began to place boxes and containers of food out on the island.

"Business is good. My boss keeps me busy."

"I bet he does," Jackson answered. "I haven't talked to your boss lately."

Jackson pulled a beer out of the refrigerator and passed it to his guest. "Well, I'm sorry about that. We could sit down and talk about your relationship with God."

Jackson took a drink from his own bottle. "No, not right now. I'm too cynical. Someday, maybe."

"That doesn't sound too concrete," Dan answered sarcastically. "What's Ari doing in there?"

Jackson yelled toward the bedroom. "Honey, I'm home, and I have food. Are you joining us soon?"

The double doors flew open in dramatic fashion, and Ari arrived. From head to toe, he looked like the super international agent he truly was. He straightened his black tux sleeves on his coat and pulled at his white shirt. Gold cufflinks shined in the living room's light. Their shine was only rivaled by his dress shoes, and his smile. His dark hair was perfect. "You two kids staying in tonight?"

"Wow, where are you going?" Dan was reviewing him as if he were under inspection.

"I have an embassy function. One of the princes is in town, and then he heads to New York City for some United Nations gig. I may go with him."

"Did Jackson fill you in completely about the names in the paper, and Dev's suspicions about Khalid?" Dan had no time to play with these two; they were out of his pastoral league. He had turned his back on that world years ago, and he had never for one second regretted his decision.

"Yes, my friend." Ari shook his head and poured himself a scotch. He drank the liquid in one gulp. "This situation isn't good. We have information about your dear friend, Brad Keeting."

"Dev already told me about Brad working for Khalid," Dan admitted.

Jackson motioned for Dan to sit down on one of the island's bar chairs. "You might as well get comfortable. I'll fill you in while the prince here goes to the event. We have more information, and it isn't pretty. You need to promise me one thing before we start."

There was always a catch with these two, well at least with Ari. Dan remembered some of the "deals" they had made with him only to find themselves in adventures they never wanted. "What?"

"Dev, heck, all of them, can't know that Ari or I are here, not yet. Dad knows, and now you. We want to keep it that way." Jackson had the same tone as Dev when he was deadly serious. His voice sent a shiver down Dan's back. It had been a long time since he had participated in any special operation. He hadn't missed the danger one bit. The only person that scared him recently was the church's wedding coordinator. He had nicknamed her Agnes the Hun.

"Are you two dating or something?" Dan laughed at the suggestion. His laughter stopped abruptly when neither Ari or Dan smiled.

Holy Moly! He'd picked that up from Lily.

Ari winked at Jackson, then blew him a kiss. "Oh, for heaven's sake, Ari. Stop it. No, Dan, we are not dating." Jackson handed him a plate and a fork. "Besides, Ari is not my type. He is way too controlling."

"But I thought you liked it when I made all the decisions," Ari whined.

Jackson pointed at the door. "Out. You have somewhere to go. Dan and I are going to be adults and analyze this entire mess. I'll fill you in tomorrow."

"I know when I'm not wanted. Good to see you again, Daniel. We will discuss your change of profession some other time. A priest? My heavens. It is as implausible as me becoming a rabbi." He was still shaking his head in disbelief as he exited.

"Grab your food, and let's head over to the table. I have a few things I want you to see on my computer, and I definitely want to hear what you found out from your pentagon buddies about that newspaper article."

Dan agreed. He found some of his favorite foods and headed across from Jackson's computer. "We have a few people in Congress who don't like us heroes."

"That's really nothing new. Remember the previous administration's little guy with the red eyeglasses who said most of the soldiers were too dangerous to be out on the streets in civilized society?"

Dan smiled. He remembered him. His name was Percival Snodd, with two 'D's'. "Society doesn't seem to be civilized anymore." Just last week he had performed a funeral mass for an elderly woman in his parish. She had been robbed in her own home. The teenager was mad when she only had fifty dollars and beat her up mercilessly. She died from her injuries two days later. Dan cussed under his breath.

"What did you just say?"

Dan looked out to the lights displayed in the window. "Nothing. I was just thinking about the people in the world and how you just can't help everyone."

"No, but we can stop some of them, damn it. Now, take a look at what I've found out so far. Then, I want to hear what the General told you." Jackson pushed the computer in front of the priest. They began to compare notes and formulate a contingency plan. It was nearly one in the morning when they finished, just in time to greet Ari as he entered the suite.

"Good, you're still here."

"How was the party?" Jackson's light smile faded as he surveyed Ari's face.

"There's a new emissary in town. He currently has diplomatic immunity, and I confirmed it with the prince. He said to tell both of you hello."

"Don't say it." Jackson was already speculating the very worst scenario.

Dan looked from one man to the other. He hated when agents like them could speak without talking. "Just spill it. What the hell is going on?" His voice was raised, almost desperate in its demand.

"Khalid. Khalid is here. I also saw Dan's friend, Brad Keeting. The congressman who gave the newspaper the story is good friends with Khalid. I believe he is the concerned constituent. This whole thing is now an international mess. I recognized a few of your State Department's officials, and they didn't look very happy. I can't touch him, and neither can any of you. He is on your soil, within arm's reach, and we can't touch him. There's not a damn thing we can do."

Dan said a silent prayer as Jackson and Ari began to argue about options. There were many "what ifs" and "we could". *Lord, we thought this was all behind us. The war is never gone from our minds, our thoughts. Now this evil man has come to hurt us, to hurt others, and those we love. Lord, you are the only answer.*

"Daniel, any ideas?'

He heard the question. "I suggest we pray." That was met with quiet consternation. He could see their lack of belief in their eyes. "Then I suggest we don't keep this to ourselves. Perhaps we keep everyone in the dark about you two, but we all need to know. We all need to be on high alert. Paul has already told his wife and girls. JT and Dev need to be told. Perhaps our extended families, siblings, parents. Oh, Jesus."

"The priest just cussed," Ari murmured.

Jackson shook his head. "No, he's praying."

"You idiots. What do we do about Lily?"

"She's tough. She'll be fine. The Boy Scout can tell her what to look out for." Ari suspected she could handle more situations than the priest.

"I agree with Ari." Jackson didn't understand the priest's hyper-concern.

"Didn't your dad tell you? You are going to be an uncle."

Jackson's mouth gaped open. "She's going to have a baby?"

"That's usually what that means." Ari smiled, his eyes twinkling. *My, the Boy Scout certainly doesn't waste any time. Good for them.* "We can do this. We just have to be smart. I'll meet with JT tomorrow. The CIA should know by now that Keeting has jumped sides, or perhaps he hasn't. Who knows? This will be complicated with immunity, but we can do this."

Ari thought of Lily and the baby, and then his thoughts were of his own wife and little girl. "Not only can we do this, we have to do this. There is no choice but death, and that is not my choice for myself or any of us. You go home, Daniel."

Once the priest headed home, Jackson lounged on the sofa. Ari made himself a cup of coffee and sat across from him in a huge leather chair. They both stared out the huge windows, seeing D.C. in all its glory.

"When were you going to tell me?" Jackson questioned.

"As soon as I knew for sure."

"Do you really think Khalid has thrown down the glove?" Jackson glared at Ari. *Was this always one huge chess game with this man?*

"Oh, he's thrown down the glove, and we have been challenged. He has that congressman in his pocket, and maybe a few more. He has his consulate on his side, perhaps even some of your State Department officials are enamored with him. He can be quite charming, but we have the home field advantage. He is now here. He is in your home."

Jackson shut his eyes. If he shut them fiercely when he opened them would the world have changed? "I don't want him in my house, with my friends or my family. I have a nephew or niece coming to live in this house."

Ari took a sip of the warm liquid. "And so, with any rat, we set a trap."

"Let's not use one of those traps that releases the rodent away from the house. That's been done before and hasn't worked."

Ari marveled at his view of the majestic spotlighted memorials in the darkness of the late hours. Dev and the Americans had trusted Khalid once. Usually, it only took one time before he burned you. There was no grey when it came to Khalid. There was only black or white, even when they were children. Ari smiled; Khalid frowned. Ari had friends of every faith; Khalid was intolerant of other religions. "No. This time the trap must come down upon his neck. There should be no mistaking this undertaking. And if someone must go to prison, it will be me. I have absolutely nothing to lose."

Jackson heard the coldness of his friend's voice. Ari's face was hard, resolute. There would be no changing his mind. "You think if you do that, they'll name the baby after you?"

Ari's dark thoughts were interrupted. "Of course. Lily loves me, you know. I think Ari Pierce sounds absolutely grand." He flashed one of his signature smiles.

"No way in hell, no matter what you do, will my brother allow that."

Ari took another sip of coffee. It was so easy to irritate a Pierce. That seemed to be his only amusement lately. His smile vanished, his eyes darkened, and his jaw pulsed. The darkness overtook him. He would bring Khalid into the light, and he would finish this game they had played all their lives. Not one more child would die because of him.

An hour later, after a little more planning, Ari stood alone in his bedroom. He removed an old cigarette case. It held his only personal items, photos of his parents, grandparents, wife and little girl. *Chaya, my little one. You need to be an angel for Lily's baby.* He kissed the photo and did so again on his wife's face. *My love, I may be seeing you very soon. God help us all.*

Chapter Eight

1. Wear flats from now on
2. Pack celery anytime I leave the house
3. Dev thinks the celery is healthy
4. Add peanut butter to the celery
5. Call Gretchen
6. Need more post-its!

"Exactly why did you fire your church wedding coordinator?" Lily was driving Dan and herself to meet Dev at the townhouse. Dev and the realtor were making one last walk through. Besides, Lily had forgotten to hand over her set of keys for the new owners. She seemed to be forgetting a lot of little things lately. Jack called it "baby brain" and claimed that his wife had the same ailment when she was pregnant with both boys. *He is such a nice man.*

Anytime Lily needed Jack to go to the doctor's office, he was there. He was probably the greatest living father-in-law on the face of the earth. Anytime she needed her latest food fetish, he was in the car and down to Ben's, her favorite ice cream drive thru. Currently, her favorite flavor was peanut butter ribbon fudge with a hint of potato chips. She added the chips as a crunchy accent.

"Do you want the priestly answer, or the real one?"

"Humor me, give me both."

Dan laughed. As the passenger, Dan was enjoying the scenery of historic Alexandria. Lily had really caught onto the frantic driving skills needed to survive the beltway. "As the pastor of my church, there does come those times when I feel that a volunteer has done so much for the church that they deserve a break, perhaps an opportunity to turn in some other direction to serve the Lord."

"That sounded really good. Now, spill. What's the real reason?"

"She was a pain in my backside," Dan admitted. "She actually told one couple that I didn't know what I was doing. Last week, she allowed a photographer to sit on the edge of the altar to get a photo. What's worse is it was during the blasted ceremony!"

Lily giggled. The priest was really worked up by this woman. Lily had met her once when Dev and she had arrived to pick Dan up after a wedding. She wasn't exactly the friendliest coordinator ever, but Lily was used to tolerating Gretchen. *Ah, Gretchen! I need to call her, then I can listen for forty minutes to every juicy piece of gossip in Kansas City. She'll make me forget all the gas I've been having. It's probably the celery's fault. That's what eating healthy gets you!*

"You are sure Devlin is going to be fine with you helping me out on the weddings I have scheduled until I get someone else in there?"

"Of course, he will be." Lily had just lied to a priest. *Do I need to go to confession for this, Lord? Don't pregnant women get passes sometimes, especially when they are helping out one of your employees? Work with me, Lord!* Dev had thought it wouldn't be a good idea when she had originally said that Dan might need some help, but he was still worrying about her doing too much. She didn't dare tell him how exhausted she had been after she'd helped his aunt.

Dan's finger pointed toward the street in front of them. "There's a lot of police and fire trucks up there."

Lily saw the police line in front of her. They were setting up barricades.

"Dan, Dev's down there." Lily's voice was soft and full of fear.

"Drive down as far as you can. Maybe they'll tell us something. It probably has nothing to do with Dev."

Lily did as she was instructed and was stopped by a patrolman.

"Ma'am, you can't go any further. You'll have to turn around."

"My husband is on that block. We need to meet him. Maybe we could just pick him up."

"What house are you headed to?"

"Three ten. It's just two houses down, where that hazmat truck is sitting."

Lily felt her stomach jump, and it wasn't the baby doing it. She felt Dan touch her shoulder and lean toward her.

"Officer, I'm a priest. Could I help in any way?"

The policeman looked over to the priest and nodded. "Actually, Father, could you get out of the car and take a look at something for me?"

Dan thought that was a weird request, but possibly he could discover more about that hazmat truck. "Sure. Lily, you just sit here, and breathe. I'll be right back."

"Yes, ma'am. Just park it right here. Sorry for the inconvenience."

Lily watched the two figures stand in front of her car. There was some pointing and bowing heads. The two men were not praying. She was sure of that. That was the only thing she was sure of. Dan shook the officer's hand, came over to her door, and opened it.

"Come on. He is going to take us down there. But you have to be good." Dan offered her a hand as she slowly removed herself from the car. She grabbed her purse. Maybe she could still return the key to the realtor if they were allowed close enough to the townhome.

"I'm always good." She offered a meek smile. They walked slowly behind the officer. She noticed some black, dark vehicles, ones that were unmarked. They didn't belong in the neighborhood, but neither did the FBI or Homeland Security vehicles. She noticed two DEA cars. She said nothing as they came closer to their home. In her head she was praying and using profanity simultaneously.

The hazmat vehicle was directly in front of the townhome. Dan held her arm at the elbow. He was silent. A man in a suit headed toward them.

"Mrs. Pierce, everything is under control. Your husband is being decontaminated right now out of caution, but he will be out in another five minutes. This is just procedure. I'm sorry, but we can't allow you any further." He smiled after his statement.

"So, something has happened to my husband, but he is okay?"

"Yes. He can explain what happened after we are finished with him."

Lily looked at Dan. She grabbed his arm in urgency. "Dan, I don't feel well. Geez, I'm acting like such a baby."

"No, it's okay. Let's get you seated." Dan looked at all his options and found just one. "Sit on the curb here. I'll get you up later. Here, sit on my jacket." He removed his black coat and draped it over the concrete. He carefully lowered her to the curb. He squatted in front of the now very pale Lily. "Just focus on me, and how amazingly handsome I am. You are now doubting your choice on the man you selected as your husband. Of course, you could've had JT too, but that wouldn't have been very wise."

"You would never have left the priesthood," she whispered. She heard someone asking for water and a bottle quickly appeared.

"You sound certain about that."

"Pregnant women are always right about everything, especially when you think they are going to pass out."

"Lily, keep looking at my face."

"I'm looking at your collar. You know I almost married a minister. I've had clergy as friends all my professional life."

"Including an ex-fiancé. I wonder where he is."

"I just want to see my husband." Lily strained her neck in a vain attempt to see Dev. She did see the realtor. The woman was speaking with an investigator of some kind. "Was there a gas leak? Did someone put a bomb somewhere?"

Dan's usually soft tone became stressed. "Why would you think about a bomb?"

Lily tilted her head, looking like a disbelieving child. "One word--Khalid. I know things."

"Woman, what are we going to do with you?"

"Just keep me breathing, Danny, please."

"Father, I can sit with Mrs. Pierce. I know Dev through the DEA. They'll allow you to go down now." Lily looked up to see a very athletic looking woman, in a dark suit. *Do they all go to the same place to get that stupid suit? It must be next door to the place where they all learn how to not tell you the truth.*

"Lily, I'm going to find out what is going on, and I'll check on Dev. Are you okay with that?" Dan touched her shoulders softly. "Lily?"

"Yes, go. I'll be fine." She took a drink of water. The woman took a seat next to her.

"My name is Ava. I was actually at West Point with Dev."

Lily turned to look at her. "Really? And now you are with the DEA?"

"Well, yes," the woman said, a little surprised that Lily had caught on that quickly. "But I chose to get out of the field before Dev so I've been up here for the last few years."

"Were you deployed in the Army?"

"I was, actually, but I wasn't part of the team, well Dev's team. We heard about them though. I went in a different direction, but I was in Afghanistan. I know all of them, and I've heard so many stories about all of them. How are they treating you?"

"Like I'm the little sister they never knew they wanted." Both women shared a nervous laugh.

"I know Dan didn't remember me when I came up. You'll have to tell him it was me, Ava. They nicknamed me Ace. Do you have a name yet?"

Lily sat a little straighter, proud. "I do. It's Sweet Pea. JT gave it to me."

"You mean that idiot is still alive?" Now Ava looked a little green around the gills.

"Ah, you know him. Yes, he is still kicking. He's the brother I never knew I wanted."

"Wow, JT is still alive." Ava seemed to repeat the sentence to convince herself of the information. "We had some good times." Her voice trailed off.

Lily saw something. JT had a past with this woman. The baby kicked. "Ouch." Lily flinched. Ava grabbed her arm.

"Did something just happen?"

Lily sighed. "The baby just kicked really hard. I'm not used to this."

"I'm not sure anyone is used to that, or ready for it." Ava's voice was comforting, her eyes soft and clear.

"Did you go to the school where they teach you to divert the subject's attention away from the dangerous situation too? I know my husband went to that school. He was probably the head of his class." Lily spoke plainly without any emotion. Ava's head dropped in shame.

"Apparently, I'm not a very good student."

Lily disagreed. "No, you are very good. I truly just caught on. So, tell me about JT and you."

Ava's entire body straightened. Her back was straighter, her arms clutched her bended legs. "Dang, I think we need to hire you."

"I have been told that before," Lily said confidently. *When did this confidence come to live in me?* She looked down at her wedding ring. Thankfully, her fingers weren't swelling, yet. *Oh, yeah, it was the day I married him.*

"I seriously don't think we have enough time." She looked over Lily's head to see two figures walking towards them. One had a collar on his shirt, the other wore FBI sweats. She motioned to Lily to see her husband.

Lily broke out in tears. She tried to push up off the cement, but it was impossible. Ava quickly aided her, lifting her up in one swift move. She was the ridiculously crying wife, falling into her husband's arms. But she didn't care. Her relief was overwhelming, and her hormones were flying in the Alexandria air.

Dev wrapped her up in his arms, holding her as tightly as he had ever held any one human being. He swore he could feel the baby kick. "I'm fine, honey. You are fine. It's okay."

Dev felt a small fist hitting him lightly on the chest. "I don't know what has happened, but don't you ever do that again."

Dan and Ava found the demand highly amusing. It was then that the priest realized who he was standing next to. "Ava? Ace? Wow, I didn't know it was you."

"It's been a few years and about twenty pounds over my fighting weight," she admitted.

Dan hugged her fiercely. "Well, you look wonderful. Let's go over here and catch up so Lily can continue to beat on her husband in private. Gosh, Ace, it is so good to see you."

Lily and Dev were left alone, as much as you could be private in the middle of a terrorism crime scene with dozens of agents and first responders running around. "Lily, honey, it is all over."

Lily pulled away and starkly reprimanded her husband. "Don't lie to me, Dev. I have this feeling it is only beginning.

This time, and you know I'm right, you cannot and will not keep me out of the loop. Now, what happened?"

"I pulled up to meet Barbara, and she was standing outside the house. She had just picked up something. She waved. I went to the door, and she said I had a delivery. The box was sitting there when she arrived. She thought it was interesting that I knew someone in Turkey. I looked at the address, and I knew there was something wrong."

"No ex-girlfriend in Istanbul?"

"No. I just had this feeling."

"Of course, you did," Lily muttered.

Dev's one brow rose. "I told Barbara to call 9-1-1. I ran with the box and placed it in the trash bin. I rolled it to the edge of the sidewalk, away from our cars, and I called my friends at Homeland. They brought the FBI, my DEA people, and a few other assorted agents from other secret alphabet groups."

"What was in the box, Dev?" Lily stared coolly at her husband. He'd described every detail except the most important one. Her arms were crossed, resting on top of her stomach.

"Nothing too significant."

Lily squinted her eyes into very small slits of optical disbelief.

"Fine. There was ricin in the box."

"Excuse me? Ricin? Isn't that poison?"

"Yes."

"More explanation, please?"

"Can we wait until we get home?" Dev saw the FBI evidence team pulling away with their very valuable evidence.

"I suppose so. I still have my key for Barbara."

Dev slipped one arm around Lily to guide her to the car. "I will stop at her office tomorrow and hand it to her."

"And you'll check on her," Lily suggested. Her arms uncrossed as she began to relax.

"Of course, honey. You go to the car, and I'll have Dan join you. I still have to get my car."

"What about your real clothes?" Lily happily lowered herself into her driver's seat. *My back is killing me. That was a bad choice of words.*

"I'm not sure we will ever see them again. I've literally given the clothes off my back for my job." Dev laughed; Lily did not. "Do you still want to go for Italian like we planned?"

"Am I still pregnant? Of course, I do. You can fill in all the information you left out while we eat. Besides, I promised Dan. He loves the lasagna down there." They were heading to the restaurant where she had met Dev's dad for the first time. It had been his mother's favorite place. And she was hungry, again.

Lily waited patiently while she watched Dev talk to Dan. She grabbed her bag of celery and munched away. Her eyes narrowed in an attempt to read their lips, but somehow Dev knew exactly what she was doing. They turned their backs to her. *How rude! You are in so much trouble, buddy!*

The baby was slightly pushing on one side of her belly.

"Geez, kid. Enjoy the damn celery." The month of August couldn't come soon enough if this was going to continue. "I know you're hungry, but your spy daddy is being very secretive. I promise you pasta very soon, oh and those breadsticks. You are going to love those. They bake them on-site."

Lily picked up her cell and pressed on the speed dial. "JT? We need to talk. There's been a situation. I'm sure you'll hear about it later tonight. Call me tomorrow."

Chapter Nine

1. Find something to wear to the wedding
2. Bring extra flat shoes
3. Pack water, chocolate, and a banana
4. No more celery--too much gas!

*B*y the time Lily had the bride walking down the aisle, she was more than ready to go outside to enjoy some fresh air and to have a snack. She grabbed her bag. She already had the perfect place picked out near the front of the church. Dan had recently installed benches near the statue of the Blessed Virgin Mary in the rose garden. It would be a peaceful location to take a few minutes to relax. She made sure she told the ushers where she would be just in case there was some emergency. Her replacement of Agnes the Hun was smooth, seamless for Dan. But Lily's feet and lower back were giving her more discomfort than usual. As she headed out the door toward the garden, she saw the man standing near the parking lot.

The extremely handsome man needed a haircut. *This baby has no chance of ever having straight hair.* Dev's hair actually curled when it was longer and less military looking. He appeared to be dressed for a picnic or patio party in his khaki shorts and light blue polo, and he had sandals on. For a change, he was casual looking, and she was dressed for a wedding.

"Hi Boy Scout." She flashed a very relieved smile. She could use a shoulder rub. *I really need a back rub, but that would look strange in the church's parking lot.*

He raised a sack from her favorite sub sandwich shop high in the air. "I thought you might need this, Sweet Pea."

She appeared to be embarrassed, shrugging her shoulders. "You know my nickname."

"I know a lot of things, like your favorite sandwich, your favorite side of the bed, and that you are probably starving and tired right about now."

He continued to walk to her, flashing that smile of his that made her heart melt. "You know me very well, sir."

"Where were you headed?" He kissed her on the forehead, grabbing the bag from her shoulder.

"To the garden, and you are so right. I'm not in playing condition. I used to still have energy after a day of weddings, but today I'm pushing it to live through three hours."

Dev remained unusually quiet until they reached their destination. They sat next to each other on a bench, and Dev unpacked her lunch. "I didn't say anything when you told me you were going to help out Dan, but I thought this might happen. You are carrying a baby in there." He pointed at her ever-enlarging belly.

"I just don't know how I'm going to make it until this baby comes. I hate hormones. It's not even that hot today, and I'm suffering. This breeze feels good. Hand over that sandwich."

"You have water in the bag, right?" Dev reached down and pulled out a bottle. "Here. I bet you haven't had enough water either."

"Yes, mother. I'm okay, just tired. Yum, chicken and swiss."

Dev was still unwrapping his own sandwich while Lily was digging in. "And I brought extra dill pickles for you."

"Have I told you how much I absolutely love you?" She kissed his cheek quickly, then turned her attention back to eating.

"So Sweet Pea, what is Danny calling you? I mean he labeled the other lady Agnes the Hun."

Lily wiped the side of her mouth. "Lovely Lily. I like it very much."

"That's because you are pulling his butt out of the fire by helping him out." Dev watched late guests briskly walking into the church. "They're late."

"Where is that wedding we are going to next week?"

"Fredericksburg. You should just keep this bag packed all the time." He could see her extra pair of shoes, more water, snacks, and what seemed to be another pair of underwear. *I'm not going to ask.* "I think this is the first time I've been invited to a co-worker's daughter's wedding."

"That's because we are getting older," Lily murmured. "I feel it every day when I wake up. In another month, you're going to have to lift me out of bed before you go to work." She rubbed the front of her. The baby was kicking again. *You liked the sandwich. Me too. Your daddy is so thoughtful.*

"I will happily do that for you." He glanced at her face. He was mesmerized by her face. He knew she was miserable, but she had never been more beautiful. It wasn't a glow; it was confidence. He loved that look on her.

The silence was soothing as they sat on a bench surrounded by roses. "Honey, I appreciate the lunch, but I get the feeling you are here for another reason."

Damn, how does she do that? There were cartel gangs and terrorists who couldn't read Devlin Pierce, but Lily could, every time. "I wanted to bring you lunch. I wanted to check on you, and I need to tell you something. Unless you've heard from JT." Dev searched her eyes closely. She shook her head negatively. "The box the other day--"

"From Turkey?"

"Yes, well, I guess someone thought we still lived at the townhouse." Dev swallowed hard. "Lily, the box wasn't addressed to me."

"Dumb terrorists wrote the wrong name on the address?" Lily snorted slightly, but Dev wasn't laughing. He took her hand in his and held on tightly.

"It was addressed to you, to Lily Schmidt Pierce."

The baby didn't kick, but the mother-to-be suddenly was sick to her stomach. "Oh, my Lord."

"Lily, you need to leave this to the professionals." Dev could see the gears working in her head, and he didn't like it for one second. "Honey, this is way above the Nottes and their drug deals. Don't try to be Jessica Fletcher this time."

"I've never done anything without you, well I haven't intended to do it without you. But you have to, you need to keep me in the loop this time. We have too much to lose this time." She patted the top of her stomach.

Dev pulled her closer and rubbed her back. "We aren't going to lose anything, or anyone. Believe that."

His hand was comforting and supportive. Lily closed her eyes. *What is going on?* Her thoughts carried her miles away. If she'd never met him, she'd be at a wedding somewhere in Kansas City right now. Her feet wouldn't be swollen, and her back wouldn't be hurting. She wouldn't be fifteen pounds heavier, well, she might be if it had been a bad, chocolate-filled winter. She would work, Abby and she would go out for dinner and a few drinks, and she would go home. Alone. Jessica Fletcher would be her date for the remainder of the night until she fell asleep. But Agent Pierce had walked into the shop after that drug-laden shipment of hydrangeas had mistakenly been sent to her.

Lily smiled. The memory took her back to that day, to the first view of his twinkling eyes. He had said his mother's favorite flower was a hydrangea, but he didn't even know what the full bloom looked like. She'd known he was lying from the very first time they had met. He was masterful at turning a tale, but now she knew him. He had just said to believe him. She did.

Lily turned her head to see his face. "Dev, is it Khalid?"

He leaned his chin on her head. "It has to be. He is making it personal. He's in the States."

Lily understood. *Khalid has come to our home. He needs to go away, far, far away.*

Chapter Ten

"It is so cute here." Lily marveled at some of the Civil War era brick buildings as they travelled the downtown streets of Fredericksburg, Virginia. "We need to come back down here and walk around, after the baby comes." She pointed at a baby shop.

"History is around every corner. It is one of my favorite Virginian towns. There's a battlefield up the hill. I'll drive you by on our way out. Across the Rappahannock River, is where George Washington's mother and sister lived, I think. Don't quote me on that."

"You don't know for sure, Mr. I-know-history?" Dev shrugged as his wife laughed.

"The Civil War was my expertise in school. I respected the history. It is so unimaginable to realize they fought each other here. We are driving over where they all walked, perhaps where they died. It wasn't until September 11th, when war came to our shores again." Dev attempted to concentrate on his driving. He needed to find a parking place near the church, so Lily didn't have to walk very far on those uneven brick sidewalks.

And now Khalid has come here to do God knows what. Lily shook the thought from her mind. She needed a diversion, and this wedding would serve perfectly to push away any thoughts of that evil man.

"Found one," Dev announced as he made a turn in the middle of the street.

"What? What are you doing?" Lily hung onto the side of her door.

"I found a parking place, just a block down from the church." He slowly parallel parked perfectly.

"I love a man who can parallel park."

He winked at her as he turned off the car. "I have many skills."

"I know, I know. Now get me out of this car."

Dev was soon at her side, opening the door, and lending a hand down to her. "Now, be careful here. The bricks are unstable. The tree's roots are buckling the sidewalk.

Lily breathed in deeply and began to lift her body out of the vehicle. With his other arm, Dev supported her back.

"I am miserable," Lily complained as she straightened up. "That car ride was a little longer than I expected. I should've put a pillow behind me."

Dev shut the door and locked the car. "We can get back in the car and head to a restaurant or that ice cream place you love." Dev kissed her on the cheek. As large as she was getting, he was beginning to wonder if there was more than just one baby in her body.

Lily raised one brow. "How did I miss the ice cream place?"

"I believe you were gazing lovingly at the wine shop, babe." He knew she'd glare at him, and she did. "Seriously, honey, we can skip this. They'll never know."

"No. I'm dressed. We're here, and I'm thinking they'll have wedding cake. Besides, we sent in our RSVP. It would be rude to not show up, and they've already paid for us."

"Always the wedding professional, Lily?" He offered her an arm for the precarious stroll on the brick. "My lady?"

"I feel like a beached whale," Lily complained again as she saw her reflection in a shop's window. The lightweight blue dress she was wearing kept her cool but billowed like a ship's sail. She saw those women who featured their baby bump, and she did have a few clothes that did the same. Today she needed air to flow, everywhere. She wasn't delivering flowers so she could wear a dress. *I can't even pick up a box or see one if it's on the floor right in front of me. Feet? Are you there?*

"But you're a beautiful beached whale, and you aren't that big." Dev offered a toothy smile.

She smirked. "You are so gallant, dear sir. Your southern roots are certainly showing, in fact," she said as she reached up to run her fingers through his longer-than-usual hair, "I'm seeing a few grey southern roots right here."

"Ha, ha. Let's get you in the church before you get too hot. Steady on these stairs."

"These aren't stairs. It's Mt. Everest, and I'm a yak carrying everyone's gear."

Lily welcomed her seat even though the old church's pews were not the most comfortable. There were no kneelers. *I need something to put my watermelon feet on. At least Dev put me on the aisle so I don't have to try to move through these tight pews. How did those ladies fit those big hoop skirts in through them?*

Lily wondered how Abby was doing today. She had two weddings today. But she had two helpers now assisting on a part-time basis. Abby was really excelling, with Gretchen's help now and then. Amazingly, the two could get along rather well. However, Abby had admitted any day with Gretchen was a two shots of tequila day before bedtime.

She smiled. *Lily's Flower Shop* was still flourishing. She looked around at a few of the guests, studying their clothing and jewelry. One young lady being ushered down the aisle had the tallest heels she'd ever seen. She winced just thinking of the pain.

Her husband reached over to hold her left hand as he continued to read the program. She gazed over at him, studying one of those grey hairs, moving on to the tight muscle in his jaw. He was bored. His left leg was shaking nervously. He looked dapper in his navy suit with Lily's addition of a fashion-forward blue and coral paisley tie. *Dev has probably never said the word paisley much less worn it.* She giggled to herself. She had also made him wear a barely striped shirt. He looked less like a DEA agent and more the businessman on the Metro on a Monday morning.

But his well-polished dark shoes still were Army through and through. *You can take the man out of the Army, but you can't take the Army out of the man.* Looking down at their hands, the United States Military Academy ring on his finger provoked her. It was taunting her, saying "I had him first and I'll always have him."

Lily, you are losing it. The baby kicked, hard. "Ow," she whispered.

"Okay?"

"Your baby just kicked me; field goal hard."

Dev bent his head closer to her ear. "My son is bored, and so am I."

"Your daughter is just hungry. Besides, you are the one who said we should go. It is one of your boss's daughters. And we reserved."

Before Dev could reply in defense or debate the sex of their child, the bridal party processional began. Lily examined every single bloom. The boutonnieres were simple with small spray roses and a touch of waxflower. The corsages on both mothers were simple gardenias. Lily could smell their fragrance from her pew. She stifled a burp.

The bridesmaids followed next with bouquets of pink roses in different hues. *Lord, twelve bridesmaids? That'll fill up the front of the church.* A young flower girl dropped white rose petals down the aisle. There was a pause before the bride's entrance. On the arm of her father, the young woman in satin and lace passed by Lily on her way to her groom. The bride carried a simple gathering of gardenias and white roses. She looked very young, but she was indeed glowing, or it was the temperature in the church. Lily began to fan herself with the program.

Lily closed her eyes. *Breathe, do not pass out. It isn't that hot in here. It is as cool as a winter day. Nope, still hot.*

"Welcome to this beautiful, joyous joining of Thomas and Catherine. Please be seated."

Gladly, Lily wanted to sit down, but she thought she knew that voice. She strained but could only see robes and the bride's very large dress. Lily was one of the last to sit down in hopes she could view the minister. Once she saw, she sat down quickly.

"Oh Lord."

"Is the baby kicking another field goal? Three points or an after-touchdown kick?" Dev asked, hoping his attempt at humor would lessen her pain.

She shook her head negatively.

"So, what is going on?"

"It's, it's my minister," she stammered.

Dev frowned. *Her minister? Her minister?* "You mean God Boy? The minister is the guy you almost married?"

"Yes." She squirmed to gain comfort. Now the baby began to kick again.

"What is he doing here?"

"Well, I don't know," Lily snapped back. "Right now, he is marrying this couple."

Dev shook his head. "Life is never dull with you."

"Nor with you." She turned and stuck her tongue out at her husband.

"In church, Lily? Bad girl." Dev's smile widened. The woman sitting behind them laughed. "Gretchen is going to love hearing this story."

"No, she doesn't need to know. Ever." Bowing her head, Lily was attempting to become invisible. Never did she think she would ever see him again. Hopefully, she could evade any confrontation by becoming as small as she could possibly be. *Oh, sure. That's never going to work. You barely fit in this pew.* Surely, he wouldn't make an appearance at the reception. *With my luck, he's a best friend of the couple or of the parents. Oh Lord, and I'm not praying!*

The service was over. The happy couple and then the bridal party walked past her. Lily had an urgency to get out of the pew and head to the nearest bathroom. She whispered to Dev that she needed to go and began to negotiate her body out of the pew.

The minister, her minister, met her in the aisle. He had followed the bridal party down the aisle.

"Lily?" His eyes immediately fell to her very large belly.

"Hi Grant, got to go." She scurried past him as fast as her pregnant feet would take her. She moved quickly from embarrassment but mostly because her bladder had a human bowling ball sitting on top of it.

Dev was left alone, staring at Lily's former fiancé. "Dev Pierce, Lily's husband." He extended his hand out and it was greeted with a handshake. "I need to go with her. Excuse me."

Lily had made it to the restroom in time. At least she had beat out the other women lining up for relief. She saw a very pale face in the mirror. She poured cold water on a towel and applied it to her forehead.

"You feeling all right, dear?" An elderly woman was patting her arm, her concern was all over her face.

Lily smiled weakly. "I just saw my ex, and I'm pregnant."

The woman removed her hand quickly and stepped away.

Lily thought about her words. *Holy Moly. That came out all wrong.* She wanted to follow the woman and give some sort of explanation that included the word husband, but it was too late for that. She took a deep breath in and then out again. She repeated that activity three more times.

All right, you've got this. You have a wonderful husband, and you are going to have his baby. Grant shouldn't bother me at all.

Dev was leaning against the wall near the women's restroom, arms crossed against his chest. He had already spoken with a few people from work and had spoken with the father of the bride. If they needed to leave, the man would completely understand that Lily wasn't feeling well. But Dev wanted to stay. *This is going to be fun. What are the odds that Lily's ex would be the officiant?*

Lily came out, looking a bit bewildered. When she saw Dev's stance, his head lowered and a thin smile on his lips, she knew he was going to take great delight in her discomfort--and she wasn't talking about the baby!

She pointed a finger at him sternly.

"Don't, just don't."

"But this is so amazing," he laughed. "Don't you think? What are the odds?"

She began to walk away as quickly as she could, albeit, slower than a grazing hippo. "If you ever want a sibling for your child, just stop it," she muttered.

Dev, still cackling, came from behind to take her hand. "Are you saying we will never have sex again?"

Lily continued to carefully navigate the church's steps. She successfully made it to the sidewalk. "No, you may lose a part of your body that is integral to performing that action if you make too much out of this."

Dev winced for effect. "Yikes. I'm done. There is no more to be said."

She looked up at him, searching his face. "Really?"

"Really." Once they arrived at the car, he opened the door for her and assisted her in.

Lily remained suspicious. Dev never gave up. The ploy to sucker her wouldn't work.

"It was a surprise," she admitted.

"We shared a quick handshake before I followed you." Dev was intent on his driving, slowly passing through the crowd of well-wishers, extending into the street. "I can stop for ice cream. It's a couple of hours before the cocktail party begins."

He was being nice, sweet, lulling her into a false sense of security. She took him up on the offer though, ordering a small chocolate milkshake and an order of french fries. Lily removed the lid carefully, grabbed a french fry and stuck it into the chocolate ice cream.

"Mmm, this is so good." Lily chewed slowly, relishing every small bite.

Dev admired his wife's zeal for all things ice cream. His gaze followed his wife's hand as she dunked another fried potato into her creamy drink. He admired her, but he didn't understand her. "Who are you?"

Lily looked up from her delightful snack. "Rhut?" She licked her lower lip from the salt and sweet.

"Have you always done that, or is it just the pregnancy making you do weird things?"

Lily wiped her mouth. She cleared her throat and took a breath. She didn't need brain freeze on top of a kicking baby. "This is not weird. I have always done this." She was serious and partially indignant. "You can't blame everything you consider odd behavior on this baby. The poor kiddo is going to get a complex."

Dev smiled, shaking his head in defeat. He rested his hand on her shoulder. "What are you really thinking? No joking now. I really want to know."

Lily sighed. "I really don't know. He was in my past, and it's hard sometimes to even remember those days. You've made me forget some very bad days." She patted her stomach. "Besides, I have been blessed in the last few years."

The color was returning to her face with every chocolate coated french fry. "Now, that's better." Dev rubbed her shoulder. "Our past gave us our future, and it is a wonderful one."

"That was nice."

Dev began to chuckle. "But don't you wonder what he thought when he saw you in your current state?" He pointed down to their ever-growing child.

He received a strong shove in his ribcage. "Devlin!"

"You love me, and aren't you happy you broke up with that jerk?"

Lily quickly kissed him on the cheek. "Yes, I love you, and I don't want to talk about him anymore. Got it?"

Dev knew when it was time to stop poking his pregnant bear. "Ma'am, yes, ma'am. Now eat your food. We have a dinner to get to."

Chapter Eleven

1. Make sure I eat some vegetables
2. Stay away from the shrimp
3. Stay off my feet
4. Eat wedding cake
5. Definitely eat cake

*T*he cocktail hour was in full swing by the time Lily and Dev arrived at the stately Virginian club where the wedding reception was being held. Lily insisted her husband "go cocktailing" while she examined the decor, the flowers, and the wedding cake. She strolled through as though she was making the final examination of one of her own weddings. She picked at a brown edge on a bloom. She quickly threw the petal in her purse. Then she looked around to see if anyone was watching her. *Lily Pierce, start acting like a guest and stop working. It's not your wedding.*

"I saw that." It was a familiar male voice, and it came from behind her.

"You can take the florist out of her weddings, but you can't take the weddings out of the florist?" She smiled shyly as she turned around to face her favorite priest. "What are you doing here?"

Looking very much like the priest he was in his basic black suit and white collar; Dan kissed her cheek. "I know the bride's dad from years ago in Afghanistan. I also baptized their first grandchild last year. Where's your hubby?"

Lily pointed toward the bar. "He is having a great time because he knows he has the perfect designated driver. He deserves a good time."

"That's very generous of you. So where is the food?"

"Ah, a man after my own heart. They've been passing some little meatballs around, but there's an appetizer bar over there."

Dan gallantly extended his arm to lead her on. In seconds they were plating stuffed cherry tomatoes, fruit and vegetables, and the most amazing egg rolls. They found their dinner table and settled in while Dev continued to enjoy himself. Lily popped a red grape into her mouth.

"Do you know the baby loves these things?"

Dan shook his head as he watched Lily relish a grape. She took so many simple things and made them appear to be so important. "I can't wait to meet this child."

"Me too." Lily rolled her eyes. "Today was not the easiest and being pregnant didn't make it any easier."

"The humidity was pretty bad today."

"That was the least of it. The wedding was lovely until I ran into the minister, literally."

Dan laughed. "Did you hurt him or her?"

"I had to go to the bathroom, so I exited the pew right after the bridal party and **smack** the minister and I met. The minister happened to be my ex."

Dan almost choked on his shrimp. "God Boy?"

Lily dropped her crostini in disgust. "You know about that nickname?"

"We all know, Lily, and we all call him that, well except for JT. He has another name for him."

God loves JT. "It wasn't the most comfortable encounter. Of course, your friend thought it was pretty funny." Lily paused as she looked over to her husband. It was as though he could sense her as he looked up and mouthed "are you okay" across the room. She nodded and pointed at her companion priest. *I love that man so much. How is it possible that he does something every day that makes me love him more every day?*

The priest patted her hand. "You know you've given him plenty of grief about his former girlfriends."

Lily looked as though she were a child caught in a little white lie. "I know, but he has given me so much material to work with, besides it all would've been hysterical if it hadn't been at my expense. I feel miserable, and I don't walk anymore. I waddle. Then to have to go to the bathroom and end up walking right into the man who broke my heart. It was just a little more than I was anticipating for today's activities."

As if to place a punctuation on her explanation, the baby gave her a swift kick even the priest beside her could see.

"Wow, he has a kick."

"Or she does," Lily answered quickly. *Why did all of them assume this was a baby boy?* "Maybe she'll be the first female football player at West Point. Wouldn't that be something?"

Dan ate another shrimp before he could answer Lily's question. He knew deep down that Dev might not think that was the best idea. West Point wasn't for their daughter, heck maybe not even for their son. As for the first female football player, if he received free tickets he might support that idea.

"Father Dan? What are you doing here?" A man behind him patted his back. He turned and stood up to greet another wedding guest.

"I know the father of the bride. Great to see you away from one of our committees." Dan shook his hand and seemed to be happy to see him.

Lily's mouth gaped open; no words could escape. She was staring at the duo. *A priest and a minister meet at a wedding reception. Holy Moly, why is he here? Lord, what did I do to deserve this? This really isn't fair.*

"Lily, let me introduce you to--" Dan turned to see a speechless, in shock, Lily.

"Grant."

Dan's head turned as though it were on a swivel. *What the heck?*

"Hello, Lily. It is so good to see you. Again."

"Ah," Dan whispered. "Grant and I know each other from an ecumenical group, and you know him from when he was in Kansas City." *Grant is God Boy. Lord, you do work in mysterious ways. Remind me to never cross you.*

Grant saw the realization on the priest's face. "I'm assuming you know how I'm connected to Lily."

"Oh yes," Dan admitted freely and then laughed. "I don't think you've met Lily's husband, Devlin Pierce. He's right behind you." Dan pointed at the looming figure, a figure whose eyes were burning a hole into the minister's body. *Little does he know Dev can do so much more to him.*

Grant was at ease. "Oh, we met at the church after Lily and I literally ran into each other. Can you believe it? After a few years and over a thousand miles, we end up here together." He gazed around Dan to smile at Lily.

"I wouldn't exactly say together, preacher." Dev's voice was slightly louder than it should be. Dan winced and Grant's smile vanished. Lily felt pretty special right now. Even with a human bowling ball inside her, she was everything to her husband. She just knew it. She didn't doubt it. Grant had never been jealous of anyone's attention toward her.

Grant's nervous laughter finally filled the air. "Oh, yes, right. You are right. I just meant that it was such a pleasant surprise to see Lily again, and she's having a baby. How wonderful."

Dev passed by Dan and Grant, laying a protective hand on the back of Lily's shoulder. "My baby and yes, it is wonderful."

My gosh, my husband **IS** *jealous. How delightful! Stop it, Lily. Poor Dev shouldn't feel this way, but I'm so sorry. I do love it!* Lily reached up and placed her hand over his. "It was a surprise to see you, Grant. You look like you are doing well. You look happy."

"I am, and I'm happy that you're happy."

Dev moved to sit next to his wife. "Well, now we know we are all happy," he muttered so only Lily heard. She patted his leg and kissed him on his cheek.

"Down, boy," she whispered. "You are so terribly cute when you are jealous."

Dev spoke through clenched teeth. "I'm not jealous. I don't like him, and I don't trust him."

"That just proves you are a good judge of character. I wish I had figured that out sooner."

"Would you mind if I sit with you all?" Grant was asking Lily and Dev.

Dan answered quickly. "Sit. Are you alone tonight?"

"Yes, my wife is out with some of her friends."

Lily took a drink of water and met Grant's eyes with hers. "You are married?"

"Yes. We've been married almost four years now."

Grant reached for his water glass quickly and broke from her gaze. He knew she knew. He was thinking this could be the longest night of his life.

Lily took another drink of water. *Are you kidding me? We dated for almost three years until I finally received that ring, and then we broke up less than two months later. Was he already dating her? He was already dating her! Would it be wrong to see if JT could possibly do something to the minister? Perhaps Grant could get lost taking a hike and never make it out of the Shenandoah Valley?*

As if saved by a bell, an announcement from the father of the bride stopped the idle, yet informative chatting. The bridal party would be coming in and dinner would be served. The guests were to take their seats.

The reception continued without any faux pas or incident. The table conversation was light, no in-depth discussion of any kind. Dev noticed Lily was just pushing her food around, a clear sign he would have to stop at the nearest McDonald's on the way home.

Dan and Grant were intent on some committee discussion. Dev heard the word "Afghanistan" and his interest peaked. "Excuse me, what about Afghanistan?"

"I work with an international association that funds schools for girls in Afghanistan," the minister announced proudly.

Dan nodded. "It is a great group, Dev. We ran into them a few years ago in Kabul, and they were doing some good work."

"Hopefully, you protect them." Dev's glare was meant for the minister. He did remember the group. Dan and he had run into one of their teachers, a scared young woman from Philadelphia who had no language skills and no understanding of the danger for a little girl to just go to school under the threat of the Taliban.

"We can only do so much." That wasn't the answer Dev wanted to hear.

"So much is usually not enough, and it ends up with some young girl beat up, mutilated, raped, or killed. God's mercy is if they do murder her."

Lily dropped her fork at Dev's over-the-top factual statement. "At least they are doing something?"

Her elbow accidentally hit her husband's rib cage. "Ow, yes. Something, I guess, is better than nothing."

"You should come to our fundraiser. It's over the Fourth of July holiday. You'll learn more about the group and actually speak to those who have served over there. Of course, Dan and you have such personal observations. I'd love to hear about it, what you saw and did."

Lily could see Grant was trying, perhaps trying way too hard, to be amiable. Dev was having none of it. *Is this the same husband who was kidding me earlier today? What is under his skin?*

Now, Dan dropped his fork. He answered before Dev could do more damage. "It's hard to talk about all of that, Grant, besides, most of it is classified, and if we tell you we'd have to kill you."

Lily and Dan laughed. Dev took a drink of his bourbon. Grant took a drink of water. Dan had to do something about whatever the hell was going on. "Dev, I just saw Captain Garland over by the bar. We should say hello. Come on." He stood up. He ordered Dev to get up with his stiff stance, no words needed.

Dev immediately left his seat. "Right. We should say hello before he leaves. We'll be right back."

As soon as the duo departed, Grant took Dan's seat. "How are you, Lily? I've been worried about you."

Lily snorted. "That's a joke, right? If you have been worried, why didn't you call, email, or maybe even send an old-fashioned card?"

"You're right. I guess you kind of figured out tonight that I was seeing Marisa while we were engaged. I'm so sorry."

Lily folded her arms over her belly. It was nice to have a built-in shelf. "No, you're not. You never have been sorry until you were caught. Geez, I thought it was bad enough when you dropped me while my dad was dying. Now, you're admitting you were cheating on me too."

Grant began to touch her arm, but Lily moved her chair over slightly. "I explained to you at the time I just couldn't be there for you. Cancer bothered me."

"And I explained to you, that you were going to be an incompetent minister if you couldn't handle death. Death kind of goes with God, Grant. You should know that by now. Oh, and I'm pretty sure cheating doesn't place you on the good little minister's list either."

"Lily, I am so sorry. My first mistake was asking you to marry me."

Lily unfolded her arms, raising her hands to her mouth. "Finally, you are telling the truth. You are a real piece of work, and I cleaned that up. Why did you then?"

"Because you were such a good person. You really did turn my life around. You were sweet, honest, and so loving. I didn't deserve you, but you taught me so much. I asked you to marry me because I knew that's what you wanted. Besides, we had such fun together."

Lord, what did I ever see in this big baby? Thank you for giving me Dev. "Enough." Lily touched him for the first time, her hand touching the arm of his suit. "You had fun. It was what you wanted to do, your fun. My husband planned our wedding and our honeymoon, but he concentrated on places and things *I* love. He is unselfish and steady. If you're taking a path to an unknown destination, he's the one I want by my side. The past is the past. I have a wonderful life. You have a wonderful life. I won't allow you to make me feel bad about myself again."

"I never did that." He moved his face closer to hers so only she could hear.

Lily finally smiled. "No, I did. Shame on me. But because you walked away, I now have a wonderful husband, and I'm going to have a baby. And just to make you feel even better, I haven't shed a tear for you in years."

Grant's voice caught in his throat. "Good. I can see your husband is very protective."

"You have no idea how protective he can be. So," Lily cautioned, "It has been good to see you. Now, if we see each other again, we can just smile and be polite. Everything, and I mean everything is over."

The band saved Lily from any additional discussion. The bride and groom were heading to the center of the room. Lily turned to watch.

"They are going to have their first dance. She is lovely," Lily commented. Her back was to Grant. She took a deep breath, suddenly feeling a weightlifting. *I can't believe I wasted so much time mourning him.* "Grant, isn't she pretty?"

"Yes." He said nothing more. There was nothing more to say. Lily was indeed finished with him, and she had moved on with a child coming and a husband who was now standing behind them.

Dev placed his hand on Lily's shoulder, and she reached up to hold his. His blood pressure had stabilized. *What the heck happened to me?* Dan explained that his behavior was totally out of line. *But there's something about this guy, and it isn't just the fact that he almost married Lily.*

"Dev, what do you do for a living? Are you still in the military?"

The priest held his head in his hands as Grant asked the questions. *Here we go again.*

Dev looked down at Lily's former fiancé. "I do some things for the military, now and then, but I work for a government agency."

Dan looked up, surprised at Dev's response. He winked at his friend. *Well played, but why?*

"So just a bureaucrat, pushing papers?"

"Oh, he pushes all right!" Lily joked. "Honey, as soon as they do those special dances, can we dance? Then, I may be done. It's been a long day, and the baby and I need to go to bed."

"That sounds great. My wife is the lowest maintenance woman I know, so I usually do anything she wants. It's also great to be at a wedding with a woman who isn't in love with weddings, except for the cake. Do you know what I mean?" Dev didn't wait for an answer. "You know, Grant, it really has been great meeting you. As Dan explained I need to thank you for being such a jackass."

The priest's hands returned to hold his head. At first, Grant said nothing, and then he laughed. Lily, her back still to the minister, smiled lovingly up at her husband. *You do everything I want you to do? That's new.*

"You don't know how many times I threatened to track you down and tear you apart for how you treated her. But since you are a minister, and you are doing God's work, I've decided to allow you to keep breathing." Dev slowly lifted his glass and took a drink. He received the reaction of fear he wanted. Then he smiled. "Just kidding, Grant. It has been great to meet you, really."

Dan peeked out from his hands. There was nervous laughter all around. "Grant, Dev is a real funny man. You can relax."

Lily turned quickly. "Or can you?" She laughed so hard she released one of her now famous snorts. "Come on, we can dance now." Dev placed his glass on the table and shook the minister's hand.

"It really has been great meeting you." The couple walked onto the dance floor and vanished into the crowd.

"Well, that went better than I guess it could've gone." Grant needed something stronger than water, but he took a drink anyway.

"I'm assuming Lily and you talked." Dan was evaluating Grant on a different level after Dev expressed his concern about the man.

"We did. She is such a special person."

Dan turned to find his friends in the throng. "We all think so. We have a group of friends, and we are all very tight. When Dev brought Lily to meet us, we all just became a family. She is our soul."

"Says the priest," Grant joked.

"I'm not kidding. She made us whole. There is something about her."

"Yes." Grant saw the Pierces dancing.

"And we would do anything for her, at all costs."

Grant loosened his tie. "She is very lucky to have friends like you."

The priest nodded. *They were lucky to have her.* "You said something about a benefactor for the gala?"

"Yes, he is going to pay for the entire event. He's also making a substantial investment in the charity. We can talk about that Tuesday at the committee meeting."

"Good. As long as you are happy with everything. I know this means a lot to you."

"Actually, my wife is the one who told me about the girls in Afghanistan. I don't need to tell you about their plight because you've seen it firsthand, but she became involved after seeing a few news stories. Then she discovered that one of her brother's friends has been over there and is currently working with the charity in some capacity. It is such a worthwhile cause."

"Yes," Dan muttered as he watched Dev and Lily dance to a slow song. "So, was the brother's friend a teacher there?"

"I don't think so. I think he was an independent contractor of some kind. I know he worked for the good guys."

"There's been so many in Afghanistan and Iraq. Sometimes it is difficult to tell the good guys from the bad ones. Do you know where he was stationed?"

"I'm not sure. He dropped by the house the other day though. It was so informative to finally meet him. He'll be at the meeting Tuesday to tell us more about what we can do for the charity. His name is Brad Keeting. Have you heard of him?"

Dan stared into his empty glass. He needed another, but he shouldn't. *Damn, Dev is right again.* "No, I don't believe so, but I have a very poor memory. Maybe Dev knows the man. Did you say Brad Keeting?"

"Yes, that's right. He's such a nice guy."

"And he dropped by your house just the other day?" Dan smiled as Dev looked his way.

"Out of the blue. Of course, I'd already been working with the charity, but to actually meet someone who has done the work of God over there, was the best. I learned so much."

"Did he put you in touch with this new benefactor?"

"Well, yes, he did. How did you know that, Father?"

Dan chose his words carefully. "Just a lucky guess." This would be one meeting he wouldn't attend, but he'd be watching. It was time to call a friend. "Sorry, Grant. I have to take this call." Dan grabbed his cell phone and pretended to answer. "Hold on. I need to take this. Tell Dev and Lily I'll be back as soon as I can."

The minister nodded as he was left alone at the table. Finally, he was feeling as though his ministry had a purpose. The priest seemed very interested. He knew the other ministers and priests would be just as impressed. He still remained an outsider even though he had been in Fredericksburg almost three years now, but this would shine a light on his mission doing God's work. Besides, it was one thing Marisa and he could share. God only knew how little they did share.

Grant found Lily on the dance floor with her husband. They looked very happy, maybe mismatched, but apparently, they had something in common. He couldn't believe she had left her shop back in Kansas City for some government guy who shuffled papers. *Why didn't he re-locate? His job is no big deal. That shop was her life, her parents' legacy, and she gave it all up for him?*

Marisa wouldn't give up that much for him. She hated the obligatory minister's-wife-must-attend church meetings, and she wouldn't even stay awake to greet him when he arrived home tonight. Of course, it would be late. He pulled out his own phone and pressed one button.

"Hi babe. I'm going to be leaving this reception in five. Can I stop by?" He waited for the answer he needed to hear. "I can't wait to see you."

Dan arrived back at the table. Grant ended his call quickly. "Everything all right?"

Dan nodded. "It all will be."

"Well, now I'm the one who had a call. I need to get going. I have a very ill church member who needs a few prayers. I told her I would stop by on my way home. Please let Lily know I said goodbye."

"Of course. I'll offer a few prayers too for the woman."

"What woman?"

Dan's eyebrow raised. "The woman who is ill, the one you are going to visit?"

Grant faintly smiled. "Oh yes. Sometimes I truly believe I'd lose my head if it weren't connected to my body."

The minister scurried away. Dan took a drink of water. He motioned a server for a cup of coffee, or two. Now, he needed to get Dev alone, away from Lily. *Grant, buddy, you have no idea how close you are to having your head separated from your body on a permanent basis.*

"Where did the minister go?" Lily tapped Dev on the arm as he asked Dan.

"He had an emergency, well he said he did. I don't believe him, but it doesn't matter. Devlin, I need to talk to you."

Father Dan's seriousness gave Lily grave concern. "What about? What's wrong?"

"Nothing. I want to go down memory lane, and there's a couple of guys over by the bar who know Dev and wanted to see him."

Lily looked straight into his eyes. "You need coffee, and I don't believe you, Danny."

Diversion was needed right about now. "Look, Lily, they are going to cut the cake. I hear it's a white cake with some sort of white chocolate and cream cheese filling." Dan pointed at the five-tiers of decorated goodness.

It was as though she was in a trance, Lily following his finger, walking toward cake. As soon as she was gone, Dev sat down.

"That'll hold her until she gets a piece. You can't get between Lily and a good wedding cake. What's up?"

"You make me crazy."

Dev checked Dan's empty glass. "You do need some coffee."

"It's coming, but so is the second coming of our Lord Jesus Christ, and for some that needs to come sooner than later."

The coffee arrived. As soon as the server retreated, Dev wanted answers. "What the hell is wrong with you?"

"God Boy is a problem. I'm not sure what all is going on, but this benefactor for the charity has an associate. He is a friend of the minister's wife's brother. The man was just at his house a few days ago, and he will be at this ecumenical meeting we have on Tuesday."

"Fine. A bunch of ministers and priests get together on Tuesday night, and is there a joke in here?"

"You could say that my friend. It is a very sick joke. I've called in reinforcements."

Dev's eyes were tiny slits, concentrating on the nervous upper lip of his friend. "Danny? Should I be worried?"

"I hate it when you are right, absolutely hate it. You are a damn Boy Scout always prepared." Dan stopped rambling and touched his friend's arm. "Brad Keeting is the associate, and I can only take a wild guess as to who the benefactor is. This means they knew Lily used to be engaged to that idiot."

"Khalid. The box was just to get my attention, now we begin to play the game. Who are the reinforcements?"

"You aren't going to like this."

Dev raised his eyes to the ceiling. "Oh, no. Don't say Ari and my brother are here."

Dan cocked his head to the right playfully. "Well, that went well."

Now Dev was the one who held his head in his hands. He only hoped there was a long line for cake.

Chapter Twelve

"You are awfully quiet," Lily commented. She hadn't heard one word out of her husband since they took the ramp onto Interstate 95. He usually had something to say if she were driving in Northern Virginia traffic, and he was sitting in the passenger seat. *He didn't have that many drinks, did he?* She noticed Dev and Danny huddled as though they were going over secret offensive plays for this year's Army-Navy game. They were all smiles and no conversation, and they were drinking coffee when she returned with her second piece of cake.

She knew something was off when Dev commented how nice the bridesmaids' dresses were, and Dan admitted that color looked good on all of the women. That's when she asked her husband to go get her another piece of cake. "It'll look like you're getting your first piece, honey, please." She didn't even have to beg him or make a deal that she would walk a mile tomorrow. He rose and walked quickly over to the cake. Alone with the priest, she thought he might open up. Instead, the cleric commented on the song the band was playing. She had played along. But something was definitely off.

Now her husband was quiet. She concentrated on her driving. "Make sure I get the right exit, Dev." Still nothing. She thought she heard a positive grunt. Ten minutes later he did tell her to turn on the next exit.

"Honey, are you drunk?"

"What? No, I'm fine. I guess I'm just tired."

He's thinking. I have no idea what he is thinking about, but his mind is somewhere else. "Dev, I'm thinking about leaving you." *That should make him open his mouth.*

"Fine, honey. I think that's great."

Something was definitely wrong. "Ari and I have planned this escapade for months. He is taking me to Casablanca. He whistled, and I decided I just had to go with him."

"I am listening, Lily. Ari, really?"

The road was familiar to Lily by now. They'd be home in a matter of minutes. "So, it was okay to say I was thinking of leaving you?"

"Sure. You can think about it, but you won't do it." His monotone answer concerned her more than his previous silence.

"Are you going to tell me what is going on?"

Dev glanced at his wife, his pregnant wife. Paris had been an adventure, mixed with a little danger, but this, whatever this was, could be a matter of life and death. She was in the crosshairs because of Khalid's hatred of him. He had done this to her. She was innocent, but she would serve the sentence. "We need to talk when we get home. If you aren't too tired."

"I knew it," Lily yelled. "There is something going on.

It's Grant, isn't it? There is something going on with him. He just isn't an idiot jerk, he's a criminal too." She seemed delighted in her delusion.

Dev relaxed as she ranted. She made him laugh even in the most difficult situations. "Lily."

"What? Can I put the handcuffs on him? That would make me so happy. Perhaps you could take him to Guantanamo for some reason? Am I making you laugh finally?"

He reached over and rubbed her shoulder. "Yes, honey, I'm laughing. Thanks."

"How can I help you and your team of secret agents save the world, yadda, yadda?"

"I'm thinking." Well, she already knew that.

Dev was talking as they headed to bed. It was small talk, but Lily would take that for now. Dev had checked his cell phone several times. As she was dressing for bed, she heard him texting. He was conversing with someone.

Dev had finally changed for bed and was brushing his teeth when Lily positioned herself on the edge of the bed. She had dressed perfectly for a conversation with her husband. He turned off the bathroom light and walked slowly into the bedroom.

"Can we just go to a later Mass in the morning? I'm really beat." He finally lifted his head to see his lovely wife, in her Scooby-Doo pajamas. "What the holy--"

"You don't like these sexy gems?" She stood up, modeling the clothing in front of him. "What do you think, Shaggy?"

Dev shook his head but smiled. "Velma or Daphne?"

She grasped his hand and led him to the bed. "Neither. Shaggy and Scooby. They solved the mysteries. Do you want to be Shaggy? I really want to be Scooby. We could use them as our code names." Dev gave her a little shove to help her into the bed.

"Lily, I need to tell you a lot. I'm thinking about how we can play this."

"So, the game is afoot, Sherlock?" Lily reached over to grab her moisturizer. In these pajamas, the cream could only be used on her hands. *Even my hands are dry! This baby is sucking every oil out of my body.*

"Your ex thinks Brad Keeting is a great guy, and we, Dan and I believe that the benefactor of his charity and that party he is so proud of is--"

She closed her eyes. "Don't tell me. Let me guess. It is Khalid. Khalid is definitely here."

"Danny told me tonight that Ari saw him at an embassy event. He's a diplomat of some kind with immunity."

She disregarded his statement completely. Lily opened her eyes wide. "My boyfriend, Ari, is here?"

Dev frowned. "You look way too happy. Yes, Ari is here

and so is my brother. Can you believe he made Dad take a vow of secrecy?"

Lily touched her husband's face. Dev's concern was intense. *What isn't he telling me?* She scooted over. She grabbed his arm and physically maneuvered it around her. "Just tell me."

"I told you that box was addressed to you. Brad Keeting weaseled his way into your ex's life, into this charity that apparently is his whole world right now. There's been a lot of research going on, and it hasn't been focused on any of us. It's all been on you."

Lily sidled up until there was not one inch of space between their bodies. She could hear his heart beating just a little faster than usual. He was worried, but only for her. "You figure out a plan, and we will go with it. I'll do whatever I need to do, besides, this will give me something to think about besides what labor pains feel like."

Dev held her tighter. "Have you figured out how to breeze through those yet?"

"Nope. This baby's birth may be the one thing I can't control."

Tenderly, Dev reached over, laying his hand over their baby. "I am so sorry. I have no words to tell you how much I wish I had never brought you into my world."

Lily placed her hands over his. He was crying. Her heart couldn't take it. He removed his hand to wipe at his face.

"Babe, I have an idea."

"Good, because I have nothing. We all need to meet over at Dad's tomorrow. What's your thoughts?"

"I talked to Abby the other day. Gretchen and she want to come for a visit. They want to decorate the baby's room for me."

"But," Dev interrupted. She placed her finger on his lips.

"Just listen. We will allow them to come and do their magic. You can't stop a speeding train like Gretchen. She's been bugging me ever since I missed her in Kansas City. You know she wants to see how large I've gotten. Yay me! So, we let them come, they decorate, and then--"

Dev was hanging on her every word. "And then what?"

"Then we set Khalid up with Gretchen. She'll talk him to death. She'll tell him that story about that sailor in Hawaii, and how they used those doughnuts, malasadas, to do something between two consenting adults. He won't be able to take the immoral visuals. One terrorist will be gone within, what two days? Do you think he could last that long if she wore those leather pants with the cheetah print tunic? Her cleavage in that top is unbelievable."

Dev's hold relaxed. "I give him less than a day if she adds those stilettos."

"That's a given with Gretchen, honey. You should know better, Mr. Delicious."

Dev kissed her soundly. "I'm beat, or I would be showing you just how delicious I am."

"I have a post-it note over by the bed. I'll schedule it for when you are available?"

"You do that, but somehow, some way I'll remember. Goodnight, honey." He kissed her again, turned out the last light and was asleep when his head hit the pillow. Lily wished she had learned her slumber skills from the Army.

Lily had a kicking baby and many thoughts in her head. Dev had changed her life, had given her a life that made her feel whole. There wasn't a morning, even when she threw up, when she doubted her decision to be with him. As long as the baby was going to keep her awake, she might as well think. She needed to make a list. She needed more post-its. *So, Khalid researched me? Maybe it's time I research him. I bet he's never gone against a wedding florist before! If she could become friends with Gretchen Malloy, she could defeat a terrorist*

Chapter Thirteen

1. Bring the lasagna
2. Bring my stomach med
3. Maintain complete Zen-like calm
4. Smile
5. Just keep my mouth shut for once!
6. Prepare for Saturday's wedding at the vineyard

By the time Lily and Dev arrived at Jack Pierce's home, there were several cars parked in the drive, but there was one spot left for the pregnant woman. "I love your dad." Lily pointed at the makeshift sign with an arrow marking the spot. "For pregnant women only. Unless JT has a secret he has been hiding, that's for me."

"His pecs are getting huge," Dev joked.

When they came into the house, the silence was frightening. The couple took their food to the kitchen and lined their additions to the countertop already filled with salad, bread, pasta and assorted meats and cheeses. She heard murmurs from the den, Jack's throne and makeshift psychiatric office. Dev had already passed by her and headed that way.

The room full of men was louder when he made his appearance in the doorway, and then Lily heard several comments that turned her fear and apprehension into calm and acceptance. "Where's Lily? I only came to see her. Hey, where's my sister-in-law? How's she doing? You did bring her, didn't you? I'm not staying if she isn't here. She has to be part of this."

"Calm down, I'm here." She walked slowly into the room and bowed as far as she could. She extended her arms out around her growing circumference. "Is this what you wanted to see?"

The first to greet her was Ari. He embraced her with arms wrapped tenderly around her back. "You have never looked so beautiful, my dear friend."

"And it is good to see you alive."

"I'm alive too, and I'm your brother-in-law. There should be a little love for me." Jackson kissed her softly on the cheek. "I can't wait to be an uncle. Congratulations."

Jackson held Lily's left hand, and Ari held her right one. They both looked so appropriately different, not the suave super agents with tux and bow ties. Rather, they looked like they were at home on a Sunday evening. The rest of the team was there too. Each one was casual, but Lily could see a difference in each one of their personas. JT was more serious than usual. Dan, attired in street clothes, was stone cold, and Paul had the greatest transformation. His usually soft grey eyes were distant. Dev was popping his watch band. Paul twisted his wedding ring.

Paul hugged Lily as though she were a piece of very rare china. "Jill is working tonight, or she'd be here, Lily.

She wants you to call her tomorrow to tell her how you are doing. She has a few helpful pregnancy hints."

"I can use any hints she has. Believe me." Lily looked around the room full of men. "All of you look like you need to eat something, and I know I do," Lily announced. "Let's eat before you do whatever you are going to do." Her father-in-law gently touched her shoulder.

"Lily, you should go first. You are eating for two."

She smiled in an attempt to lighten the mood of the undead. "This is the best time of my life. I have permission to eat for two. I should've gotten pregnant years ago." Jack smiled, but the remainder of the men were somber. *Wow, tough room.*

After quiet conversation and several updates on what each one was doing, the group began their meeting. Lily took a back seat near Jack. She watched the team, plus Ari and Jackson, begin the planning of reconnaissance, and the plans for information sharing. She listened. She saw with clarity what she always knew to be true. Dev was in charge. The Boy Scout finalized the decisions; he was the moral conductor. Not even the priest held that title. Even Jackson and Ari bent to his orders. It was a study in leadership. But something, that little voice nagged at her. *Don't say anything, Lily, just listen and watch. Nope, I've got to say something.*

"Gentlemen." Her one word stopped Dev in mid-sentence.

"What, honey?"

"Could someone explain to me why Khalid has taken such an interest in waging some sort of historic vendetta against Dev? I mean this is an international smuggler, drug lord, and terrorist. Why is he worried about some DEA agent in Northern Virginia and his very pregnant wife? Inquiring minds, like this one, want to know."

Jack Pierce reached over to hold her hand. "You know, Lily does have a point. Dev, what put you and maybe all of the rest of us on his radar?"

"Dad, I told you about Paris," Jackson interjected quickly.

The older Pierce shook his head. "No, I don't buy it. He got everything he wanted, well except that one art thief who is still alive."

"Bernard Notte," Lily whispered. *I wonder when he is going to pop up? It would be just my luck that I go to the store one day, and there he is standing in the cereal aisle. I know his son is still in prison.*

Dev stood silent. Ari attempted an explanation. "You know Khalid killed my wife and little girl. He is a sick man. He can't leave it on the battlefield."

Paul stood up. "None of us can leave it on the battlefield, Ari, but you don't see any of us plotting the murder of our adversaries."

"But we are." Dev's three words lingered in the air. "I'll say it. We all know it goes back to Afghanistan, and then beyond. After that first encounter with him, and all the subsequent missions when we were just one step behind him as he massacred old men, children," he paused and looked toward his wife, "and pregnant women. He has torn up pieces of the world. He has killed dreams. He is the devil personified."

Lily put her hand up for Dev's attention. It wasn't as if she was still in a classroom, but she needed more information. She suddenly had acquired everyone's attention. Besides, she needed to lighten the moment.

"Excuse me, but why is he specifically involving all of you? I mean, did you steal his goat, or blow up his favorite bomb maker? Why isn't he going after some SEAL team or a Ranger, or some specific general?" Her questions only garnered somber faces, no smiles, and no laughs.

"It's been done, Lily. You just didn't hear about it." JT lifted his glass of ginger ale for a drink. "It was done over there, but last year, three members of a specific SEAL team were killed in Virginia Beach. The newspapers were told that the shooter was a disgruntled civil servant. The truth was they were killed with a bomb. The signature of the bomb maker was a terrorist from Syria. A general outside of Ft. Hood was killed. He was targeted by the son of a Taliban leader. There are more, but Khalid gets his kicks from all of this. He knows Dev is a straight-shooter, and we all have a history with the maniac. But we are going to fight back."

Lily shivered at JT's statement. "Is the history too long to tell me? A little background might be helpful."

Now Lily's words lingered. All eyes focused on Dev Pierce, the unflappable DEA agent who was now twisting his own wedding ring. Lily watched as his hand stroked nervously through his hair.

"She's right, Dev," Ari said quietly. "You need to tell her, but maybe later? Lily, would that be sufficient, if your husband tells you privately?" His eyes were almost pleading.

"Yes, of course. Dev?"

Dev nodded. "Later will be good. Now, are we good on what we have decided so far?"

There was a unanimous affirmative answer, almost as though they were affirming a direct order. The team looked over a few documents Ari had acquired before Dan announced that he needed to get back to the rectory. He had an early day to start the week. JT kissed Lily on the cheek and followed Dan out. Ari and Jackson had work to do downtown at one of the embassies, and no one questioned what exactly that work would entail.

Paul helped Lily in the kitchen when he received a phone call. "Yes, I'm her husband. She's at work tonight. What? When? Where have they taken her? How serious is it?"

Lily grabbed Paul's hand. Something was desperately wrong with Jill. "I'll be there as soon as I can. Dev, it's started. Jill has been hurt. I've got to go."

"Dev, you have to go with him," Lily ordered. "I'll stay here tonight with your dad."

Paul was exiting the house, but Dev ran after him. He looked back at his wife. "Are you sure?" Lily nodded. "I'll call you as soon as I know something." The car was pulling away, with Dev driving, before Jack Pierce could get to the front door to close it. He firmly locked the deadbolt.

"Well, it's just the two of us now, Lily. Let me tell you a little about what I know. Let's get me a glass of wine, and you--"

"I would like, well, I'd really like a rum runner, but I'll take a strawberry soda straight on the rocks."

"Coming right up." Jack joined her in the kitchen and began to prepare their drinks. "How about over ice cream instead?"

Lily felt like a child, clapping her hands in approval. "Yes, please." She poured his wine while he concocted her ice cream soda. They returned to the den. Jack took his position in his recliner, Lily kicked off her sandals and positioned her feet up on the couch.

"I've never been afraid of any of them," Lily began, "but tonight, I could see just how lethal they could be. I looked around and saw JT as this huge machine of war. He has muscles upon muscles. Paul became a quiet mercenary; Dan reminded me of a loose cannon. You would never know what could set him off. Jackson truly looked every bit the FBI agent in search of the criminal, and Ari was a cold-blooded international spy."

"And your husband? What did you see tonight?"

Lily swiped away a tear. "I saw a little boy who grew up in the United States. He thinks it is the best country in the world. He grows up to be a soldier and a good man. I know he is very good at what he does, but I saw something else tonight. I saw a leader. I saw an unrelenting warrior who will protect those he loves with his life. I'm afraid that I will lose him physically, or to those thoughts that he never shares."

"Ah. Dev will tell you everything, I hope. I know a little. It happened very early in the war. Khalid was a leader in Afghanistan working with the United States to defeat the Taliban. But he had other ideas. JT was with his SEAL team. There was this little girl--"

Chapter Fourteen

"Lily is sound asleep on the couch." Jack Pierce opened the door to his son. "How is Paul's wife?"

"She survived surgery and is in intensive care at George Washington Hospital. Paul's mom brought the youngest daughter. I called some friends to check on the one girl in college. She flies in tomorrow. We don't know much more than that, not even what happened."

Dev continued walking through the house until he stood over his sleeping wife. He adjusted the throw that his father had placed on her. He needed to tell her how beautiful she was when she was asleep. *When she isn't talking.* He grinned. *What am I going to do with her?* He wanted to kiss her senseless.

"Do you want some coffee?" Jack whispered. "I made a pot about thirty minutes ago."

"I'd love some. You have any eggs and bacon?"

"Sure do. Sit down, and I'll fix you something. You look like hell."

Dev rubbed his chin. He needed a shave. "Thanks, Dad."

"Jackson apparently found out where they had taken

Paul's wife. The Israeli gentleman and Jackson took Paul's car there. Did you see them?"

"Yes. They dropped by. We all made Paul drink some coffee and eat something." Dev rubbed his eyes. He hadn't been this tired and worried in a long time, but there was no controlling the situation they were in now.

"That was some kind of a meeting of the minds." Jack was already cracking an egg into a skillet.

"This is all so unbelievable. First, our names are let out by some government official, printed in one of the largest newspapers in the world, then Khalid appears at some embassy party, Lily sees her ex after all these years, and he thinks a thug like Brad Keeting is amazing. The minister is an idiot."

The bacon began to sizzle. "We all knew that. He left Lily."

"You know, Dad, I always wondered who made her feel so bad about herself. Maybe some family member made her doubt her worth, but I'm pretty sure that guy is the main reason. When I met her, and sometimes she still falls back into it, she was so confident in her work, but personally she was a mess."

The father turned around to face his son. "You didn't help when you left her, when you couldn't figure out what was right in front of you."

Dev took a sip of hot coffee. "That's on me, yes. I try to make up for it each and every day. Now, I'm bringing this on her. My past is going to hurt her."

"You did nothing wrong. It was war."

Dev could still see the young girl's face. She clutched the book he had just given her. Her eyes were glowing. She was still smiling as the bullet found its target in the middle of her forehead. She fell dead. He had turned around, gun ready, and met Khalid as the enemy for the first time. Khalid yelled for him to go, that this was his country, his people. Dev had wondered about Khalid's loyalty on several occasions, but the commanders thought he could be trusted. Until he couldn't be.

"I gave her a book," Dev whispered. "Her crime was she was a little girl who loved books, who loved to read. She wanted to be a teacher."

Jack placed the plate in front of his son, placing an arm around his broad back. That back held all the worries that his son conveniently kept hidden within. Jack was comforting a grown adult who was still his little boy. "And your mom gave you that book. You packed it in your bag when you left for West Point. You hid it away in your duffle bag when you headed over there. That poor book was in bad shape."

"But not to that little girl. It was her everything, and Khalid took it all away. He took away her life and her freedom."

Jack released his embrace. He poured himself another cup of coffee and sat across from his son. "This man is a psychopath. Why the heck is he taking the time to bother you?"

Dev's fork hit his plate. "Dad, he holds me, and my team responsible for the loss of his brother."

"Again, I'll repeat, it was war. But are you all responsible?"

Dev's eyes looked down as he remembered that day. "Yes. His brother was a teenager, a teenager who banded with the Taliban. When he pointed a gun straight at us, I took him out before he could kill my team and the family we were visiting."

Jack Pierce said nothing. This was the first time he had heard this part of the story. He knew Dev and the guys had struck up a friendship with a family. They had eaten in their house and had played with their children.

"So why now? Why has he waited all these years to find you?"

Dev took a couple of bites before answering. "Because now I have an Achilles heel, and she's sleeping in the den."

"Ah." Jack Pierce had complete understanding. "So, he's been watching you all this time?"

Dev shook his head. "No. I just think it was pure coincidence. Perhaps we just all happened to be on the same plane, flying to Paris. He had been following me once we arrived. He saw Lily and knew immediately how he could hit me. It's Shakespearean for him, the retribution. He has played his hand with Paul's wife. He is escalating." Dev paused. He began to look around the house. "Dad, you need to be careful too. I want all these windows checked. Make sure you tell your postman to leave the deliveries in the driveway or near the box, not at the door. Danny and I will come over and update the security system."

"No, Dev, I'm not going to live like a victim. I'm too old for that crap. If something happens to me, I've had a great life."

"Jack Pierce, you have to be here for this baby." Lily entered the kitchen. "Don't even think that you won't be here, mister. I need you. Who is going to take me to my doctor's appointment? Who is going to take me out for pie after said appointment? Who is going to treat me like a queen? If I don't have you, I only have the mother hen over there." She pointed at her husband. "That is just not acceptable. You will allow them to do their security thing. You will be careful. You will take this seriously. But you will live your life. I'm going to live my life, and Khalid will not win. What time is it?"

Dev looked at his watch. "It's almost four in the morning."

"Is that breakfast on your plate? Why didn't anyone wake me?" She stared at her father-in-law. "I could go for breakfast."

As if he had been shot out of a cannon, Jack jumped out of his seat. "What would you like, Lily? Dev had eggs and bacon, but I can make you a waffle, pancakes, french toast, whatever you'd like."

"Wait a minute," Dev interrupted. "You only offered me eggs and bacon. I didn't know french toast was an option. Why does she get choices?" He pointed indignantly at his smiling wife.

"Because she is the incubator for my grandchild." One sentence closed Dev's mouth.

"Well, there is that," he muttered. Lily came to his side and kissed the top of his head.

"Yes, there is that. I'm thinking french toast and sausage. Jack, do you have sausage, patties, not links? I love those patties. The baby does too."

Dev watched the scene as Lily continued to discuss food. If his father didn't want to fix french toast, frozen waffles sounded fine as long as he had whipped cream. Apparently, the baby preferred whipped cream on top of waffles. *Who knew that my baby prefers whipped cream to syrup? Lily, only Lily. I have to do everything to keep her safe even if that means I have to kill a man in cold blood and serve the rest of my life in prison. I will. I will do anything, Khalid. It is time to look the devil in the eye for the final time.*

"Dev? Dev?"

His head shot up. His father was calling his name.

"Do you want some french toast too? I'm apparently making sausage patties as well."

"Sure. Yes, Dad. I need some more coffee too. I have to go to work in a couple of hours." He looked at his watch again. Monday morning was here. Lily hugged his shoulders, leaning her head beside his cheek. Dev looked at his wedding ring as he reached up to touch one of her hands. *It's time to end this war.*

Chapter Fifteen

1. Have my go bag packed
2. Assure Dev I'll be fine
3. Check in with Paul and Jill
4. Contact bride to set timeline

"Dev's aunts look identical," JT commented as Lily and he took a short walk to their destination at the vineyard.

"Well, they did in that photo you saw on the wall, but now you can tell them apart. Dev's dad said he always knew who was who. He also says that the two of them couldn't stand each other until a few years ago."

"That sounds about normal for siblings, especially twins."

Lily rubbed her stomach. *Hmm, siblings? How about it, baby? Do you want a little brother or sister? We'll talk later.* "So, when I first met Maggie, she was pushing me to help her out here. The Pierces can be very persuasive, but that was before Dev asked me to marry him. Last year, Maureen's husband took a position near the vineyard. Maggie was feeling overwhelmed with the success she was having between the wine and the booked events so Maureen stepped up to assist with the vineyard. Maggie still has a manager who knows all things wine, but Maureen is a phenomenal businesswoman in her own right. What's more important is that Maggie trusts her. Dev's dad helped here and there, especially this past fall. Once I ended up here, it was hard to say no to the family business."

JT snickered. "They keep pulling you back into the wedding business?" Lily handed him flowered initials as he climbed the ladder near the ceremony location.

His attempt at an Al Pacino imitation fell on deaf ears. Lily scrunched her nose. "JT, why exactly are you here with me?" Lily asked her question as she shielded her eyes from the sun. She was watching from the bottom of the ladder while JT hung the monogram on an oak tree. The tree shaded the wedding ceremony arbor by the pond on Aunt Maggie's property. It was the perfect location for vows, with just a short walk to the reception barn.

"Tell me if this isn't straight before I get down, will you? You know why I'm here with you. Dev was called out of town, and he insisted, well, demanded that you have someone with you at all times. I'm staying through tomorrow. Next up on the schedule is Jackson. He's coming over to spell me, and he'll be with you until Wednesday when Dev returns. Is this straight?"

"Yes. It's perfect, the flowers, not the situation. I'm a big girl. I think Dev is going a little crazy over all of us. What are you swatting at?" JT's hands were flailing away over his head.

He descended quickly. "Damn bees. Those flowers are drawing them. What's next, boss?"

"I think we are good. That's the only thing we needed to do for the florist. Now we just wait until the guests begin to arrive. You think Dev is going a little crazy, don't you?"

JT folded the ladder and carried it with one arm. "Yes and no. I get it, but I don't understand it. Truthfully, I've never been in love with someone as much as he is with you."

Lily held onto his other arm. "That was awfully sweet of you to say."

"No, it's the truth. The Boy Scout is lethal when love is involved. I've seen him when he thought he was just in like a lot and that was awful. You, lady, are on a totally different level."

The baby kicked. Lily stopped walking.

"Is the baby coming? Oh my God, the baby is coming." JT began to panic. "Who should I call? What do I need to do?"

Lily grabbed his arm tightly. "Stop. Let me breathe. The baby is not coming. He's just kicking."

JT's jaw dropped. "It's a boy?"

"Will you stop jumping to conclusions! Sometimes I call the baby he, and sometimes he is a she. It's just the pronoun I used today. I have months to go."

"No, you said it's due in August."

Lily breathed deeply. "Yes, and it is only the end of May. Just chill. Geez, you are such a nervous Nelly. Were you this way when you were in the Navy?"

"No. I know warfare. I don't know love, women, or babies. Let's get you up to the house and off of those." He pointed down to her Miss Piggy feet.

"You order me around like Dev does, except you don't growl." Lily continued to waddle to the main house.

JT grinned. "Do you want me to growl? I can do that very well, Sweet Pea."

"Nope. This is a wedding day. We need to be happy."

JT assisted her up the few steps. "I don't like weddings."

"Keep that to yourself, please," she whispered. Lily pulled a post-it note out of her pocket as she took a breather on the porch. "Do you know that your dear crazy friend, my husband, put this note on my belly the morning he left?"

"Do I want to know what it says?" JT opened the door.

"It's fine. It just said he loves me." Lily giggled.

"And you are okay with him posting it on your belly?" JT could see Dev's writing on the small note.

"Yes, I love a man who uses post-its in the right places and can plan any attack. As they entered the house, Lily heard wailing. The sound, a mix of disappointment and desperation, was coming from the bride's suite. The bridal party was dressing there, preparing for the early photos.

"What on earth?" Aunt Maggie asked Lily as they met in the foyer.

"We just got in here." Lily looked up the steps as though it was a mountain too tall to hike.

"I'll go up. Go rest." Aunt Maggie headed up the stairs. Lily and her companion headed to the nearest sofa and chair.

JT forced her over to the couch. Lily sat, and JT lifted her legs for her.

"You will stay here. I'll go get you some water. I'll also get your bag so you can forage for your snacks. I know you brought them. Are you still going through chocolate like a visitor to Hershey?"

Lily blushed. *Holy Moly, JT knows me too well.* "Nope. Now it is salt, but I really have to watch it or I end up with the inflatable ankles."

JT soon returned with a cold water bottle and her bag. He marveled at her packing skills as she removed another pair of shoes, a shirt, a pair of what looked to be shorts, a brush, a makeup bag, and finally, a bag of chips. "I knew I had it in here. I have another one. Do you want it?"

"I don't eat that crap," JT commented. He emptied his water bottle in two gulps.

"I don't eat that crap," Lily mimicked. "You seem to forget I have seen you on Army-Navy game day. You eat plenty of crap."

"That's different. You eat garbage during a football game."

Lily ended the discussion, sticking her tongue out at her friend.

Aunt Maggie walked into the room, holding a bouquet in her hands. "Lily, the bride says this bouquet isn't right, that it isn't what she wanted. Can you do anything to save this?"

The bouquet was made of all white roses. It was pretty but very vanilla. Lily looked at the construction. "I can tear it apart and start over, but I don't know what she wants."

"Honey, she is desperate. I'll bring her down to explain it. You just stay here with your legs up." She left the bouquet in Lily's hands.

"I wonder why she didn't ask me to fix it?" JT could barely get the statement out of his mouth as he began laughing.

Lily rolled her eyes and lowered her legs. "I can't be lounging here when the bride comes in, and you, you remain quiet. That is an order, SEAL."

"Ma'am, yes ma'am." He saluted her quickly. He would remain quiet. He would be her handyman and her runner, but he would be a mute handyman and runner.

JT stood out of habit as the bride entered the room. Her mascara had run down her face. One of her lashes was hanging off to the side. Her lipstick was smudged. She looked more like a woman who had been out all night in Las

Vegas rather than a bride two hours before her impending wedding ceremony.

"Lily, I have a photo of what I wanted it to look like." She handed the paper to the pregnant ex-florist. Lily looked over the design.

"You wanted more flowers in here than just the roses?"

The bride nodded her head. "It is supposed to look like a garden bouquet. I just wanted a few white roses, not this. I wanted the bouquet to look like the table decorations in the barn. I don't know why the florist did this. Can you do something, please?"

Her pleas were not ignored. She sat next to Lily, more tears freely flowing. Lily patted her leg. "It's going to be fine. Anything will be better, right?" As soon as the bride nodded, Lily knew she could work it out, with the help of one of the Navy's finest.

"You go upstairs and get ready. I'll take care of this."

As soon as the bride departed, Lily gathered her team of two. "JT, I want you to go to the barn and grab three of the table pieces. I'll need those. Maggie, I need any supplies you have such as wire, tape, clippers, anything. I'll also need a table here to work on, maybe some paper on the floor? It'll be easier for me to just work from the sofa, if that's okay?"

"Of course, honey. I'll get those supplies, and I have a tarp I can spread out. JT, move that table over there in front of Lily." JT did as he was told. He headed over to the barn and returned with four arrangements, just in case. Aunt Maggie had a box with various supplies.

"Oh wow, you even have some wire cutters," Lily exclaimed. JT marveled at how she began to work. She dismantled the entire bouquet. She picked through the blooms of the arrangements for the needed flowers. Once she was finished rifling through the table pieces, she began to assemble the bride's bouquet.

"JT, you can take these flowers back to the barn."

"I can't even see where you took the flowers out." JT picked them up from the table.

Lily smiled. "That's the idea."

By the time JT returned to the house for further direction, Lily was almost finished. She was wrapping the bouquet with the satin ribbon that had been on the original.

"That's beautiful, but I know nothing about flowers." He couldn't believe how rapidly she could completely change everything about that bouquet. Lily never became nervous. She was unflappable. *She's a secret weapon.*

Dev's aunt agreed with JT and soon brought the bride back down to Lily. When she returned, her wide smile gave Lily the answer she needed. "That's it. It is perfect. How did you do that? You have saved my day, Lily."

"Wonderful, now finish getting ready." Lily brushed it off like it was just one of those things. Well, it was. *I used to do this all day long. It really isn't a big deal, but to her I guess it is.*

Now that the crisis was averted, the bride and Maggie left JT and Lily alone. JT moved Lily's makeshift worktable over into the corner for a later clean up. Lily pulled peanut butter and cheese crackers out of her bag and began nibbling.

"You really can't help yourself, can you?"

"Rrut?" Crumbs fell onto Lily's chest. *It's so nice to have my own dribble shelf.*

"You, you have to help. You love helping. Dev told us about you, but I really didn't believe him until I met you. You are as good as gold."

"JT, I can be awful. I have been mean to people along the way."

JT chuckled. "Right. Who have you been mean to? Was the guy trying to steal your purse?"

Lily placed her remaining crackers into a plastic bag and sealed it shut. "No. He was stealing my heart, and I sent him away."

JT landed with a thud in the chair. *What on earth was she talking about?* "Your awful former boyfriend?"

"No, I wasn't nasty to him until the other night. I have been mean to Gretchen the wedding coordinator. Not really mean, but I've been cold. But I was mean to Dev. I didn't believe that he cared for me. I just didn't think it was possible. I wanted him. I wanted everything he was offering. But I didn't think he was ready, and I guess I wasn't ready either. I just told him to go. And he did."

"He was an idiot." JT's answer surprised Lily. "Lily, he should never have left you. If I had been him, I would have opened that shop's door, kissed you soundly until you couldn't breathe, swept you up into my arms, and I would've given you any life you wanted." Lily was hanging on his every word. He had her exactly where he wanted her. "Then the music would've been playing, the jets would have flown over us, and we would've jumped on my Harley. The open road would've been our home, the love sustaining us." JT raised one brow as he watched her mouth gape open.

Lily rolled her eyes. "Geez, you had me until I realized you blended *An Officer And A Gentleman* with *Top Gun* and maybe a little of some old war movies, but how did you know he came to the shop that day when it happened?"

Damn, she caught everything. "Dev told us," he admitted. "He couldn't believe you told him to get lost. Man, you blew up his ego."

"Then, all that was left was the real Dev. That is the man I love." Lily winked at her companion. "I love you guys too, just differently."

"Thanks, Mom. Now, what else do we need to do?"

"We need to keep this shindig on time. The photographer should be with the men right now. If you could go back to the barn and make sure the cake is there, I'd really appreciate it. Also, check in with the caterer and our wine staff. They should have the large bar open by now. Finally, the parking valet area should be in place, ready for the guests. That's it."

"Dang. I used to think I was good at logistics, but you put me to shame. Going, boss. Call me on the cell if you need me." He stood to leave, but Lily called him back.

"Could you also make sure the officiant has shown up?"

JT saluted and was on his way. Lily pushed back on the sofa until her back was supported. She let out a sigh. Weddings were a ton of work. She didn't miss that part of her former life. *Poor JT. He is now a wedding coordinator. Watch out, Gretchen!*

Lily waited twenty minutes and headed out to the large porch. JT was running back from the parking area. "Everything is good, boss. The cake is here. The caterer and wine staff are ready and in place. The parking guys are good. Guests are coming. The photographer has been doing his thing, and he is ready. He says to tell you he didn't get to work with the girls because they weren't on time."

Lily nodded. "That's understandable. What about the minister?"

"He's right behind me, only I run faster." JT pointed back at the man in the suit walking toward them.

"Holy Moly," Lily said loudly. "I do not believe this." She was paralyzed.

"Can you believe this, Lily? You haven't seen me for years and then twice in one week?"

JT's head seemed to be on a swivel, looking at Lily first and then at the stranger. In his second look at Lily, a realization occurred. "God Boy?"

Her nod gave him the answer. As the man in the suit, a smile across his face, came nearer, JT's left hand clenched.

He took one step, then another, closer to a man he had only heard of in stories. He had hurt Lily, that was the story.

"You. You will stay ten feet away from her at all times." JT shoved the minister back. "You will not say anything to her unless you are spoken to. You will do your job today, and then you will leave as soon as possible. Is this understood?"

Grant smiled the smile that used to melt Lily's heart. He directed his attention to Lily. "You have a bodyguard now? Will you call your dog off?"

Lily looked over JT's head to answer. "He isn't a dog. He's a SEAL. I would do what he says, Grant. There's a lot of land out here where one could get lost, maybe never return. Just keep that in mind."

Grant's smile vanished. "What did I do to deserve this?"

"You are not to speak to her, man. I told you the rules." JT pushed his hands against the minister's chest.

"You wouldn't understand if I told you. JT, leave him alone." Lily remained on the porch; her arms folded. She could feel her hands begin to shake. She tucked them under her arms on top of the baby.

As JT backed away, he pushed one more time nearly sending Grant onto the ground. "Just do your job, preacher. I'm sure you have places to go after you marry this couple. You could go home or visit that little number you have on the side."

The minister was now the one paralyzed with fear. "Excuse me?" His voice quivered.

JT continued to walk toward Lily. "You heard me. You have places to be."

"Lily," Grant pleaded. "I need to talk to you. It's a matter of life or death."

"You always were melodramatic." JT joined her on the porch. They both looked down on the little man. "Remember that time you told me you had a criminal record? You claimed you were a reformed drug dealer? Geez, you had a parking ticket in front of a hospital."

"I can't talk about it right now, but I have to explain to you what is going on. I have to do this wedding, and then we have to talk. Please."

JT nudged Lily's shoulder. "He does grovel very well. From what I've discovered he juggles many items at one time too. I'll tell you about it later."

"Hmm, that sounds interesting." *What the heck, JT? What do you have on him?*

"Please, Lily."

Lily searched JT's eyes. He nodded his approval. "Fine, we, the three of us, will talk after the ceremony. Dev's aunt can make sure the reception runs smoothly."

Grant shook his head. "Does she hate me too?"

"She doesn't know anything about you." Lily looked at her watch. "You need to go to work. The ceremony is over there. The bride is upstairs in this house. The groom is by the barn. If you need anything, just yell, well actually, just ask nicely, and JT will get you anything you want." She pointed to the group of groomsmen speaking with some of the arriving guests. It was only thirty minutes before the ceremony would begin.

As Grant walked slowly away, Lily finally let out a huge breath. *Have I been holding my breath?* "JT, would you like to explain to me what all that was about?"

"No."

JT headed back into the house without offering any explanation. Lily followed on his heels. "JT, what was all that about?"

He stopped in his tracks abruptly. Lily ran smack into his back. JT turned and steadied her with his hands on each of her shoulders. "I was just having a bit of fun, but when we talk later, you need to be sitting down. Jackson and I have been doing a little research on your minister. Let me just say that we haven't told Dev."

"Why not?"

JT kissed her on the top of her head. His adopted little sister had no clue what her husband could be capable of doing when provoked, heck, even when he was nudged just the right way. "Because if Dev knew what we found out he'd kill the minister. We will allow him to live and use him as bait to pull in the big fish."

JT walked away from her toward the kitchen. Lily stood by the door, motionless. She cocked her head to the side, recounting some of the words that had just been thrown around. *Maybe Grant is in over his head? Maybe he hadn't lied all the time? What was that about a wife and something on the side? For once, I'm not the bait, not the little mouse waiting for the trap to close. Grant, get ready to squeal... squeak, squeak.*

Chapter Sixteen

The bride and groom kissed, the guests clapped, and everyone was happy, except one. Minister Grant Sharpe's happiness in front of the newly married couple faded quickly as he walked away from the scene. He had intended to visit at the reception, but he followed JT's lead to the side door of the house. He entered and saw Lily sitting at the large farmhouse kitchen table. She was eating grapes.

JT pulled out a chair opposite her and ordered him to sit. The SEAL sat next to Lily. "Let me begin. Sir, you have a problem, don't you?"

"Yes." With no emotion in his voice, Grant looked at Lily. "Lily, I don't know what you know or don't know, but I'm in trouble. I'm being blackmailed."

Lily leaned over and whispered in her friend's ear. "Is he really, or is he just being melodramatic?"

"He really is." JT's whisper was intentionally loud.

The minister sighed. "Yesterday, Brad Keeting came to my home. At first, we went over some of the details for the charity event. I was looking at a donation of one million dollars from our benefactor. I couldn't believe my good fortune. We could really do God's work with that money."

JT laughed. "And, tell her what was in it for you."

"Fine. Brad gave me an envelope filled with cash. He said it was for me, for all my good work. There was also a photo with the bills. He explained that there was fifty thousand dollars in there, and a photograph of my friend."

JT extended his hand in the air. "Get to the good part."

Grant pounded his hand on the table. "This is my life. If you know so much, you tell her."

"Fine. I will." JT turned to Lily. "The photo was of little Grant here playing house with a coed who happens to be his girlfriend. His wife doesn't know yet, but Brad will happily make more photos public if the minister doesn't tow the line. This charity is a sham to clear drugs out of Afghanistan through Turkey and into Belgium for shipment into Europe. A couple of our friends have been working in Belgium and figured it all out."

Lily speculated on who the two friends could be, and she began to mentally place this puzzle piece with the others. Grant Sharpe was definitely in way over his head.

"Your minister here really was telling you the truth years ago. He did have a criminal record. He was a drug dealer, and he was friends with another punk named Garrett Notte. He was the one who taught Garrett everything in the beginning. Is this all making sense now?"

Lily raised her hand to her forehead. "Oh boy. This just keeps getting better." She looked over at the man she thought would be her everything. She saw nothing. "What the hell is wrong with you? You couldn't handle cancer because you were too busy trafficking drugs? You have a wife, and she just isn't enough? You had a nice little church, but you had to go for glory at all costs. Now, you are paying the bill. Why should I help you? Why should anyone help you?"

"Because," Grant's voice quivered before he continued. "Because they'll ruin me, maybe even kill me. I'm supposed to get close to you."

"If they knew me at all, they would know I wouldn't want you close to me ever again. Did you explain that to them?" Lily's voice was unemotional.

"No. I didn't think you would feel that way."

"Wow, this guy is a real piece of work. He has more ego than me," JT admitted. "Lily, Dev knows nothing about any of this. We have a plan, but you'll have to be in on it for it to work. I hate to pull this idiot's back side out of the fire, but we need to use him to get the big fish."

"Fish don't eat mice, or rats." Lily paused. She stared at the man she used to love. "Big cats eat rodents. This cat has claws. He has murdered people and created nightmares for others. Grant, for once in your life, do the right thing."

The minister nodded.

"Then let's go to work." JT pulled devices from the end of the table. "Give me your phone, preacher. From now on, you are mine."

Lily looked up to the ceiling. Usually, a line like that would be so romantic, but as JT placed a small transmitter of some kind into Grant's phone, she knew what she had known since she had fallen in love with her husband and his merry men--she wasn't in a romantic comedy, she was living in that Tom Cruise movie she had always thought would be so exciting.

"Grant, I just need one answer from you." Lily's voice was unwavering and without any emotion. "Just what is it about you that you can't be satisfied with what you have? Why isn't anything enough for you?"

He sat silently. She studied every feature on his face. He was a nice guy. He could be a nice guy. But she hadn't been enough for him. Now his wife wasn't either. His congregation wasn't enough. He needed to do something big for the glory of God. But Grant still didn't realize that God didn't need the glory.

"I was trying to do good, Lily."

"No, well maybe, but you were doing it for yourself. It has always been about you." Lily pushed away from the table and stood slowly. She needed to walk around to relieve the pain in her lower back. "You've met my husband and now JT. You know Danny already. These are men who try to do good. Through all of this, you may want to study them, to be like them. It might serve you well."

Lily patted JT on the back before leaving the kitchen. JT shook his head and smiled. "Preacher, she's the only reason why you are still breathing, that, and we need to use you. If it was up to me, I'd snap your neck in a New York minute."

Grant gulped and loosened his suddenly tight tie. It was a toss-up as to whom he was more frightened of, the bad guys or the good guys.

Chapter Seventeen

1. Answer Gretchen's voicemail
2. Make sure Jack can go with me to the doc's
3. Get to Mass on time
4. Who is my next babysitter?

*L*ily had indeed made it to church on time. She would have to deal with JT when she arrived home. He would be angry and most likely disappointed in her behavior. She'd made sure he was in the shower when she took off in her car, leaving him behind. He didn't want to go to church with her, and she didn't want to force him into it. So, she bolted.

Dan was the celebrant for the morning Mass today. Lily sat peacefully in the pew. She had caught his eye when he began the service. During the homily, he was speaking about one of St. Paul's letters to Timothy, and he paused. It took him a second or two to continue speaking, and it seemed like from that time on he was constantly looking over at her. *Geez, Danny, I'm fine. I don't need another hovering mother hen, especially not a priest.* In the last week, clergy hadn't been her favorite people, well at least one in particular was proving difficult. She didn't need another one shadowing her every move.

Lily didn't want to kneel anymore, but she sat comfortably in the pew after communion. Just a couple of prayers remaining, and Mass would be over. She would deal with the angry SEAL as she made him his favorite blueberry pancakes.

Dan stood for the final prayer. He looked toward Lily and smiled. He'd figured out a rescue. "We all know that May has been the month of our mother Mary. I have a friend here this morning, and with your indulgence, I'd like to offer a mother's prayer for her. She will have her first baby this August. Lily, please come up here."

What the holy? Darn, I can't use profanity in church. Sorry, Lord. She nodded negatively, but Dan insisted. Finally, slowly, one foot in front of the other, she waddled up to the altar. He came down to greet her.

She was not expecting this. His charming smile was met with blazing eyes glaring at him. He brought her to the center aisle. "Lily, please bow your head for this blessing. May our mother Mary be with you during this time. May our Lord look upon you and be with your child, keeping this baby safe as he or she grows and nears arrival into our world. In Jesus' name. Amen."

Dan finished the Mass's prayers and insisted Lily leave with him down the aisle. "I don't know what you are doing, Daniel, but this is overkill," Lily hissed through clenched teeth as they walked to the back of the church and into the lobby.

"Do not, for the love of God and that baby, leave my side. No discussion, Lily, not this time."

Lily realized that something was very wrong. This time, she would not offer any discussion. She would do exactly as she was told. If Dan was concerned, then undoubtedly there was a good reason. He wasn't a reactionary like the rest of them.

So many parishioners congratulated her. Dan was told how wonderful it was to bless Lily. Lily remained bewildered by the entire activity, but Dan was all smiles. As the last of the attendees exited the church, Dan headed to the sacristy.

"Come on in here while I remove my vestments."

Lily took a seat while Dan pulled the garments over his head. With military precision, he neatly hung the vestments. Beneath, he wore simple black pants and a white tee. He placed his collar and black shirt on quickly. "Did you drive here by yourself? Where is JT? Waiting for you?"

Lily sat near the door, but she wasn't sure she could bolt fast enough. "Remain calm. Remember that you are the pastor here."

"You left him at the house, didn't you?" Dan's disapproving expression sent goosebumps down Lily's back. "You know, I'm not sure he even knows where my church is. What were you thinking?"

Lily stood up quickly. *I am not five. I am a grown woman, but a priest is yelling at me. I feel like I'm five.* "I thought I could safely go to church by myself." *What would Dev do? Oh, right, divert in a true Pierce fashion!* "And what was the blessing all about?"

"I'll drive you home in your car. Come on."

Dan gently tugged at her elbow. "No answer, Father?"

"Lily, sometimes, just sometimes, you don't need to know every damn thing."

Lily stuck her finger in his face. "Such language in a church is not acceptable, Danny. You need to say three 'Hail Mary's'."

Dan stopped suddenly as he looked out into the parking lot. "Change of plans. We will come back for your car later." He guided her to the other side of the church.

In complete confusion, Lily pulled back. "I'm not going any further until you tell me what is going on? Have you lost your little priest mind? This hasn't been my best week with clergy."

Dan physically came in front of her. "Lily, I'm driving you home. There's a man standing at your car in the lot. That same man was sitting behind you during the service. I'll call in to have your car gone over. I don't trust anything."

Lily was tired of the intrigue. She glanced at the man. "I shook his hand during the sign of peace."

"There's nothing peaceful about him," Dan grumbled.

Lily was attempting to be strong, but it was so tiresome. She decided to give up on getting along. "OH. Fine. Let's go."

As the priest and his friend exited the church, heading to the rectory's garage, he heard a familiar voice. "Danny, good to see you again. Nice change of uniform. Black looks good on you."

Dan's plan had failed. He turned on his heel and faced Brad Keeting. Khalid's bad boy had moved away from the car and was walking, his hand stretched out for a greeting shake.

"Keeting, it's not that great to see you." Dan stood rigid. He felt exposed, completely naked without any way to protect Lily or himself.

Keeting shrugged and put his arm to his side. "And you must be Dev's wife. I believe I missed you in Paris at the gala."

Lily smiled sweetly. "I'm happy you did, but there were so many people there, so many interesting people."

She watched the stand-off between the priest and the terrorist's sidekick. She half expected Clint Eastwood western movie music to play. They said absolutely nothing. "Mr. Keeting, are you Catholic, or interested in becoming Catholic?"

Dan's double-take toward her made her realize that she had no idea why she asked that question. "I mean, why else would you be here?" She added a sweet smile. If he was going for intimidation, he would fail with her.

Keeting chuckled. "I used to be religious but fell away from the church. When I heard that Danny the Ghost was a priest, I wanted to see what kind of a church he ran."

"I see. It's a great parish. Dan is a wonderful leader. I'm sure you already knew that."

"Yes, Mrs. Pierce. I remember that he did have some skills. They all did back then but times change."

"Not always," Dan muttered. He was standing even straighter if that was possible. He had widened his stance, and at any second, he would do his very best to remove Brad Keeting from the property. Beyond his nemesis, he saw the last parishioner's car drive out of the lot. It was now just the three of them. Lily had stalled long enough.

"Keeting, I've got to get her home. Take care." Softly, he tugged on her arm and began to walk toward the garage.

"I take care with everything I do, Danny boy. I'm sure I'll be seeing you around, and you too, Mrs. Pierce. Tell Dev I said hello. It sure is good to be back home again." Keeting didn't allow for any further discussion, walking back to his own car.

"Dan, now that he is leaving, I can drive my own car home."

"No way. I don't trust him. I'll call Jackson to get someone out here to go over it, just in case."

Lily's eyes widened. *Just in case? Lily, just shut up and do what he wants you to do. JT is going to be angry enough when I get home.*

"Fine, babysitter number two. Let's go home to number one."

JT was angry, but it was tampered down when Dan offered to make the betrayed babysitter's favorite omelet. Lily sat at the kitchen table, enjoying a cinnamon roll with a glass of milk. The baby began to kick happily, and her feet were happy she didn't have to make the SEAL his blueberry pancakes.

"Don't you need to watch your sugar?" Dan asked as he placed breakfast in front of JT.

Lily looked up as if she had been caught in a tale. "Who told you?"

"Ah hah! I wondered." Dan's smug smile told her she had fallen into a trap.

"Priests are not supposed to be so devious." She picked at the roll. It wasn't as tasty as it had been just seconds ago. *Darn him!* "I'm missing Dev so much right now. I don't think he is as bad as you two."

She pointed at JT. "That one there goes around threatening ministers and insisting I eat more protein. You are not welcoming to strangers, and now you are a sugar hater. I can't win lately." She shoved the remainder of the pastry in JT's direction. "Here. You might as well eat it. I don't want anymore." She looked like a sad puppy.

Dan was rummaging through the refrigerator's freezer compartment. He found a package and placed it on the counter. "JT, isn't Jackson bringing some groceries today?"

JT nodded and continued to eat. "I think you make omelets better than Dev."

"My husband is coming home Wednesday. I won't have to have you all around then." JT and Dan completely ignored her comment.

"JT?"

JT's head shot up. "Yes, Jackson is bringing over food."

"I'll text him and make sure he brings fruit and vegetables."

Lily stuck her tongue out at the priest. "Could you possibly have him get some of those frozen fruit popsicles? They are healthy."

Dan continued to text. "Yes. I'll tell him."

Lily stood up too quickly, losing her balance briefly. Before she reached the back of the chair, JT steadied her by grabbing her arms, and Dan perched behind her. "I'm fine but thank you." *Oh geez, I'm going to cry.* The tears began to fall.

"Let's get her onto the sofa," Dan suggested. The two slowly walked her into the living room. Dan propped a pillow on one side as JT sat her down. He quickly lifted her legs. "Just lay here, Lily. JT, send that throw over here."

"Oh, that's better." Lily's head found the pillow. "Thanks, you two. These last few weeks have been a little much for the baby and me. Being older and having a baby is stressful on its own. Add, a man you almost married, a box of ricin, a terrorist, his hatchet man, and you have the perfect cocktail for high blood pressure and spiking sugar levels. I will deny every part of this if either one of you tells my husband." She threatened them with a shaking finger.

"I noticed the mint cookies were gone in the freezer." JT's comment brought him a glare from the sofa.

"Do you all go through my food?"

"I do recon. Those cookies were in there two weeks ago. They are gone now. Dev doesn't eat that stuff so there's only one other person who could be the culprit."

"Oh, come on," Lily complained. "Two weeks for a box of cookies is an eternity. You all worry too much."

Dan knelt beside her. "Listen to me, Lily. You are everything to Dev. You saved him. You need to take care of yourself. Allow us to take care of you, to keep you and the baby safe. You will stay on this sofa the rest of today, understand?"

"Yes. Did you tell JT about Keeting?"

JT sat a little straighter. "What about that creep?"

"He paid a visit to us at church today. By the way, once Jackson gets here, you and I need to get her car. It's being checked over by the FBI right now."

"Fine. You'll update me on Keeting?"

"Sure, on the way over to church."

Lily rolled her eyes. "The FBI is checking your car out for bombs or whatever is nothing for the two of you, is it?"

They answered in unison. "No."

"In Afghanistan, someone checking for car bombs or messed up break lines is a daily occurrence." JT's admission drew Dan's ire.

"JT, she needs to relax, not worry more."

Lily closed her eyes. *If only I hadn't fallen for those lush lashes and those twinkling eyes my life would be so much calmer. But where would be the fun in that?*

Chapter Eighteen

*T*he remainder of Sunday was uneventful. Jackson arrived with three bags of groceries. Jack Pierce arrived an hour later with two more. Lily stretched up from her pillow to notice the apples, bananas and blueberries. Jack had picked up some strawberries from a local grower as well as tomatoes and some large onions. She would eat sugar, but it would be from fresh fruit.

"I can get the grill going." Jack grasped the package Danny had pulled. "Lily, I'm going to grill chicken too. Dan pulled these steaks. Will a salad and baked potato sound good to you?"

"Yes," she called from her throne.

Jackson walked near her and touched her covered toes. "I did bring some ice cream. Dad said you like mint chocolate chip so that's what I got. The peanut butter fudge is more my style--"

"Next time, please?" She fluttered her eyelashes at him.

Jackson laughed. "I'll bring some tomorrow."

Lily grimaced. "Do you have babysitting duty tomorrow too?"

"No, I'm fixing dinner for you. Dad will be with you tomorrow. You have a doc appointment, right?"

"Why do I need a calendar when I have you all?"

Jackson watched his father head outside. "Exactly. I know this is more than you signed on for, but just hang in there. What more can I do to make you more comfortable?"

Lily swung her legs down and removed the light blanket. "Help me upstairs so I can change out of these clothes?"

"Of course. I'll just walk behind you to make sure you don't fall down or up the stairs."

"Thank you." She really did appreciate his acceptance of her very little independence. By the time Lily reached the landing she had to rest and take a breath. "I don't know what is going on with me today."

Jackson rested his hand on her back. He still didn't know much about Lily, but from what he had learned in Paris, and the hour he spent with her here and there, he admired her spirit. She wasn't a complainer either. His buddy, Ari, absolutely adored her. Her expanding belly held his future nephew or niece. "You may have overdone it with all that is going on. You worked at my aunt's yesterday. Today, you really do need to rest. Let us do whatever needs to be done."

"The trash and recyclables need to go out tonight. They collect early on Monday mornings." Lily could move again. "I'm good, but I need to get out of these clothes."

Jackson followed her into the bedroom. The large suite featured a nice sitting area in front of the main windows. He found one of the chairs to wait for her. She walked into the closet and pulled out clothing. Jackson saw a wedding photo on one wall, along with other family photos. It was inexcusable that he wasn't there. Devlin and he only had each other. Distance always kept them apart, at least that's what he told himself.

He continued his examination of the blended room. He could see a mix of Lily and his brother. Dev's side of the bed had a table with a brass lamp, a couple of books, and a charger. On Lily's side, the table and lamp were the same. There was one book about babies, a bottle of moisturizer, a half-eaten snack bar, a used cold pack, and a package of post-it notes. Jackson chuckled.

"Okay, watchdog, I'm ready." Lily arrived into the room dressed in some sort of yoga pants ensemble with a large striped shirt. "No comments. I know I'm beginning to look like an Oompa Loompa."

He knew that phrase. "Willie Wonka, right?"

"Yes. You were a child once, weren't you?"

Jackson shook his head. "They all think you are wonderful, but you have a little wicked in you. You can't fool me." He walked over to the wedding photo for a closer look. "I'm so sorry I didn't make the wedding."

"But you made the honeymoon, remember?" Lily slipped on a pair of sandals. "Could you grab that book over there? That's all I need from up here for a while." She pointed at the baby book.

With the book in his hands, he guided her slowly down the stairs. She convinced him that she could relax just as well outside in one of the patio chairs while Jack grilled. After a wonderful meal, including mint chocolate chip ice cream, Lily and Jackson remained at the table while Jack cleaned up in the kitchen. Lily glanced over at Jackson's computer.

"What is that about?" Lily saw photos of who she thought was Khalid.

"Um, these are classified."

"No, come on, let me look. Something isn't right." Lily pointed at the photos. "Are Ari and he related at all?"

Jackson looked up from the screen. "Yes, on their fathers' side. Their fathers are first cousins."

"And of royal lineage?"

Jackson seemed surprised at how much she knew. "Well, yes. Ari's father made a huge mistake though. He fell in love with a French-German Jew. I don't know for sure, but I have the suspicion that she became pregnant before the marriage. It wasn't just a scandal. It was bigger than a mere scandal. It was also politically devastating for Ari's father. He was ostracized completely."

"Do you have a photo of Ari? Maybe of the fathers?" Lily thought she noticed something, something that would be so outrageous that no one would believe her.

Jackson began to go through files. "Let me check. Just look away for a minute, could you?"

Lily did as she was told. She was used to Dev leaving

the room when he received a phone call or shutting a laptop down quickly when she kissed him goodnight.

"Here. Here are the two cousins. Now, here's a photo of Ari, and here is one of Khalid."

Lily studied the screen. She noticed the similarities, but there were differences. All of the men had the same noble nose, except for Khalid. "Has Khalid had his nose broken, or had some work done?"

Jackson wondered what she was thinking. "No, not that we know of. He's never had plastic surgery. He doesn't believe in any changes to the body. He's a health nut. He doesn't drink. During Ramadan, he will not travel. He's quirky, and I would call him a zealot for his beliefs."

"Jackson, he doesn't have an aristocratic nose. See." Lily pointed at the screen. "Look at the two fathers. Ari has the same nose, but Khalid does not."

Jackson studied the photos. Lily had a point. "What are you thinking?"

"He gives Ari hell about being a mongrel, that he isn't pure. Could he be protesting too much? What if he is the one who isn't pure?"

Jackson shook his head. "No, there's no way. That would mean that his mother, and she's the one who really followed her faith, cheated on her husband. She wouldn't take the chance. She would've been stoned to death, seriously."

Lily pointed at the photos again. "Look, his ears are different. His hair is thicker. Look at his eyes. Ari's eyes are so similar to the other two men, but not Khalid's. Is it my imagination, or is Khalid a little lighter in skin color?"

What? How did she see all that? We haven't seen all of that. "Lily, you have a point, but I'm not sure how that information helps us."

"I'm assuming you all, I mean the alphabet government groups can't do anything, but if we could prove that he isn't part of the family, wouldn't he be sent home? Wouldn't the kingdom revoke his immunity and get him out of here? It wouldn't put an end to his vendetta, but it would get him out of our lives for now. He'd have to fight from thousands of miles away."

Jackson fell back into the chair. "That's the least of it for him. If it was found to be true, the kingdom would strip him of his power, perhaps money, and he'd have to go live in the caves or the desert. He would be such an embarrassment that they would make him invisible. The sins of the mother would fall on him."

"You talk to Ari about it. He may have some information we don't know about, not even your spies. Or could we just make up the rumor that he was illegitimate? Would that be enough?"

"No. We can't play it that way, well at least I can't. Dev can't either. JT, well I'm not sure how much of his career could be destroyed. Paul could be burned, and I wouldn't ask Dan to do anything like that. The State Department would become involved, and everything would go to hell."

"That leaves Ari," Lily paused and patted the baby, "and me."

"Lily, I don't know what you are thinking. I don't know you that well, but you need to stay out of this completely."

"Jackson, I need to keep my family safe." Despite Jackson and Ari's association, he was almost as straight an arrow as his Boy Scout brother. "Never mind. You are right. It was just something I was wondering. What can I do? I'm just a very pregnant woman." *No, I need someone who doesn't mind taking chances, who loves a good scandal.*

Jackson patted her shoulder. "It was an idea. I will tell some of our guys about your theory. That would be something to take him down after all these years without a shot. You would've been a great agent. Your knack for details is amazing."

Lily giggled. "You should see what I can do with post-it notes."

Later that night, with Jack in the room down the hall from her and Jackson sleeping in the guest room on the first floor, Lily felt completely secure. She retreated to the bed and thought about what she was about to do. *Dev might kill me, no, at least not until after the baby is born. I just have this feeling.* She had already texted Ari about her idea. He promised to investigate on his own. In the meantime, he was intrigued and amused. He'd even texted a 'wow' emoji. It was now time to execute one more detail.

She hit the number in her cell. She took a deep breath. *What the heck am I doing?* "Hello, Gretchen? It's me, Lily."

"You silly girl, I know it's you. How are you, bestie?"

Ignore the bestie comment, Lily. "I'm good, very

pregnant, but good. Gretchen, are you still thinking about coming in July?"

"Of course, silly. Abby is bringing that dog so we have to drive, but we are coming. We are going to completely transform the bedroom for the baby. I don't want to hear one protest from you. As her fairy godmother, it is mandatory that I decorate the nursery for my little princess."

"Gretchen, what if it's a boy?"

"No, it won't be. Just put that thought out of your head, dearie. Don't you worry, we will be there. What do you need?"

"There's going to be a party we need to attend while you are visiting. Bring one of your most attractive outfits. I need you to help me with something, and you are the only one who can do this job."

"Coordinating? You know I'm the best in Kansas City, perhaps in the entire nation."

Lily paused. She was going to ask a lot out of her friend, and yes, Gretchen was her friend. She'd even shared stories about her with Ari. Of course, he couldn't breathe at times as he laughed so hard, he cried.

"No, I need you to stop a terrorist." The sentence was met with silence for a few seconds. "Gretchen, are you still there?"

Lily heard crying. "I'm here. I've never been so happy, bestie. We are back in business again, Schmidt and Malloy Detective Agency. I guess it is Pierce and Malloy now. I'm so very honored. Will I have to hide a vial in my blouse? Do I get a gun? I'd love one of those thigh holsters. I could pretend to be the wife of that well-built Navy SEAL. I'll do anything you need me to do, even sacrifice my body and my honor."

Lily fell onto the bed. *What was I thinking?* "Gretchen, I need to go to sleep. We will talk more when you get here. It'll be safer that way."

"Of course. You never know who might be listening. I can't wait. I've missed my bestie. I've also missed Mr. Delicious. You get your rest, and we will leave the day after Abby's last wedding. We will be there by the first of July. Will that be good enough?"

"That will be perfect." Lily acted out a yawn. "Well, I better let you go. Thank you so much. Just hearing you tonight has made me feel better."

"Well of course, Lily. I always have that effect on you. You and I are just magic together. Get some sleep, dearie. I'll touch base this week."

After she ended the call, Lily pulled the blanket up over her body, and she turned out the light beside the bed. She touched the empty pillow beside her. "Dev, I wish you were here. I'm losing my mind." *I just called Gretchen out of desperation and asked her to help me take out a terrorist. I'm not a super spy. I am living in that Tom Cruise movie, though. I'm just not riding on the motorcycle with him. I'm in the clown car! What did I just do? And why do I strangely feel better?*

Chapter Nineteen

1. Don't eat any sugar before appointment
2. Look for that baby thing-a-ma-jig
3. Take Jack to lunch
4. Maybe Dev will call?

*L*ily woke to the smell of bacon. *Bacon is the most disgusting smell in the world.* She remained in bed, on her back, until her stomach settled. It was unsettling to think that her feet were down there somewhere doing whatever they were doing. She couldn't see them from this position. Turning onto Dev's side of the bed, she slowly and carefully maneuvered her body into a seated position.

Her feet were swaying in free air, not touching one bit of floor. "Come on, Lily. You can do this. All you need to do is take a shower, brush your teeth, and get dressed. You used to do this in your sleep, literally if I didn't have coffee. Oh geez, I need to stop talking out loud or one of my guards will hear me."

"Lily, you okay in there?" *Too late. Now Jackson is going to think I'm completely unhinged.*

"I'm fine. I'm just encouraging myself to move. It takes a bit in the mornings to heave myself up. If you have a crane out there, that would be helpful."

She heard laughing. "No crane out here, but Dad and I are making breakfast. What do you want?"

Cereal, no. Waffles with syrup, not today. What will stay down this morning, kid? "Could I have some scrambled eggs with a little cheese on them? They need to be really cooked."

"Sure, we'll wait about ten minutes to fix them?"

Lily found her feet and smiled. The baby kicked. The kiddo was hungry. "Jackson, you better make that closer to thirty minutes. It takes me a while."

"You've got it. Yell when you get to the top of the stairs."

Lily placed her feet down tenderly onto the floor. *My babysitters are doing their job too well.* She'd almost forgotten her lightheaded, loss of balance activity of yesterday. She'd have to tell the doctor. He'd probably say that was completely normal, but he didn't have to answer to the group of men who surrounded her, literally. She did have to answer them, to make sure they knew she was completely fine. *When does Dev get back? Can I last until Wednesday?*

Nearly three hours later, the doctor did indeed tell her that it was a normal occurrence, especially if she was doing a little too much or anxious about something. *Does a psychopathic terrorist count for a little something, and didn't she have the right to be anxious?*

As she waited for the nurse who was going to do the bloodletting for her labs, she texted Ari again. She received no answer. *He's probably doing some super-agent thing. I'm just having a baby.* By the time the nurse entered the room, Lily was feeling pretty sorry for herself. Her life had a target on it, and she had a life growing inside her rendering her completely vulnerable. She couldn't even walk quickly away from an attacker. *When they tell you to find an exit in a movie theatre, I'm not sure I would fit through it!*

The remainder of the day and evening were uneventful. Lily felt freer with Dev's dad around. He was obviously calmer around a pregnant woman than the team. Tuesday, she stayed in pajamas all day, completing all the computer work she needed to do for Aunt Maggie's clients. By afternoon, she had called five brides and one caterer. Maggie would be set now just in case Lily was unavailable the last two months of her pregnancy.

"What's for dinner, Jack?" Lily asked as she walked into the kitchen. Dev's dad was enjoying a glass of iced tea while reading.

"Someone is bringing you dinner."

Lily stood at the refrigerator. She wanted one of those frozen fruitsicles. "Anyone we know?"

Jack placed his eyeglasses on the table. "I certainly hope so. Jackson just said someone is bringing us dinner, and you get a new house guest. I'm going to Wolf Trapp with Arlene tonight."

Lily began to lick her favorite strawberry frozen treat. "Right. What are you two seeing?"

"An American in Paris. That musical isn't my favorite, but I love going to the outside theater."

Lily looked away just in case she cried. Her memory of taking Dev to Kansas City's own outside theater, Starlight, had been just the beginning of her feelings for him. "I'd like to be an American in Paris, but I agree. It isn't my favorite show either. Do I need to change for my guest?"

"I doubt it, honey. Those pajamas are cute. Who the heck is the cartoon character *du jour*?"

She looked down and pulled out the top. "Marvin the Martian and his dog K-9."

Jack shook his head. "Does Dev like those?"

Lily laughed. "I suppose so. He bought them."

Jack shook his head one more time. *Well, at least they found each other.* His son had his own bizarre sense of humor, and he did love his cartoons when he was a boy. He loved the old ones. Ironically, Dev never favored the superheroes.

"You two have a wonderful time." Lily walked slowly into the living room. She just kept walking to the door when she heard the doorbell. She didn't even think about the danger factor of opening her own front door.

Lily realized her mistake in opening the door and her selection of daytime fashion when she saw the man dressed in a suit and tie.

"Don't ever just open the door like that." Ari's tone was dismissive with just a hint of concern. He kissed her quickly on her cheek and continued in, a large bag in one of his hands. "Love the jammies. That dog was one of my favorites. Where's the kitchen?"

She pointed, and he walked through. She heard greetings between the almost strangers as she shuffled behind. She wasn't just waddling now. She needed a new word for the slowest walk ever.

"My mystery date is Ari." She directed her attention to Dev's father as Ari unloaded food onto the counter. "You know, I do have groceries. The guys have kept me rolling in them."

"I'm cooking for you." He began to open cabinets. "I'm looking for your spices. You do use spices, don't you?"

Lily felt like a stranger in her own home. If the girls in high school could see the revolving door of good-looking men, they would've always picked her house for any study project. She didn't say anything, nor did she move to assist her new babysitter, Ari the Terrible. Instead, Jack began to show Ari where the spices were located and other staples he might need.

Jack's eyebrow lifted as he looked toward Lily. "Do you want me to stay?"

Before she could answer, Ari did. "Oh no. We will be fine. Please go out on your little date."

Jack frowned; his forehead creased. "I'm not sure I feel comfortable leaving her in your hands. I only have Jackson's word that you are okay. I'm not sure how my other son would feel about you."

Ari turned around as he loosened his tie and pulled it off. "Oh, Devlin wouldn't want me here. Some days he likes me, most days he dislikes me greatly. He is especially not fond of my friendship with his wife."

Lily decided changing the subject might help. "Ari, have we heard how Paul's wife is? Since Dev is gone, I don't get much information from the guys, or Paul. I know he is with her."

"She has stabilized, but she remains in ICU." Ari removed his jacket and rolled up his sleeves to reveal his very tanned skin.

"How did she get hurt?" Lily was relieved that Jack had asked the question she had been wondering for days. "Lily and I haven't heard any details."

"There was an attack at the hospital," Ari answered quietly. He continued to open cabinets pretending to look for something, anything.

Lily and Jack exchanged questioning glances. "In other words, Jack, Ari isn't going to tell us anything."

Ari turned to face them. His face showed no emotion. "There was an attack. The facts are ambiguous at best. Dev will have more information, and I'm sure he will share it with you both."

Lily squinted at Ari and frowned. She wasn't pleased with his deflection. *Apparently, there was an international class for averting the truth.*

"Jack, please go on. Arlene will be disappointed if she

doesn't go." She touched her father-in-law's arm softly and whispered. "I'll be fine, really. Ari is harmless, well at least to me. Dev really does respect him. Go."

Jack Pierce reluctantly headed toward the front door. "You are sure? You text me if you need anything, promise?"

Lily nodded obediently. "Of course. I will text you if I need you. Go have a good time. I want to hear all about it tomorrow." After a quick kiss on the cheek, Lily playfully shoved Jack out. She leaned against the door and sighed.

Ari looked out, watching her every movement. "Are we finally alone, dear?"

Lily looked up. She had been studying her wedding band. No longer could she wear her engagement ring. Sugar and salt were not her friends. "Yes, but he really didn't want to go. He doesn't trust you."

"Your husband doesn't either. It must be a family trait."

Lily laughed as she walked slowly toward the kitchen. "I think he trusts, but wants to verify, at all times. Besides, their family excels in diverting the conversation. You are very good at it, but you could learn a few things from them. You know, here look at this shiny thing, not the real important thing over there. I need some olive oil."

Ari grabbed the bottle from the counter. "Exactly what are you going to do with this?"

Lily took the bottle and sat down at the kitchen table. "I'm going to get my ring off of my finger."

Ari clapped. "Finally, you have seen the error of your ways, and you are leaving that husband of yours."

"No, my finger is swelling, and I want to get it off before they have to cut it off." She worked the oil around the band, turning it back and forth. She pulled it off slowly. "There. Got it. Here's the bottle back. By the way, what are you making tonight?"

Ari exchanged the bottle for a full glass of water. "Drink that. It will keep some of the swelling at bay. Tonight, we will dine on a lovely steak with a reduction made with mushrooms. The steak will be topped with mixed vegetables including tomatoes and zucchini. I'll add garlic mashed potatoes for the lady's starch habit. For dessert I have fresh berries with ice cream."

If the baby doesn't do flips, I will! "That sounds absolutely amazing. You mean you can cook too?"

"Of course. I'm part French and German, it is mandatory."

"About that pedigree thing." Lily continued to look at her wedding ring. She needed Dev to get home. She missed him rubbing her back, massaging her feet, moisturizing her belly, and kissing her before he closed his eyes. *I just miss him, and it's only been a few days.*

Ari concentrated on the stove as he boiled the red potatoes and began his vegetable concoction. They would rest as he prepared the steak with mushrooms. "Jackson and I talked about your suspicions. I did enjoy your texts. I'm learning about those emojis. I like the angry one. Now about your idea, it is an interesting theory. Khalid does go out of his way to emphasize my pedigree, rather my lack of pedigree. Have you already developed some sort of espionage scenario?" He turned to smile at Lily.

Lily smiled widely. Ari had tied on her apron. She had purchased it in Paris hoping it would add to her culinary talents. It did not possess magical powers, but it did have a beautiful Eiffel Tower on the front. *At least it doesn't say kiss the cook!* Ari looked perfectly at home in her kitchen. He flipped the mushrooms in the small pan as if he did it daily. He placed a towel over his left shoulder.

"I have this gut feeling. I have an idea of how to acquire proof, but I need to wait until that charity party. His ego won't allow him not to show up. Do you think I'm being ridiculous?"

"You Pierces and your gut feelings." Ari avoided the question, concentrating on the searing of the steaks. Dev was known for his intestinal decisions. He was usually correct, but Ari struggled with what he should tell her. *Maybe honesty would be the best avenue when travelling with Lily?* "Dear, I wish it were that easy. If he really wasn't part of the family, they would recall him, well at least I could have some leverage to accomplish that." He wouldn't tell her that he had already made several pleas to have Khalid removed from his capacity in Washington, but the man had become too valuable to the Kingdom. Khalid had not one, but two congressmen in his pocket and a few defense contractors.

The Pentagon seemed to be looking the other way, ignoring Khalid's rumored and actual terrorism ties. In the beginning, he had been a valuable asset to the Americans, serving as a guide into the caves and a procurer of intelligence. But then Khalid became greedy and power hungry.

"Lily, this is really not your battle." He moved the buttered mushrooms to the steak pan. His tone was harsher than usual. Lily didn't like it one bit.

"And why not? Apparently, he has placed a target right on my little back."

Ari lowered the temperature on the pan. He threw the towel down on the counter and quickly turned to face her. "Yes, and that's why all of us are involved. You need to take care of yourself and that baby." He pointed toward her. "We cannot lose you."

They can't lose me? "Who are you talking about? Dev and who else?"

Ari lowered his eyes from hers. How had she found a way into so many hearts? "Lily, we, all of us that were in that room the other night, care about you. I believe we all care what would happen to Devlin if he lost you, and on a personal note, you have certainly given me more smiles in a short time than I have had in most of my life."

Lily's silence was a betrayal of her feelings. The tears fell down her cheeks. She truly had no words to answer him. But she needed to say something. "Ari, you all, every one of you have given me so much. Of course, I love Dev, but his father has made me feel so special and welcomed. It was hard to leave the life I had in Kansas City, but he has given me a family and a home again. JT is such a sweet man."

Ari rolled his eyes. *He does it almost better than me.* "Yes, Ari he is sweet. Paul is such a calm man, and his wife has always answered any questions I have. Then there is Danny. He has quiet courage. I believe he would sacrifice his life for anyone. Then there is you. You are that enigmatic character who will play the fool if it will help solve the world's problems."

"Really, enigmatic? Did you look that one up in the dictionary?" *Now he wants to play it that way? I'll play.* "No, I learned it from JT."

Ari shook his head. "I just need to finish these potatoes, and we will be ready. Do you wish to eat inside or alfresco?"

"Just in here. It's less work, and I don't have to walk so far."

Ari began to mash the potatoes. "Tomorrow morning, you and I will take a walk. I was told you need to do that."

"I won't need a leash."

"You are being funny," Ari replied without emotion.

"Who told you that I needed to walk? Dev? Jackson?"

The super-agent continued to finish his mashed potatoes. "No."

"What are you, some kind of a spy who just knows things?" She snorted as she laughed.

Ari didn't move from his work. He smiled, but he didn't let her see. He was told by Jackson that she needed to walk, but he did know. He remembered the walks his wife and he used to take to the market. Not only had it been good exercise for her and the baby, but the shared conversation had bonded them as they prepared for the future. That future had been cut short by Khalid.

"That was wonderful," Lily announced as she stood up slowly from the table. "I can't eat another bite."

"Good, I'm very happy you enjoyed it." Ari removed the plates and began his cleanup. "You go into the living room and relax. I know how to use a dishwasher."

"You are very accomplished, sir. By the way, what do super spies do in the evening?" Lily slowly lowered her body onto the sofa. *I move like a huge turtle!*

"I like to watch baseball."

Interesting. Lily found a Nationals' game on the television. In a few minutes, Ari joined her. She handed him the channel selector and spread her body out, a pillow under her ankles and another behind her back. "If you don't like that, find something. I'll be sleeping in a few minutes. Now that I'm full, and the baby is happy, I'm done for the day."

"I'm very happy with this game. When I was a small boy in Israel, we played every day. I believe George Brett was from Kansas City's team?"

"Yes. What position did you play?"

Ari smiled. His memories of baseball were good ones. His little buddies played in a small park behind the apartment building that was their home. They would gather every morning. They played until it became too warm, or until an alarm sounded. The threat of a missile sent them scattering into the darkness of safe rooms. "I was a catcher."

"Always in charge," Lily muttered. It was becoming increasingly difficult to keep her eyes open. "Ari, if something does happen to me, you will take care of Dev, won't you, even if you have to hand feed him?"

Ari was studying the screen. His hard stare prevented any emotional response. "I'll hire someone."

Lily nodded. "I expected that response. What was she like, your wife?"

Ari turned his attention to Lily. Thankfully, she couldn't see him breaking. He could only see the back of her head. "Wonderful."

"More, please."

"Joanna was a lot like you. She could read a person in minutes, just like you. She would study humanity, just like I suspect you have done in your work and now with all of us. She was a children's doctor. When we were dating, I would come to the hospital to take her home. There would always be some little one hanging on her legs, or they would have their arms hugging her waist. It was hard to compete with them."

"You were on another level, Ari. She must've loved you very much to put up with you." It was easier to ask Ari questions so personal when Lily didn't have to look into his dark eyes.

Ari chuckled. "Ah, yes. I was a handful. We met in a nightclub. Her girlfriend knew me from the Army, and she thought we might get along. That night, Joanna expressed to me her dislike of soldiers. In Israel, we all serve so it is hard to be so picky. She never served because she was born in the United States and moved to Tel Aviv for the position at the hospital."

Lily patted down a kick from the baby. "So how did you two get together then?"

"I brought her lunch at the hospital the next day. It was an offensive attack, and you know how irresistible I can be."

Lily raised her arm in the air and waved. "Sure, sure, tell yourself that. Feeding a woman can be the best aphrodisiac. Dev took me to Paris, after all."

Ari coughed comically. "That seemed to work very well."

"Yes, I became pregnant on my honeymoon. Laugh away, but if you feed me chocolate, things happen."

"Thanks so much for placing that visual in my mind, Lily."

"Joanna is a beautiful name. I'm beginning to think about what we will call this baby." During the last doctor's appointment Dev had attended, a sonogram was done, but they both chose not to look at it. She had the results in a sealed envelope in the bedroom, in Dev's drawer next to the bed. They would look at it when he came home. Lily patted her stomach. If the baby was a girl, Joanna would be a lovely name. Dev wouldn't allow her to call a son, Ari. Lily giggled. "How did you get her to marry you?"

"She asked me." Lily laughed loudly, but Ari continued with his story. "Seriously, she asked me. I came back from a very classified mission. She was waiting in my apartment when I returned. She said she needed to be my wife. She needed me." Ari could picture that memory very clearly. He had described in specific detail how dangerous his life was, but it didn't matter to her. Joanna needed no one, but she chose him.

"I wish she were on this earth so I could talk to her about you," Lily admitted. *Joanna would understand everything she was feeling, wouldn't she?*

Ari's view was distracted by a car driving by. "I wish you could too. She would like you very much, Lily." He stood up to take a closer look out the window. Something didn't feel right. Perhaps it had been the discussion about his wife. He seldom talked about anything personal, but with Lily, all the rules seemed to fly out the window. "Lily, I think I will sleep here in the living room tonight. I want to see how this game ends." With no reply given, he headed for the sofa. Lily was sound asleep, both hands propped on her ample belly.

He touched her hair, and she stirred. "What? Did I miss something?"

"No, you fell asleep. Let's get you upstairs. You and that baby need to go to bed."

As Lily stood, she was a little off balance. Ari used one hand on her back to steady her. "Getting my balance is a little awkward." She had one hand on his shoulder. She saw the pain in his eyes. "I'm sorry I asked so much about Joanna."

"It is good to speak about her. She made me a better person. After she died, it has been hard to be good, but you, Lily, make me want to be better. Thank you for reminding me of her spirit."

Lily leaned up and kissed his cheek. "Take me to bed."

Ari drew back. "Excuse me? Dev would kill me, one body part at a time."

Lily's laughter filled the house. She hit him on his well-muscled arm. "Crazy man, help me up the steps. Did you say you were sleeping here in the living room?"

Ari drew a relief-filled breath. "Yes. I want to watch this game, and sometimes I prefer a sofa or couch. I have a hard time sleeping through the night."

Lily could tell that there was more, but tonight was not the night to pry. Sadly, she feared there would be more nights like this when a super-agent worried about those bad people who moved in the darkness of the night.

Chapter Twenty

*A*ri was uneasy during the night. He had watched two baseball games, and he had eaten another bowl of ice cream, something he never did. Lily's pregnancy was rubbing off on him. He had heard her wake twice to visit the bathroom, but she never yelled for him or came down the stairs for a snack.

It was almost uncomfortable to be in a house for more than just a few hours. It was a lovely home, one that could and probably would be filled with happy children who played football and knew every flower in the garden. *What a life they will have!* When the sun rose, Ari calmed a bit, but he still felt as though something was about to happen. He had insisted they take a walk. Slowly they had walked and resumed their discussion of Joanna, and of his daughter, Chaya. Lily clutched his hand, and he swiped away a few tears.

Lily was working on something in the baby's room as Ari began dinner. With his apron on, he looked like the perfect house husband. He heard a car pull up. The dogs two houses down were barking. He went on alert, pulling his gun at the ready. He heard a noise at the door, holding the gun behind his back. He needed to tell Dev to put in some sort of a peep hole or a security camera so someone could see who was at the door. He was completely blind when he opened the door quickly.

"What the hell are you doing here?" Dev Pierce looked Ari up and down, smiling at the apron.

"Honey, your husband is home," Ari yelled up toward the steps.

"Really?" Both men could hear her moving to the top of the stairs.

"Your brother assigned me the duty. I would've volunteered." Ari moved to the bottom of the stairs to assist Lily if she needed it. He turned to Dev. "You look like hell."

Dev set his two bags down near his office door. "You have no idea. You are not going to believe this one."

"You'll be able to tell me?"

Lily began her walk down the stairs of terror. She needed to watch her feet, but she wanted to see Dev's face. Dev pushed Ari out of the way. "My wife, I'll stand here. You go finish dinner, honey."

"You've never appreciated me. I've tried and tried, but nothing is ever good enough for you." Ari acted out. He left to offer them their privacy.

Dev stopped Lily, reaching for her hand. "I missed you so much."

Her face said it all, a large smile crossing her face and a few tears stuck on her eyelashes. "I missed you too. You look tired. Kiss me."

Dev took her into his arms and kissed her soundly. The baby seemed to be pushing out further, but he held her as close as possible. After a lengthy kiss, he held her in his arms. Her head rested on his chest. "I was worried about you the entire time I was gone."

"That's not good for you. You make mistakes when you are thinking about me."

Dev stroked her hair and leaned his chin on top of her head. "I'm assuming you have been well cared for."

"You have no idea. I've had Danny, your dad, Jackson, and now the Israeli, French, German, Arab menace. *Oy vey*!"

"Yiddish?"

Lily stood back from her husband and led him to the sofa. "I need to sit down. He's been very good to me. He has fed me as though I'm a queen, and yes, he made me walk today."

Dev was distracted by the man in the kitchen, in his kitchen. "What is he doing?"

"He's making dinner. Tonight we are having some French chicken dish, green beans, a summer salad, and he baked something for dessert."

Both of Dev's brows rose. "Ari cooks?"

"Very well. He also vacuums, dusts, changes sheets, and he cleans bathrooms. I seriously can't lean over anymore. I believe my feet have left, and my belly has its own zip code. Look at this." Lily pointed at her stomach.

"He cleaned the bathrooms? I would believe it if you told me he blew something up."

She softly hit his arm. "I thought you were a mother hen! They are like wardens. I missed you."

Dev attempted to view the action in the kitchen. "What is he doing?"

Lily sat back on the sofa. Her husband was more interested in the spy in the kitchen than the wife in the living room. "Go." Dev left her side and headed to speak with Ari. Less than thirty minutes later, the threesome sat cordially at the table eating a delicious dinner.

"I'm going to miss this French food." Lily savored her last bite of chicken. "Did you make the salad dressing from scratch?"

As Dev continued to study their dinner companion, Ari was taking great delight in upsetting the Boy Scout. *It's just too easy!* "Yes, I did. I'll leave the recipe for you. I'll have to return and cook a few of my favorite German recipes."

Lily nodded enthusiastically, Dev did not. "That won't be necessary. I can get her a cookbook."

"It's more fun if I come back and show her." Ari took a sip of wine and looked over the rim. He winked at Lily. Bothering Dev was more delicious than the meal could ever be no matter the nationality. "But I must leave tonight now that you are home."

Dev reached for the empty plates and began to clear the table. "Yes, you must."

"You are being very rude to Ari. He has done so much, Dev."

Dev never turned around to address Lily. He continued to fill the dishwasher.

"I'm pretty sure he is upset that I've replaced him for the last few days," Ari whispered.

"I believe you are right, Ari." Their whispered conversation immediately had the effect they wanted.

Dev returned to the table and took a drink of his beer. "You two do realize that I'm here. I can hear you."

The other two answered "yes" in unison. "Shall we move to a softer place for me?" Lily began to move from the table. "Geez, I move but my stomach is still back at the table."

Dev tenderly reached behind her, guiding her into the living room. "Chef, you may serve dessert for Mrs. Pierce. She will be on the sofa."

Ari bowed from the waist. "As you wish, sire." He arrived a few minutes later with three plates, each holding a slice of pear tart.

Dev took a bite. His eyes shut automatically. "Are you kidding me? You made this?"

"I have many hidden talents, Pierce. You should know that by now. We've known each other for how many years now?"

Ari made this tart? Unbelievable. I need to step up my game. "Too many," Dev growled. "I'm not sure you saw the coverage last week, but Hezbollah was acting as a drug cartel, shipping used cars filled with drugs into the Baltimore area."

Ari remained silent. *They are becoming quite creative. It is difficult to stay one step ahead.* "They need money and new outlets. The terrorists have become used car salesmen. The next thing you know they'll have a coffee shop drive through for your shipment of drugs."

"I heard rumors that drugs may be funneled through the embassies. Our friend has a lot to move thanks to that operation in Paris."

Lily watched the two men as though it were a ping pong match. They continued to talk about drug cartels and terrorism. *Baby, don't listen to daddy or Uncle Ari right now. Think happy thoughts like ice cream, bananas with whipped cream, peanut butter cookies, tasty seasonal strawberries--* "Did someone ask me something?"

"I asked if you wanted another serving." Ari stood in front of her, looking down at a somewhat confused face.

"No, I'm fine. It was delicious." She handed her empty plate to her waiting servant.

"And it is healthy. You need to watch your sugar intake in the last trimester."

Ari's absence allowed Dev a few minutes of privacy with his wife. She looked tired, but her ankles weren't swollen. She lifted her glass of water, and Dev noticed something out of place, actually it was missing. "Where's your wedding ring?"

"I took it off. My finger was beginning to swell, and I didn't want someone coming at me with a hacksaw to get it off." *Hmm, you are feeling a little out of control, aren't you, husband? Let's see how you like it?* "And where is yours?" She pointed at his naked ring finger.

"In the box upstairs, remember?"

"Yes." *Dang it, I forgot. Dev never took his wedding band or the West Point ring. Divert, Lily.* "How is Jill? I've heard so little."

"She remains in ICU, but she's doing better. I'll check in with Paul tomorrow. I did hear that your car passed inspection."

"Yes. It's in the garage. Two sets of alphabet groups cleared it, and I think your brother went over it again the other night. Jackson has trust issues. Oh, he also changed the oil."

He had missed Lily's non-intentional "nail-it-on-the-head logical comedy. "You think? We all have trust issues." Dev looked toward the kitchen. "If you recall, I'm not as trusting as you."

No, you are not. In the beginning, you didn't trust me either even though my life ended up in jeopardy. Stop it, Lily. The past is in the past. But Dev's past was front and center in their reality today.

"Dev, what happened to Jill? I can't seem to get an

explanation. I know whatever happened, happened at her job."

Ari held a full glass of red wine in his hand as he sat in the chair opposite Dev. "Are you going to tell her?"

"Of course." Dev was lying, but now he was pushed into a corner by his supposed ally. "A man asked for Jill. He had a young girl with him. He said he came to the Children's Hospital because Jill had told him about what great work they did there, and his daughter had a rare disease. He said he was Jill's friend. When she arrived at the desk, saw the little girl and her father, she just thought she had forgotten him. His greeting was friendly. When he shook her hand, his left hand brought out a six-inch knife, and he stabbed her as he yelled in Arabic that God is good. The little girl ran as did the man. Security went after them, but they were picked up by a black sedan one block away from the hospital. That's why you have your babysitters."

"Which reminds me, Devlin, I have a few suggestions to upgrade your security," Ari commented calmly.

Dev's brow rose in suspicion. "Is it legal?"

Ari made a face, something in-between disappointment and offense. "I suppose the electrified door is out of the question?"

Dev's brow rose even higher, closing in on his hairline. His wife was chuckling. "Do not encourage him or you will have a burning door by next week. I'm shocked he hasn't land mined the front yard and set up a wire perimeter in the back."

Ari snapped his fingers. "Darn, that was on tomorrow's post-it note."

Lily snorted and both men focused on her. "You two are so good together. I don't need any entertainment with you both around."

"Honey, some of his outlandish ideas are based in factual ability. He's probably done it before." Dev headed to the refrigerator for another beer.

"Dev, I set up that monitor system in the baby's nursery. I found the box. I hope you don't mind." Ari had also found an elephant mobile. Fondly, he remembered how Chaya's eyes would follow the mobile they had hung over her crib. He had watched her for over an hour one afternoon as she cooed over the butterflies above her. The next day he had left for Afghanistan. By the time he returned, she was standing in her crib, jumping to reach the pink and purple flying objects. "But I made a few modifications, so it is harder to hack into."

Dev finally replied as he returned. "Thank you, I think. I was worried about having enough time to install it properly."

After a sip of wine, Ari killed the tender moment with a flippant remark. "It only took me an hour from start to finish. You Army boys are a little slow." He couldn't resist tweaking the American.

"Don't you have somewhere to go?"

"Dev," Lily rebuked. "Do you have to be this way?"

"With him I do. You don't know him the way I do."

Ari drained his glass and stood up. His laughter lightened Lily. "It is okay, dear. Devlin and I have this unusual relationship, our friendship wrought in battle. If we aren't fighting, even with each other, we aren't alive. It becomes increasingly more difficult for me on a daily basis to feel, to feel anything. Dev gives me joy. The more uncomfortable he becomes, the better I feel. But your husband is correct. I do have somewhere to go and work to do."

As Ari retreated from the room to gather his bag, Lily stood slowly. "I swear, Dev, do you even know him?"

"Do you?" Dev's voice was a little higher than usual, in defense not anger.

"I think I do." Lily's voice trailed off. She knew so little about Ari. He truly was an iceberg. You only saw the tip, glistening in the sunlight. Below was the hidden danger of the jagged ice filled with brutality, revenge, and fatalism. "He would die for any of us if he thought that would protect our lives."

Dev gulped. *She does know him. How did Lily do this? How did she see the soul of someone so quickly? It took me two years before I sort of trusted Ari.* "You are right. You need to know that if Ari and I didn't go at it like we do, we wouldn't be us. The one would think the other was ill. It's survival skills, honey."

Lily understood, but sometimes Dev could be abrupt. That night at the wedding reception, she had seen him as a green-eyed monster. He hadn't been very cordial to her ex-fiancé. *Well, I wasn't either.*

Ari rounded the corner, bag in hand. "My lovely Lily, please take care of yourself and that baby." He leaned down and kissed her on the head. Then he winked. "Make sure you take care of little Ari."

Lily and the super-agent shared delight in Dev's booming voice. "Over my dead body will my son be named after you."

Ari kissed her cheek and faced Dev. "That could be arranged, my friend."

"Get in line and take a number," he mumbled. "I'll walk you out to make sure you are really gone."

Lily began to surf through television channels. "Play nice, boys."

As soon as Dev closed the front door, his demeanor with Ari changed. "I haven't heard anything from JT about Keeting. Have you?"

"No and nothing from your brother. Perhaps the CIA won't even play well with their own agents? Besides, Keeting is a cockroach. He will survive no matter what." Ari placed his small bag in the passenger side of his rented car.

"Unless there's a zombie apocalypse."

Ari smiled. "My friend, you do have a sense of humor. I've been wondering why he was at Danny's church. Any ideas?"

Dev leaned against the car. "I know he likes a game as much as Khalid. Danny and he have history. I can only hope he was there to warn Dan. But my theory is that they want us to think Lily is the target. Maybe she really isn't."

Ari returned to the driver's side to face Dev. "Then how do you explain Paul's wife and her accident? We all know she was targeted. We all know Lily was targeted with that ricin delivery."

Dev shook his head. His thoughts were literally miles away in Afghanistan during another time. "But there was that released list of names. I'm looking into that congressman."

"Tread carefully, Devlin. It would be hard for me to investigate a member of the Knesset."

Dev completely understood. There were always those rumors that Ari floated so easily here and there because he had friends in very high places. Dev Pierce didn't have those contacts. He had friends but some friends would back away when uncomfortable questions were asked.

"Have you heard about your wife's latest idea?"

Dev's head fell to his chest. "Yes."

It gave Ari so much joy to see Pierce without his usual control over most people. He had not one ounce of power over his lovely wife. Especially in Lily's condition, it was difficult to tell her no. He understood that. "Why must she solve all of this? As in Paris, she had this uncanny skill to put the pieces together in an organized puzzle, even if that international puzzle had pieces missing."

As Dev raised his head, his face lightened. "She likes an organized finished product. Everything must be right. She has to organize what she can and be in control."

Ari pushed around him to the car door. "And she married you? Tsk, tsk, I thought Lily was smarter than that. However, her scheme made me think about a rumor from my childhood. When Khalid was finally brought in, did you Americans acquire DNA samples from him?"

"No, at least I don't think so. It was so early in the war, but I'll check. We didn't set up that lab in Iraq until 2005. But wait a minute, after the resurgence, he was picked up near Jalalabad. I know he was processed, but he ended up in Pakistan. I'm sure some payoff was involved. After that, he was never captured again."

"He was licking his wounds and regrouping." Ari knew exactly where Khalid had been, in Israel killing his wife and daughter.

Dev noticed Ari's demeanor travel into the darkness of his thoughts. He also knew where Khalid had been and what he had accomplished. The last time Dev had seen him on the battlefield was in Syria. "Even if I do find his DNA, maybe from a swab or a water bottle they collected, what can you possibly do with it to prove what?"

"Lily has a theory," Ari explained. "If I can compare his DNA to mine then we may have some options. I'm sure she'll explain it to you. She's becoming quite the little sleuth."

Dev agreed. "Your DNA compared to his?"

Ari opened the car door and slid in. "His father and mine were brothers. I know my mother was never with any other man. He was her one love, a man who gave up so much for her. But there was this rumor about Khalid's mother. The same could not be said. I'll make a call home, or it may be time for me to *go* home. Perhaps our Lily will solve it all again."

"There will be no living with her if that happens."

Ari's laughter was shared with his companion. "And you can't live without her. I'll keep in touch. Take care, my friend. *Shalom.*"

"*Shalom*, Ari." Dev watched the car pull away. He slowly walked back into the house. He couldn't live without her. *I won't live without her.*

Chapter Twenty-One

1. Tell Dev that Gretchen, Abby, and Mort are coming
2. Tell Dev how the last doctor's visit went
3. Check if he can come to next visit
4. Open the sonogram results?
5. Ari used butter. Need butter and milk
6. Definitely tell Dev Gretchen is coming

*I*T almost seemed normal the last few weeks with Dev home. Khalid was only a rare thought of concern. As Lily enjoyed her husband's bare chest as her pillow, she made lists in her head. She needed to write a few things down, including a complete grocery list. Her baby brain was beginning to fog her memory. *Post-it notes are necessary!* Dev's arm tightened around her shoulder. They were quietly celebrating the opening of the sonogram results envelope. Now they could make more plans.

"What did the doctor say?" His voice was soft and low.

"Everything is fine, especially for a geriatric pregnancy."

His chest moved lightly in a muted laugh. "Stop worrying about that. It is just a label, and we all know you don't fit in a box."

"Maybe I'd fit in a large storage crate down by the docks?"

Dev rested his head on his wife's. His other hand reached for her belly, lightly patting his child. "You are beautiful. We are so lucky that this is possible."

"I know. My sugar is a little high. My salt is too so I need to drink more water. I also need to keep up the walks."

"I'm not surprised."

Lily stroked his chest. There was nothing better in the world than waking up with a half-naked man. Lily smiled. *It is good to be me, well when I don't have swollen ankles and fingers, or have to pee every ten minutes! And when can I see my feet again? I used to like my feet.*

"Honey," Lily began. "I need to tell you something. I'm not sure how you're going to take this."

"We already know about the baby. What? Are you running away with Ari?" Dev was joking, of course, but she better not be running away with the agent.

She lightly struck her husband's flat stomach. "No, don't be ridiculous. JT would be my obvious choice. He allows me to do anything I want."

"That's not even funny. What is it then?"

Lily stretched her neck, kissing him full on the mouth. "I love you so much. I need to tell you that--"

"The doorbell is ringing. Keep that thought, and I'll be right back. It's probably Dad or Jackson." Dev jumped out of the bed and left the room.

"Do you think it's safe to answer the door dressed only in your pajama bottoms, Dev? You might freak out whoever is at the door if it isn't your dad or brother." Her yelling was not responded to in any way. He had already bounded down the stairs and was at the door. She heard a familiar voice. "Oh no. Holy Moly!"

"Well, hello, Mr. Delicious! My, you look, um, well rested."

Lily squirmed out of bed as quickly as possible, throwing on her robe to cover her light nightgown. Gretchen was here! She was early. *Of course she is! Geez, Dev is going to divorce me, but he'll wait until the baby is born.*

Dev was speechless. "Gretchen?"

"Mort and me too! Hi Dev."

Dev looked behind the diva to see Abby and the dog. *What the bloody hell?*

He had no words. His mouth gaped open. His shock was evident even to the dog. He had never been this surprised in battle or on any DEA special operation. Never. Ever. "Honey? Will you come down here?" His voice quivered a bit. *Was he experiencing fear? Nah, it was only Abby and Mort, and Gretchen. Gretchen! Yes, she makes me afraid. She has luggage next to her feet. Oh dear, Lord, no.*

"I'm here." Lily slowly made her way down the stairs. Abby squealed and pushed past Dev to hug her former boss, her very pregnant former boss.

"Oh my gosh. Look at you. Gretchen, come look at Lily. She is so, so--"

"Huge?" Lily asked.

Gretchen patted Dev's chest as she came to Lily. "No, you are beautiful, absolutely stunning. Oh my. You are going to have a baby."

She quickly wiped away a tear.

Mort toured the house. Dev remained at the door. He tipped his head out to see if any other surprises were around the corner. Instead, he saw a few more pieces of luggage and an SUV with Missouri license plates. The vehicle was filled with more luggage and boxes, lots of boxes.

Gretchen tenderly grasped Lily's hand and led her into the living room. "Your home is lovely. You haven't finished decorating, have you? Of course not. You just moved in, and now you have the baby coming. Well, I'll do what I can while I'm here. Let's sit down and see what you've been up to. Devlin, would you be a dear and gather our bags from the porch?"

"I'm a bellhop now?" Dev grumbled. *Why am I bringing their luggage into my house? Why is she here? No, no, no.* He growled as he brought three pieces of luggage into the foyer and closed the door. "Honey, when were you going to tell me that we were having visitors?"

Lily looked up at him from her center spot on the sofa. "Um, I was just telling you when the doorbell rang." She pursed her lips into a child's pout.

Dev shook his finger at her. "Don't do that face. You know you are in trouble."

"Of course she is," Gretchen admitted. "She is being targeted by some mad man, and she needs to prepare for this baby. We are here to assist in both. I'm obviously qualified to assist in the investigation, and I'm overqualified to decorate a baby's room." Gretchen looked around the room. *That lamp in the corner would not do, nor would that cabinet.* "And I can add a few touches here and there to the rest of the house."

"Lily." Dev said only one word. Abby looked up at him as if she was guilty as sin of...something. Gretchen's look seemed to be one of defiance. He felt as though he was the outsider. *But it's my house!*

"Dev, maybe you should go get dressed?" Lily was noticing Gretchen's gaze. She looked like a lion ready to devour a piece of raw meat. Dev looked down at his attire and nodded. He said nothing before leaving the women.

"Do not travel with a slobbering German Shepard," Gretchen complained.

Abby smiled. "She wasn't that bad. There was that one incident with Gretchen's Louis Vuitton rolling bag."

"Wasn't that bad? That roller is over three thousand dollars. That drooling DEA dropout dog thought it was her new chew toy."

Next, Gretchen complained about the hotels along the way. Apparently, the morning breakfast at one hotel chain had too many carbs. Abby enjoyed the biscuits and gravy. Gretchen continued to complain about the lack of thread count on the sheets at another location. Lily smiled from ear to ear. She had missed this, and she noticed that Abby was the perfect foil for Gretchen's insane comic relief, even when the woman didn't realize she was being funny.

"I did like those free drinks at that one place," Gretchen admitted. "Lily, they give you these tickets. You receive one drink for one ticket. I found a few tickets left behind on one of the tables, so I used them. That night the mutt didn't bother me."

Abby poked Lily in the side. "Mort slept with her every night. She's not telling you that."

Gretchen changed the conversation. "Enough chit chat. We have work to do. What shall we do first? The furniture won't come until tomorrow, but we do need to paint first. Let me see what we are working with. Is the room upstairs?"

Dev bounded down the stairs preventing Gretchen's search for the nursery. He had quickly dressed in a pair of shorts and a DEA shirt. "Gretchen, let's get some breakfast first. We haven't eaten yet. How about you all?"

Mort barked. She was in support of food. Abby grimaced. "I am hungry. We were so excited, we just got here as fast as we could."

Dev's eyes were twinkling as he passed his wife and gave her that look she loved. "Thank you, honey. That would be wonderful. We should have something in the fridge."

Damn, Ari! Dev was more than disgruntled over what food items were missing from the refrigerator. He knew his dad and Jackson had brought groceries, but the crazy

French-German-Israeli-Arab had used just about all of the butter and most of the eggs. The only option was pancakes. He searched the freezer. Thankfully, the turkey sausage was still there.

An hour later, breakfast was completed for everyone but Lily. She was still savoring her pancakes. Abby helped him do the clean-up as Lily and Gretchen visited. "You didn't know we were coming, did you?" Abby asked as she closed the dishwasher's door. Gretchen was so eager to get to Lily they had left Kansas City a week early.

Dev smiled. "It is a pleasant surprise. Lily was just about to tell me something, and I gather your visit was that something. Jeremy is going to be excited to see you."

"Yes. He's coming later tonight if that's okay."

Dev leaned against the kitchen counter. "Of course. It'll be great to see the little nitwit. Although, I hear he has been stellar in his classes. He is going to be a fantastic FBI agent. We'll grill, have a real party."

"Lily said you just returned? Now you have been invaded. I'm so sorry. We could stay at a hotel."

Dev placed his arm around Abby's shoulders. "Stop it. You are family. You and Mort are. Gretchen is that crazy aunt you never allow in your house, but obviously, it is too late now." They both watched Lily and Gretchen as Gretchen talked and Lily listened. "Just too late. The vampire has been invited in."

Lily's laughter at one of Gretchen's outrageous stories was heartfelt. Dev pulled Abby closer for a hug. "Just look at her. She is pure joy; Lily, not Gretchen. She's hanging on every ridiculous word and eating her pancakes." Lily clapped at the finale of the tale.

"I'm ridiculously happy right now. All my favorite people are with me." Lily's announcement drew a warm hug from Gretchen. Abby and Dev wondered if Lily was having a sugar high emergency.

"You know when they talk about a pregnant woman glowing, I'm thinking in my wife's case, it's just the sugar." Dev felt more relaxed at that moment than he had in several weeks. Surrounded by Mort, Abby, and even Gretchen, he knew she would be safe. The two women may not be trained soldiers or spies, but they worked on weddings every week. He knew they could handle any emergency.

"I want to see this nursery immediately. We just can't fritter the day away." Gretchen stood up and bounced her way out of the room. As usual, she didn't wait for anyone.

"Honey, you need to tell her," Dev warned.

Lily stood up slowly, holding her pregnant stomach from the top and bottom. "You tell her. You can't stop a typhoon named Gretchen. You should know that, Mr. Delicious."

Abby shrugged her shoulders as she followed the other two women. "Dev, you know she's right. I don't know what Lily needs to tell her, but it really doesn't matter at this point. Gretchen is going to do what Gretchen does."

Dev's head bowed down in true Magnum fashion. He added a growl. He followed too. Abby and he took a few minutes to give a little attention to the very patient Mort.

Upstairs, Gretchen was formulating a plan. "This room is perfect. The color on the walls is a little bland, but I can work with it. You'll probably want to repaint in a year anyway." Gretchen was picturing where the crib would go and the bassinette.

"Gretchen we weren't thinking about this room. In fact, we--"

Lily was cut short with Gretchen's hand to her mouth. "This is the room. It is the nearest to yours. I already have my design plan. It will not be changed."

"But Gretchen, we've already--"

"Shush, Lily. I have decided."

And so it has been decreed. Geez, Gretchen is more commanding than any of the men in my life. I've missed her so. Have I really?

"Abby," Gretchen yelled from the top of the stairs. "We need to unload the car. Chop, chop."

Dev placed his hands up in surrender. "You heard her, Abs. You are to unload the car."

She shouted down one more time. "Devlin, you could help her, can't you?"

Abby punched him in his side. "Oh, Devlin, you can help me, can't you?"

"I need to go into work later," Dev grumbled. "She should be down here unloading her car."

Abby laughed as they headed outside into the Virginia summer heat. "Do you know Gretchen?"

"I know, I know. Show me your things so I can stick them in the guest room suite on the first floor. Let's get to work."

Lily entered her bedroom to finally dress for the day. Gretchen followed her. "Now, what are we doing about that terrorist? You do have a plan, don't you?"

Lily began to make the bed. Gretchen lounged in the chaise near the front window. She looked down to see Dev and Abby quickly unloading the boxes and luggage.

"There's this charity party. I figured you, being you, could get close to him and gather some DNA."

Gretchen sat up straighter. "Lily, are you asking me to exchange bodily fluids with this man?"

Lily immediately blushed. She had forgotten Gretchen's mind traveled in a different direction than most. "Holy Moly, no, Gretchen. Get your mind out of the gutter. Besides, his nationality, his religion won't allow you to touch him. We need blood, spit or hair with a follicle on it. I'm assuming there's no way he will allow us to swab his cheek."

Gretchen laid back once more in relief. "And what is the end game? Why are we getting his DNA?"

"I have a suspicion that he may not have the lineage he thinks he does. If I'm correct, he could lose his diplomatic immunity and be turned out of the embassy and the United States. The guys want him dead. I want him gone."

Gretchen frowned. She had chipped a nail. "Lily, I agree with your men. He won't be truly gone until he's dead, right?"

Lily looked up from the pillow in her hands. Dev's head rested on that pillow. They'd fallen asleep in each other's arms last night as she watched yet another Jessica Fletcher mystery. "Gretchen, I just want him gone until this baby is born. Then, if he is still on this earth, maybe one day someone will neutralize him. I just need some time for us to get this baby here, and to offer my husband just a little bit of safety."

"Dearie, you do know your husband is a DEA agent, right? You met him while he was undercover. He is usually in danger."

Lily bit her lip. *Don't cry in front of Gretchen. Hormones, take a rest.* It was too late. Tiny tears found trails of anguish down her cheeks. "I have this gut feeling that this dangerous game is just a game to rile Dev to do something stupid. This terrorist would give his life up if it meant Dev would spend the remainder of his life in prison. He is just poking him, poking all the guys to do something stupid. Besides, I just want normal."

Gretchen flew out of the chair to hold Lily in her arms. "You know very well that normal is highly overrated. Where's the fun in normal? Don't you worry. Your bestie is here now. The Schmidt and Malloy Detective Agency will be at work. We can take care of one little terrorist. How hard can it be?"

Lily's head was cradled in Gretchen's ample bosom.

"Gretchen, it usually takes an army to get rid of people like him."

Gretchen petted her hair. *Thank God, Lily has allowed her hair to grow a little longer. It's still so curly.* "So, where's that SEAL? He can help me gather a little DNA anytime he wants to."

Lily laughed and sniffed at the same time. And Gretchen was back.

As if ordered by the gods, JT arrived to babysit while Dev went into the office. He also brought chicken, steaks, corn on the cob, farm fresh tomatoes, and the biggest strawberries Lily had ever seen. He knew a man. *Of course, he did.*

Lily had to warn Gretchen that no touching was allowed. JT could've dressed in a few more clothes. Instead, he wore his usual workout shorts, tight to the skin. His shirt was light enough in color you could see every ripple and bump. Gretchen's eyes followed him everywhere when he came into the room and when he departed. Coming or going, JT was at the center of her attention. Abby was busy unloading boxes upstairs. Gretchen was just ogling. Lily needed two large post-it notes with **STOP** written on them. One would be placed on JT's chest and the other strategically on his backside. *That should do it! Right!*

Thankfully, Dev arrived home as JT started the grill. He kissed Lily, interrupting some talk about pink curtains. *Pink curtains?* "Honey, I've been called back out into the field. I leave tomorrow morning again."

Lily would not cry. She refused to do so; hormones be damned. "I understand. Who is to babysit me?"

"Well, Gretchen, Abby, and Mort will be here, so I feel good about that."

That was interesting. "No strong men? Are you using me as bait again, husband?"

"No. I wouldn't do that. I think Dad, Jackson, and Danny will probably take turns spending the night. Please keep Gretchen away from the priest, heck, and away from Jackson. Oh, and don't even allow her to speak to my father."

Lily clapped her hands. "That would be perfect! Honey, you could have Gretchen as your stepmother."

Her joke had hit his mark. His scowl served as his answer.

"Fine," Lily laughed. "I'll keep her away from all the men in my life."

"She can have Ari," Dev added. "I would pull up a chair and eat popcorn while watching that show."

"Very few know how evil you can be, Agent Pierce." She kissed his cheek and touched his lips with her hand. "You need to play nice with others. I keep telling you that."

"I know, I know. I better rescue JT from Gretchen." Dev could see the two on the patio. "She keeps reaching for things in front of him. What is she doing?"

The baby kicked soundly. Dev even saw the movement.

"She's being seductive. Go rescue your friend before anything happens out there." She waved her husband away. The baby kicked again. She attempted a few short breaths to take the edge off. *I know. You're upset because Daddy is going away. We will be okay. I've been okay before. I can do this again. But now I have you. We just need to get you here, baby.*

Chapter Twenty-Two

$\mathcal{D}$ev was a passenger in a DEA car the next morning. As it turned the corner, Lily stood in the yard acting as though she was the strongest person in the world. She was no Hercules. Her world was in that car headed toward the interstate. He had just come home, and now he was gone again. Making the turn to come to her house was a truck full of baby furniture. She had tried three times to tell Gretchen that the furniture wasn't necessary, but she wouldn't listen to her pleas. There was no way to harness the storm that was Gretchen. *What am I going to do with this stuff?*

Lily was restricted to the downstairs sofa. Mort, the DEA dropout German Shepherd, was content to sit on an ottoman in front of her, resting her head on Lily's belly. Except for the noise and muffled discussion coming from upstairs, the house was surprisingly peaceful. Lily was enjoying the time to read through a baby magazine while petting Mort's head.

The coordinator was in her glory as she directed the movers to the upstairs nursery. Lily watched the action from a living room chair. The furniture was extremely high quality. She giggled at the thought that she was shocked there was no leopard or animal print of any kind. Of course, there was still time for curtains and pillows.

"Pick up something, please. No slackers here," Gretchen ordered. One man slid empty-handed into the house.

Mort's ears pointed straight up, and she began a low growl.

Lily looked down at the dog as Mort suddenly jumped off her perch and stood in front of her human. "What is it, girl?"

"I'm not a mover. I'm here to see Lily." Gretchen eyed him suspiciously. He looked familiar. Perhaps he was the son of someone she knew at the club? Who would she know in Virginia? *No, it can't be. It is the minister!*

"I'm in here." Lily's voice led his way to her chair. She assured her protector that she was safe. "Mort, sit." The dog responded by sitting at her feet, lowering to a sleeping position. "Grant, what are you doing here?"

"Do you have any updates for me?" He appeared frantic, sweat on his brow, his hands were shaking. "Please tell me you all have figured out something."

"Grant, I'm not privy to what the guys do or don't know. Just this past weekend, your buddy Brad sat behind me in church and then was standing next to my parked car. I don't need to worry about you. If you haven't noticed, I'm having my first baby with my husband. I need to just worry about us."

The minister sat in the adjacent chair. He leaned back and shut his eyes as though he was in prayer. "I'm sorry. I didn't think about all of that."

"We've already established that you never have believed you've done anything stupid. If you did, you wouldn't be in this position." Lily paused as he finally opened his eyes. "How is your wife? Have you told her what is going on?"

"Are you crazy? Of course not."

Lily shook her head in dismay. "That's not a smart move. Honesty has never been your strong suit, has it?"

Oddly, Grant Sharpe relaxed a bit. He had forgotten how Lily could be very sharp tongued when she needed to be. But he had come today to her, for her to save him. "Lily, I am so sorry for what I did to you."

Perhaps Lily's eyes were deceiving her, but he looked as though he was sincere. *Do hormones make you believe ex-fiancés?*

"Thank you," she answered softly. "You need to understand something. It wasn't what you did, Grant, it's what you didn't do. You weren't honest. You weren't supportive. You didn't love me the way I deserved to be loved. You weren't there for me when I was in a crisis. My mother's death rocked me. Then when my father was dying from cancer, just like your mother had years ago, you told me you couldn't be around. His death devastated me. I felt as though I was alone. Of course, I had my family, Abby, and some of my clients and friends, but I didn't have you. But I thank you for being you. You walked away, and eventually; Dev walked through my door. Even when he is gone, he gives me more support than you could ever give another human being." *Finally, all the words came out of my mouth the way I wanted them to! Now, I'm really finished with him.*

"Ouch." Grant only uttered that one word. She was completely correct. He offered support to his church community, but that was his job. Sadly, he knew he needed to change his life; he had needed to for a very long time.

"I need you to do something for me though. I need to have a few friends with me at the charity event. Let me provide a boutonniere for your benefactor. We need to make him feel special." Lily had a plan.

"I thought he was the bad guy."

"Oh, he is," Lily said casually. "But he still needs to be made to feel special. I'll need to bring at least two more people."

"Fine. I'll just make sure the registrar knows you are bringing a group, how's that?"

"Perfect." It would be perfect if her suspicions were fulfilled.

"Sorry to bring this back up, but what am I going to do? Those photos will ruin me. My past coming forward will prevent my ministry from continuing. I'll lose my church, my wife--"

"Your girlfriend, and perhaps your pot stash?" Lily didn't wait for an answer. "JT said he would help you. He will, despite you, he will help. Is Brad still on you?"

"For your information, he has cut off my pharmaceutical drugs."

"Ha." Lily's short loud laugh was heard by one of the movers. He stopped and looked. He proceeded up the stairs with a white chair that seemed to feature a pink rose pattern. *What is Gretchen doing? I need to stop her, but she promised we'd go out for ice cream later.*

Grant ignored her disdain. "He wants me to get close to you, maybe get you to say something incriminating."

Lily frowned. "Like what? That I still love you or something?"

"Maybe something a little more provocative."

Lily looked down at her body, and then she smiled. "You have got to be kidding. Do you know me?" *Grant does know me, and he should remember I would do nothing to jeopardize my life, my marriage. Besides, I fell asleep on my wedding night. I won't tell him that.*

"I'm as big as a whale, and quite frankly, have you seen my husband? You are a nice-looking guy, but you are nothing, sorry, compared to my husband." He wasn't. He was at least two, if not three inches shorter in height. His eyes didn't twinkle either. They never did.

"What about something financial?"

Lily twitched her mouth back and forth as though she was searching for an answer. "Nope."

"Maybe you slept around after I left you?"

Lily grabbed her head. If she grabbed it, maybe it wouldn't explode? "I was a nun, a very celibate nun. I know clergy who have better love lives than me during that time. I went on one date with a bartender. Geez, why am I telling you any of this? Grant, listen to me." She turned to face him. "JT will help you. You need to talk to him. I am off limits. If Dev knew you were here, well, it wouldn't be good. I will tell him when he gets home."

"Lily, please. They are making me--" Grant grasped his hands tightly. This time he was in prayer. Ultimately, there was no way out. He had to tell someone.

"Making you do what, Grant?"

"They forced me to become a drug contact at a high school."

Lily heard what he said, but she was still processing in her mind what he really meant. "Are you telling me that you are dealing drugs to high school students?"

"Keeting made me. I've been such a fool."

Lily stood up quickly. Mort growled protectively. As Lily pointed at the door, the dog bared her teeth. "Get out. Get out now. I am calling JT now. I know exactly what Keeting and Khalid are doing. A drug dealer in my house, the house of a DEA special operations agent. Out!" She grabbed Mort's collar as she lunged forward to attack the unwelcome visitor.

Her yelling also brought two sets of feet running down the stairs. Abby was the first to arrive. She said an obscenity when she saw Grant. Gretchen came forward. "I don't know what you have done now, but if Lily says out, you get out right now. Mister, now." She walked over and began to pull the humiliated minister out of the house.

As Gretchen forcefully escorted him out the door, Abby held Lily in her arms. "What do I need to do?"

"Nothing. I need to call Dev's emergency number. The minister has compromised Dev. He could lose everything because of that idiot."

"Where's your phone?" Abby began looking around the room.

"It's on the table, over there." Lily sat down quickly. The room began to spin. *I don't know what I'll do if they destroy Dev and his career. I really will have JT or Ari dispose of Grant somewhere in Prince William Forest, or maybe somewhere along the Appalachian Trail. Lord, this can't be happening.*

Abby handed the phone to her, and she called the number. Within a few minutes, the phone rang. Lily breathed deeply. "Baby, the minister was here today. He has done something awful. He was in our house."

"Lily, tell me everything."

Dev could take a punch. He could take a challenge, and he could survive a threat. Hearing his wife's explanations that she had created a threat to his career because of her past relationship was hard to take. He listened intently. She was angry. She wasn't crying.

Finally, he answered. "Here's what you are going to do. You are going to relax and keep our baby happy. You are going to call Dan and have him come over. Just talk to him. I'll call in and have someone take your statement, but make sure Dan is there when you make it. He is also an attorney.

We can't hide this in the shadows. That's what they want. We are going to call their bluff. Do you understand, Lily?"

Lily nodded. "Yes, but what could this do to Grant?"

Dev waited a second and then answered, "I don't give a damn. But he'll be fine. Honey, you don't know it, but the DEA has been working on something in Maryland, and this all might be tied together. You will call Dan, wait for him, and then the DEA will be over. Got it?"

"Yes. I can do this."

She didn't see Dev's smile. He softened his tone. "I love you, and I know you can do anything. You are part of a highly successful detective agency. I have all faith in you and in Gretchen."

"How do you know about all of that?"

"Undercover guy, remember?" He was comforted by the giggle on the other side of the call.

"Oh no, Gretchen! Could you please send some ugly DEA agents?"

His girl was back in control. "I'll tell them to send the ugliest guys we have, or maybe we have a couple of female agents? Would that work?"

"As long as they aren't her type!"

It was almost dinner time by the time the DEA supervisor and another agent entered the house. Dan sat by Lily's side as she recounted Grant's visit. She went out on a limb and told them about the blackmail attempt that forced him into what he did. The supervisor knew Dev very well and assured her that her husband wasn't compromised in any way. Everything would be fine. *He's just placating a very pregnant woman. I know that tone.*

But it was mandatory for Lily to believe him. She knew by now that there was always more to the story when dealing with the DEA. Maybe she would eventually learn some of the details, but most likely she would acquire bits and pieces of information within the next five years. Of course, she would give up trying to pry any details out of Dev. It truly was futile.

After the agents left, the three women and a priest had dinner and lots of conversation. The priest decided he would be the one to spend the night on the couch. *What was with these men and that couch? There's a perfectly good bed upstairs in the guest room.*

In the morning, Lily insisted she had to go to church. It was time to talk to God about this entire mess. Dan drove her while Gretchen followed behind.

"Has Gretchen been in a Catholic church? She won't burn up in all-consuming fire if she enters, will she?" Dan looked in the rear-view mirror to make sure she was still following him.

"Stop it. She's been in a Catholic church when she's working. Besides, you have fire extinguishers."

"Ah, I forgot about her job and the fire extinguishers. By the way, I feel pretty good about yesterday, don't you?" He glanced at his passenger briefly.

Lily leaned her head on her arm propped on the window ledge of the car. "I suppose. I'm beginning to not trust anyone. Is that bad?"

"No. I understand, but you should now understand why Dev is considered a Boy Scout. He follows the law, and he believes the law will protect the innocent and jail the guilty."

Lily squirmed in the seat. Her back was stiff. She hadn't slept much last night in an attempt to become comfortable. It was harder every night to take the stress off her body. "I hope he's right."

"He is."

"You are awfully positive about this."

Dan took another glance at the driver behind him. "I'm relieved that we have other authorities involved in this, not just our team and the CIA. The DEA has resources, and I bet they'll contact the FBI."

Lily sighed. "And they'll all discover they can't do a darn thing to remove Khalid from this soil."

"Have faith."

Lily pointed her finger at him. "I just knew you were going to say it. It's in your employee's manual, isn't it?"

Dan smiled sheepishly. "Well, actually it is." He pulled toward the rectory's garage and motioned Gretchen into the church parking lot. "Come on. Let's go to Mass and see what we can do about your trust issues."

Gretchen sat in the pew next to Lily. The very pregnant woman looked down at the kneeler. It would be a challenge to get down on it, but the larger challenge would be getting back up again. *Would I even fit in between the pew's seat and the pew in front of me? What kind of equipment would the EMT team have to use to pick me up? Would they borrow some crane from a construction company?*

Gretchen occasionally grasped Lily's hand. Lily looked down at her friend's heavily ring-laden hand. One ring nearly spanned past her knuckle. Another one had diamonds set in different heights. *Wow, that could hurt someone. Yes, that could hurt someone.*

Lily began to formulate a plan. *This just might work. I always knew Gretchen was a weapon of mass destruction. I have the perfect target for her. Thanks, Lord. You never fail me.*

Dan saw Lily's face change as he prepared the eucharistic celebration on the altar. It was as though the Lord had removed her fears. *Thank you, Lord. Please help her.*

And then she smiled, a very thin smile as though she knew something no one else knew. Dan noticed her again in the small group for morning Mass. Dev had often mentioned that Lily's mind worked in a very organized way. She thought things out and over-organized. Dan became suspicious as her smile widened. *Lord, what is she plotting now? We may need your divine intervention this time.*

Chapter Twenty-Three

1. Gretchen seems to scare JT
2. How many sets of fake lashes did Gretchen bring?
3. Need to talk to Gretchen about the nursery
4. Must eat more veggies and fruit
5. Mmm, watermelon

*A*bby had placed a chair outside the nursery that Gretchen was designing. Lily felt as though she should be the director of this crazy film, but she wasn't. She was a spectator in her own production. Gretchen was firmly in charge. Every time Lily wanted to protest, there was suddenly a bowl of ice cream in one of her hands and a spoon in the other. Lily's protests were muffled by the most wonderful flavors. She hoped her treats were off-set by the walks Abby and she were taking in the cool of the morning. Mort, the lazy canine was still asleep at Gretchen's feet. Luckily, the baby woke Lily up early enough, and Abby didn't seem to mind getting out of the house to get away from her suite buddy, Gretchen.

"It was so good to see Jeremy the other night." Lily's waddle seemed wobblier today. Thankfully, they stayed on flat streets.

"I know. I hope you don't mind, but I'm not going to that charity party. Jeremy and I are going to take three days and go on a short trip to the beach. Let's head to that street over there."

Lily followed Abby's pointed finger. "Nope, that looks like a mountain to me. Of course, you go. I'll still have Gretchen."

"What are you two plotting?" Abby took a drink from her water bottle. She had heard them whispering and organizing. Traveling with Gretchen had opened her eyes. The insane event planner was just as organized as Lily. She made lists incessantly, crossing out each item accomplished. *They scare me. I won't tell Lily how similar they are. We don't need to stress the baby.*

"Oh, we're helping with the event, just a little." Lily looked forward. She was telling one of her best friends a half lie. *We are helping.*

"Well, just be careful."

Lily stopped walking. "Careful? We aren't doing anything dangerous. I promise."

"Be careful because of the baby. Don't stand too long, make sure you drink your water, etc. What did you think I meant?" Abby's interest was piqued by Lily's defense.

"Oh, that." *Geez, Lily, you aren't very good at this. Obviously, this agent stuff isn't for me.* She looked down at her body. How could she forget about **that**? "I'll take care. I promise. How is the shop? Gretchen has created a whirlwind in the house, and you and I haven't had much time to talk."

"Wonderful." Lily noticed Abby's face light up as she said just that one word. "I have one part-time designer. She is a retired florist who lives just a block from the shop. I work around her schedule, and it worked very well during the May and June weddings. She will work again in September, October and November. Of course, I have one college girl who is my mini me. My staff is completed with three other contract workers who help deliver and clean up."

Lily grabbed her hand as they walked. "I am so proud of you. Watch out that you don't delegate so much that you have no income."

"Your accountant has been working with me. I've been careful. I keep my inventory down, and frankly, Gretchen has chosen me for two high dollar weddings already this year. We have four more this fall."

"Wow, remember when you used to hide in the backroom when she walked in or even called?"

Abby's giggle was infectious. Lily stopped walking. "I can't walk and laugh this hard at the same time or I'll have to knock on someone's door so I can go to the bathroom."

"Nice way to meet the neighbors?" Abby stopped beside her friend. "Besides, I have this new thing I do. It's called *medirita*."

Lily's eyes crossed. "*Medirita?*"

"I finish the day, after a long day of Gretchen with meditation while I drink a margarita. *Medirita!*"

Lily leaned over and hugged Abby. "I've missed you so much."

"But have you missed the life you used to have?" Abby whispered in her ear. As the women pulled back from their embrace, Lily thought for just a second.

"Surprisingly, no. There are those days when I think I could be doing something more productive, and then Dev's aunt will call needing assistance on a wedding or an event out at the vineyard. Dev's dad has helped so much, and I've met a few women at church and around here. I actually went to the library the other day. I can't tell you the last time I did that. With this pregnancy, it's all been about preparing, so even when Dev is gone, I'm busy. Right now, we have this thing with the terrorist."

"You say that like it is a normal thing."

Lily's laughter was nervous. "It seemingly is. The last few years of my life--"

Abby stopped her. "You've been a danger magnet."

"There is that. I guess it comes with being Devlin Pierce's wife."

Abby smiled. Jeremy and she remained close, but she often wondered where, literally where they were headed. "And that is still good?"

The baby kicked to answer the question for her. "It is more than good. There's not one day that I regret becoming his wife."

"No regrets," Abby murmured wistfully. "That's what I want."

Chapter Twenty-Four

"Agent Pierce, good to have you here." Dev was met with a friendly handshake from Agent Andre Freeman as he was led into the New York office of the FBI. It was a clear, hot summer day in Manhattan. Dev could see the skyline of the lower island, once spotlighting the two World Trade Center Towers.

"You have a beautiful view on this floor." It was Dev's attempt at small talk as he put the memories aside and focused on following the agent to a private office. Dev could still remember those towers in his mind. That one day changed his life.

"I hear you just returned from Israel?" Agent Freeman led him into a smaller office holding a conference table.

"Yes. I've been traveling quite a bit lately. I think I remember you from the Suarez case in Miami a few years back." Dev took a deep breath as he was directed to a chair facing the windows. *Get it together, Pierce. Keep on the task at hand, not the past.*

"That's right. I was working with the federal prosecutor's office and assisting on that sting operation off the coast of Key West. I'm sorry about this New York meeting and keeping you away from your wife. Sadly, some of the Washington FBI are too tight with the congressmen involved. Have a seat."

Agent Freeman took a seat at the head of the oblong table. He slid a file forward to Dev. "That updates you on all the intel. You know, when you suggested that maybe Khalid's lineage was in question, I thought that might be too easy. Your wife's suspicions are simple, and if proven correct, brilliant. Are you aware that the Mossad is collecting information as we speak?"

"Yes, I would imagine they are. I met with a few old contacts while I was there, and they confirmed Khalid is certainly bringing his operation here." Dev had discovered that Khalid was putting his nose in many different ventures, not just art and drugs.

Freeman opened his own file. "We firmly believe he is setting up the embassy as his base. That fiasco at the Louvre taught us a very valuable lesson. He isn't bashful with his lofty ambitions or taking chances. Funneling drugs into the United States by smuggling them in diplomatic pouches means they can't be touched. But if it can be proved that he isn't part of the royal family, then he will lose his position and his immunity. We can at least get him out of here and stop his ambitions. I've alerted the State Department, and I'll update them on the situation. If we can give them something to go on, we all can proceed."

Dev opened the file in front of him. He was never that confident when dealing with the bureaucrats. He shook his head. "It's not that easy with Khalid, it never is. So, let's say he loses his immunity. What then? He turns his operations to Turkey, or maybe Egypt this time?"

Freeman shook his head. "We think, of course all of this is hypothetical, but if he embarrasses the kingdom this time, they will take him out. At the very least, we can gain intel and seize those drug shipments."

Dev glared at that opinion. He looked outside and didn't see the twin towers. "In 2001, most of those terrorists were their own citizens, and they did nothing. Setting up scholarship funds for children who have lost their fathers and mothers isn't enough. They may remove him, but he will be back. They turn a blind eye when it suits them." *There's good people with good intentions, but a lack of options and actions can destroy so much and so many.*

"Agent Pierce, you know we can't assassinate him. That's against the law."

Dev looked down into the file. He turned over a page or two of paper, but he wasn't reading. "Hmm. We all know that."

Agent Freeman saw something in the DEA agent that alerted his FBI trained senses. "Agent Pierce, you do know we can't kill him unless provoked?"

Dev's head shot up. "Provoked? He sent a box of ricin to my pregnant wife. He sent a terrorist, accompanied by a child, into a children's hospital to kill a nurse just doing her job. He sent his guard dog into a church to threaten a priest and my wife. What more does he need to do? Oh, I know. I understand, and I've been trained to understand, and to stand down. That's the only reason why I alerted my supervisors, and frankly, why I am here. If I didn't believe in the law, Khalid would be dead by now. Plain enough for you, Agent Freeman?"

"Crystal." Freeman pulled away from the table and stood up. "I think we need coffee. Agent Pierce, it's not that we are going to do absolutely nothing. It's just that we need to be careful every step of the way." The FBI agent saw another meeting attendee waiting outside the room. "Ah, here's another one of our secret weapons." He opened the door and allowed the young man in.

"Hey Dev."

Dev questioned everything the FBI was setting up as he looked up to see the visitor. "Nitwit? Jeremy?"

Freeman saw Pierce's demeanor flip flop as Jeremy Klein entered the room. "You fill him in about your algorithms while I get a large pot of coffee.

The young man and the seasoned DEA agent shook hands. "Dev, my Pashto is getting better. This trip to the Big Apple is so cool. I never thought I'd be helping out so quickly but because of the personal nature of this operation, they brought me in. Surprise!"

Jeremy's quick speech caused Dev to smile. Jeremy's energy was intoxicating; maybe all of this might work out. "Show me what you have, Jeremy."

The computer genius quickly opened his laptop and began to acquaint Dev with his specialty. "Khalid is a creature of habit." As Jeremy began his presentation, he saw Dev nod. "I know you know that. You've followed him for years. I researched who he threatens and how he disposes of his enemies. He has broken his habits with you. He seems to delight in doing something different, even when you were following him into Syria."

Dev glanced at Jeremy. The young man knew more about Dev's paths in the Middle East than he could actually remember. "When you are tracking a killer, you aren't actually aware of borders."

"I get it, so here, look at the screen. It seems Khalid likes to provoke you. Also, we might be underestimating Brad Keeting's influence in all of this. He hates your team. You guys really got under his skin. It really goes back to that gold you all found."

Dev attempted to remain unaffected by Jeremy's statement. JT, Paul, Dan and he had agreed to never talk about that incident ever again. It was just safer that way. *Keeting never liked us, but could it really be about the gold?* The CIA operative had guessed their report was not complete, but he couldn't prove it, and he never would.

"Fine, I'm looking at my military service on your screen. What does it have to do with taking down Khalid?" His impatience was growing going down memory lane when he knew his wife could be in danger. He wasn't there to protect her.

"Now watch Khalid's path when I overlay it with your DEA missions." Dev watched the screen and was in disbelief. "He's been following me?"

"It appears that way, but it is more that you have been tracking many of the drug operations that he is funding through product or money. Pretty rad, huh?"

Dev's frown shut down Jeremy's delight. "I wouldn't say rad, Jeremy. I was thinking he was just poking me because he knew he could. We were in that office in the Louvre, and I know he could've killed me right there and then, or had his flunky do it. But he didn't."

"Where would the fun be in doing it there? He wants you to suffer like his brother did. You remember his brother, right?"

Dev shoved his chair and stood up quickly. "Are you a computer expert, or an interrogator, Jeremy?" Dev didn't need to relive the mistakes he had made.

"I'm sorry. I really don't remember what I ate yesterday, so I'm not sure what someone remembers. Some soldiers pack those memories away in a neat little bag. I didn't mean any disrespect. I'm just doing my job."

Dev walked toward the window and stared out at lower Manhattan's skyline. "I know what he is doing. He is terrorizing me through Lily. He terrorized Paul through his wife. He is threatening Dan's church, letting him know that he can come in and destroy all that truly is holy. If he had done anything to JT personally, he hasn't shared."

"JT has been hit personally." Jeremy's voice was devoid of any light-hearted tones. Dev turned sharply to address him.

"How?"

"JT wasn't really part of your team. He was taken in, but he still wasn't Army. As a SEAL, his team is very important. If he loses his team, he loses everything. Khalid is one sick puppy."

Dev looked toward the ceiling and shut his eyes. "He'll hurt JT by isolating him. He won't touch him. He will take us out one by one, and he will make him watch. We've sent JT on a wild goose chase going after Keeting." Dev swore under his breath.

"JT has gained some intel on Keeting. His movements have been very enlightening. Keeting is still employed by the CIA, but he certainly makes a lot of money on the side. They have been watching him since you ran into him in South America. Thanks to your report, they have been tailing him."

"Then why didn't they stop that massacre in Paris?"

Jeremy shrugged. "I'm still in training, but it's my understanding that they are waiting for the right time."

"That's what Washington is known for, just picking the right time according to their interests while innocent people die." *Maybe it is time for me to look for a new job.*

"That's why we are here in New York City. Two congressmen are ensnared in this entire operation. They leaked the names to the newspaper. The newspaper had this great story, and you know the rest. Those same congressmen will be at that charity event. They are on the board of the charity. We've been delving into their finances, and they have made more money than what the charity has brought in. This whole thing is all over the board with Khalid pushing all the pieces."

Ironically, Dev smiled. Puzzle pieces. His wife could fit the pieces together if she had all of the corners. But she wasn't the professional, he was. *Lily is my kryptonite, and Khalid knows it. Stop thinking like a husband. Think like a soldier, fighting to survive, fighting for everyone back home. Dammit, Khalid is here. He's in my home.*

"Do you have a plan, Jeremy?"

"We have developed a plan. The State Department has issued guidelines for us to follow so be careful, but they are allowing the FBI to do oversight. We also have the Secret Service involved. Khalid may just be targeting you all, but he may have a bigger target. The Vice President has been invited to that charity event. Um, let me find our point man, yes, you know him. Our Secret Service guy is Monroe Patton. You know him, right?"

Dev's hands unclenched. "Oh, I know him. Monroe was at West Point with us. He's tough." *Going down memory lane is all I'm doing today.*

"Your brother got me on board right away. He had a theory, and he was right about Khalid's involvement with the drug trade in South America. Jackson is assisting as a liaison with the Washington office, so they don't get their noses out of joint too much. And then we have one more character, and you won't like this one."

Dev chuckled. "Who are you going to bring in now? My first-grade teacher or Garrett Notte, that idiot drug trafficker?"

Jeremy winced. "I don't know about your teacher, man, and Garrett is still in jail, but his dad isn't."

"Jesus," Dev muttered. The timing was perfect as

a limping Bernard Notte entered the room with Agent Freeman.

Jeremy lifted his arm, his hand extended in royal fashion. "May I present our secret weapon, Mr. Bernard Notte."

"Hello, Mr. Pierce."

Memory Lane is truly a rotten path. "Notte. I hear you are going to help us this time."

"That's what I've been told, Pierce. It's either that or they leave me to Khalid."

"It would be a win either way, Notte, as far as I'm concerned." Dev walked all the way around the table to avoid the man. As they sat down, Jackson entered the room and sat beside his brother.

"We can do this together, Dev."

"Jackson, we have to." Dev said a silent prayer as he began to listen to the option and the plans. He began to make a list. Lily would be so proud of him. *You have me making a list, you crazy woman! God, we have to do this.*

Chapter Twenty-Five

1. Must have comfy shoes
2. Could I wear sneakers?
3. Need new dress for event
4. Plan out attack with Gretchen
5. Talk to Jill

"How are you doing?"

"Oh, I'm slow, Lily, but at least I'm home from the hospital. How are you? The baby is almost here, right?"

Lily rubbed her belly. Now it wasn't just a zip code, it was its own county. "Yes. Just a few more weeks. I'm as ready as possible. I hear my husband will be home tonight so that is a relief."

"Yes," Jill whispered. "I've made the decision to go to that event."

Lily was stunned. "Are you sure you are up to it?"

"Yes. I'm going to come in a wheelchair, but I'm coming. We need to show a fortified front. Paul isn't thrilled, but he would rather have me with him than here at home alone, as alone as you can be with a security car in front of your house."

"How are your daughters coping with all of this?"

Jill shifted slowly on her couch. "The oldest one isn't so thrilled. Paul has her on a short leash. She goes to her summer internship, and she comes home. The younger one thinks Dad is cool now. You know, Paul never talked about anything about his service. Even I know so little, and we lived on post most of the time while he was in."

"Paul left the Army first, didn't he?"

"Yes," Jill answered. "His last deployment did him in. It was hard for him to make the decision, but Dan was leaving for the priesthood. Mike and Tom were already dead. JT and Dev stayed in the longest." She paused to think. "I guess JT was still in when Dev came home."

There's still so much I don't know about my own husband. Will I ever know it all? "Yet, they are so close, still."

"In their own way. They have their separate lives, then they come together, and it's as if they were never away from each other. That terrorist doesn't know what he has done. They are a team again."

"And we are a little part of that this time too, Jill. I'll see you Saturday."

"Yes, you will," Jill answered strongly.

After their goodbyes, Lily looked down at her stomach. "Well, baby, I didn't want normal anymore." As if on cue, Gretchen flounced down the stairs in her own way.

"I believe I only have a few more touches and the room will be complete. I believe it is my best work." She sat down slowly across from Lily as she noticed the pensive former florist. "What's wrong?"

"Nothing. I was just thinking."

"That's highly overrated. Don't do that too often." Gretchen looked down at one of her painted fingernails. She had chipped it hanging the last bit of tulle. So far, she had sacrificed two nails to her Picasso of nurseries.

"I do, Gretchen. I have a lot of time on my hands right now. I think about the awful world I'm sending this baby into." Lily's face was sullen and pale.

Gretchen sprang from the chair. "And it is also a beautiful world full of color and joy. It's all in how you look at it, dearie. You can't think that way. I refuse to do so."

Lily looked up into Gretchen's highly made-up face. *Oh my gosh, she has lipstick on at ten in the morning, and she's wearing kitten heels.* "I know, but it is hard to do when so many things are so bad. My husband is a good guy. He doesn't deserve this."

"Mr. Delicious is a great guy. He can handle this, and we can do it! Don't forget the team of Schmidt, sorry, Pierce and Malloy are on the case. You'll have a beautiful life for that baby after Saturday."

Lily struggled to get out of the chair. Gretchen helped her from behind her shoulders. "What is it with Khalid and parties? I have to get a dress or maybe a tent."

"The man knows how to party? We need to go shopping? Wonderful."

As Lily began her slow walk to the nearest bathroom, she waved Gretchen off. "Oh yeah. I don't need to party or shop. I just have to pee every hour on the hour."

Gretchen completely disregarded her grousing. "What color do you want to wear? I'm thinking a navy color would be slimming, Lily. I'm wearing a yummy shade of raspberry, slim over the hips with revealing cleavage. I always try to focus on my assets."

Lily took a breath as she finally reached her destination. "Yah, yah, yah…"

That night Dev returned home, and he brought Jeremy with him. Dev was grilling hamburgers on the back patio, a beer in his hand, when Gretchen brought out a package of hot dogs.

"Your dad wants a couple of hot dogs."

"Fine. Just set them over there." Dev directed with the bottle. Gretchen noticed he was unusually quiet. His eyes didn't twinkle. Instead, they were dark and brooding. Gretchen didn't see Mr. Delicious. She saw the character Heathcliff from *Wuthering Heights*.

"I hope you are going to share your concerns with your wife."

Dev ignored her statement, answering her with a low growl.

"Hey," Gretchen said as she grabbed the bottle out of his hand. "You need to talk to Lily about what is going on. Don't you dare shut her out this time."

Dev flipped the burgers and plopped the dogs on the grill. "I'll talk to her later. I promise."

"What do you think is the endgame for this guy?"

"In my worst-case scenario, he wants a brother for a brother. He lost his, and it was probably at my hands during war. He wants to make me hurt, and he thinks he can do it by ruining Lily or taking her away from me. He wants all of us to feel alone. He wants us to become him."

Gretchen handed the bottle back. "How could he make you become him?"

"He's already tried to get Lily's ex-fiancé to find something awful about her, or to make her do something she would never do such as cheating on me with her ex." Dev chuckled for the first time in days. "He needs better intel, or he would know that Lily couldn't and wouldn't do that if someone gave her a million dollars."

Gretchen raised an eyebrow. She might. "So, what does he have on you?"

"My entire career, at least in his eyes. His brother's death is at my hand. I've tracked Khalid all over the Middle East. He knows my weak point. He killed a little girl just because I gave her a book. It was a special childhood book my mom gave me when I was a kid."

"Ah, anything else?"

"Gretchen, what the hell do you want me to say?"

"What does he have on you? Did you do something

that was out of character? Did you steal from him or fall in love with his pet camel?"

"I'm done talking. The burgers and hot dogs are ready."

Gretchen began to open her mouth one more time and then shut it tightly. *So, there is something? Devlin Pierce what are you hiding?*

Later that night, the house was quiet. Lily attempted to discover a comfortable position, shifting this pillow here and that pillow there. Dev stood by the bed watching his wife.

"You know, I've never slept with a pregnant woman. I've been meaning to tell you that."

Lily glared as she found just the right combination of pillows, bed, and body parts so she could sleep. "I certainly hope you haven't. Since you are the Boy Scout, I figured you hadn't."

As Dev pulled back the covers and slid in, Lily could see the concern on his face.

"I'm not always a Boy Scout. Years ago, I made some decisions that were less than perfect."

"It couldn't have been that bad," Lily murmured as she touched his chest. "Will you get the light?"

In a second the room was dark, the only light coming from the moonlight streaming in through their bedroom. "Lily, we found Khalid's stockpile years ago."

"Good. What's bad about that?'

"We gave it away to the people so they could get away from the monster."

Lily patted him softly. "I'm sure your commanding officers were a little surprised when you gave the people those guns, but they needed something to protect themselves, right?"

"It wasn't guns."

"What was it? Food?"

Dev's arm reached down from behind his head to hold his wife. "Gold. Gold coins, bars, and jewelry. We gave away his gold. What the village people couldn't carry we reported to our commanders. We made the decision among us to only report what was left."

Lily leaned up as much as she could. "Let me get this right. He isn't mad about his brother, or loss of men or drugs along the way? He's mad about his missing gold?"

"Yep."

"Okay, so he is so sick. He's made more money since then."

Dev finally stopped looking at the ceiling, placing his attention onto his wife. "But he lost control over the province; he lost those people. He lost his slaves and his informers. He lost credibility and respect. He had to start over. I'm thinking that Keeting told him how much gold was confiscated, and when Khalid figured that some of the gold was gone, he probably thought we took it for ourselves. A month later he came back to that area, and the entire village was gone. They had escaped his imprisonment. Then he knew the truth."

"Wow." Lily leaned down and kissed him slowly. "You are even more delicious now that I know you have a little bad boy in you."

Dev laughed out loud. "It wasn't that bad, except we lied on a report. We all lied for those suffering people. We didn't think twice about it. This was after his brother was killed in a nasty battle. This was after he killed little Bahara just because she wanted to read. This was after he land mined the orphanage and bombed the school. We found his gold, and we made him pay those poor people. Now you know I'm not the Boy Scout all the time."

"Oh honey, I already knew that, but that's what I love about you." She kissed him again. "If I could reach more of you, I would. In this shape, I can only reach your mouth."

His eyes finally twinkled for her. "That's enough for now. I'm just sorry you are paying the price."

"Do you really think he would be here if you weren't married, having a child, and happy? Of course not, so let's just get him out of our country and our lives. We can all do this together."

Dev brought his other hand up to lightly brush the hair from her face.

"Yes, together." *I hope you're right, Lily.*

Chapter Twenty-Six

1. Pack as much as I can in little purse
2. Candy bar in purse
3. Phone in purse with doctor's number in ICE
4. Does this dress make me look bigger?
5. You look hugely pregnant
6. Survive tonight

*J*ackson Pierce attached Lily's brooch on her dress above her heart. They were alone in the room, in the privacy of Dev's home office. The doors were shut tightly. Dev was upstairs still dressing. Gretchen was still making herself up. He could only wonder about how long that took to do.

"You know, he is going to kill you and me when he finds out everything." Lily watched her brother-in-law carefully place the pin and its secret weapon on her. "This is better than those watch bands that count your steps. This way you'll know every step I take, every move I make." Lily laughed nervously at her attempt at humor. Now, she wanted to sing the song, *I'll Be Watching You.* Jackson didn't move a muscle to even smile. It did appear his frown lines had creases upon their creases.

"He will kill me, not you. He wouldn't like anything about this idea, especially if we use the baby and you as bait."

Jackson stepped back to make sure the tracking device was working. Lily took a few steps to assist him. "It's not the first time I've been used in a sting operation. I'm choosing to do this."

"Are Gretchen and you still going ahead with your little idea?" His attention was on his small monitor.

Lily placed her hands on her hips. "It isn't just a little idea. Besides, it will keep Gretchen occupied. Trust me, without Abby here to act as a buffer, Gretchen in full measure is way more than any of us can take. She needs to feel as though she is adding her special skills into the mix."

"Well, I have to hand it to you. Your crazy ideas got the ball rolling in the right direction. Ari is absolutely thrilled. You were his favorite before, but now you are a rock star in his little beady eyes."

"Ah, I'm his favorite?"

Jackson finally looked up from the device and smiled. "Don't get too excited. The man's favorite thing to eat is some sort of eel."

Lily's stomach rolled. "Yuk. I need something to eat. Are we finished?"

The doors opened to reveal a very brooding, very handsome tux-wearing Devlin Pierce. "I like this tracking idea, but I don't. Have I told you that, Jackson?"

"Yes, many times, but you should be happy that we'll know where Lily is every second." Jackson placed the transmitter in the pocket of his tuxedo. "If she is the target, we will have her covered. You are on your own."

"I'm fine with that. I am wondering what Ari and you have up your sleeves."

As Lily left the office with Jackson following on her heel, her very low heels, he checked his sleeves. "No, nothing is up my sleeves, and I gave up magic when I was thirteen, remember?"

Dev called after them. "You took part of the dog's ear off, Jackson."

Lily was already in the kitchen, grabbing grapes from the refrigerator. "Was the dog okay?"

Jackson grimaced as he grabbed a few grapes for himself. "After the two hundred and change vet bill he was absolutely fine, except when he tried to wiggle his ears, ear, well you get the picture. I was grounded for two weeks, and I was told in no uncertain terms that I was never going to be the next David Copperfield. Now, I have learned how to make people disappear." His smile was wide, making Lily snort in delight.

"Your meaning of making someone disappear is probably not as comfortable as one would want it to be."

He slumped casually in the kitchen chair. "Well there is that. Safely, I can make a work of art disappear, and then reappear. Usually I replace the real thing with a fake thing. I return the real thing to the museum it was stolen from."

"That is magic." Lily looked up from her snack and into the loving eyes of her husband. He was worried. He was worried for her. *Lord, have I told you, thank you for this man? Darn, he does look good in a tux.* "Dev, everything is going to be fine."

"I usually tell *you* that, honey." He took just a few steps, stopping in front of her to kiss her lightly on the lips. "I don't like anything about this night."

"That's because you aren't in charge, Dev. You always hate it when you have to follow my lead." Jackson sat straighter in the chair expecting reprisal from his brother.

"You are completely correct. I have this gut feeling that I don't know everything about your evil plan. I couldn't believe it when Agent Freeman said you were heading this operation. You are an art specialist." Dev's glare was aimed in his brother's direction.

Jackson stood up slowly. He smiled. He began to walk away. "I am also an FBI agent, big brother, and I'm damn good at what I do. Deal with it. For the first time in our lives, I'm in charge, not you. Besides, you're too emotionally involved. You just need to be a husband tonight. That's your job. I'll see you two at the hotel." He waved back at Lily as he departed the house. He shut the door firmly.

Lily placed a finger on her husband's mouth. "Don't say anything. You deserved that." Dev's mouth began to form a word, and she placed the finger up once more. "Don't, darling. We need to go. Gretchen, it is time to leave."

Lily yelled for their guest as she left him alone in the kitchen. He did deserve it. His concern about this entire night was driven by his fear for Lily's safety. Khalid knew how to hurt his heart and soul. If Khalid took Lily from him, he would die. Physically, maybe he would survive, but he would be dead inside. *Jackson better know his stuff. And what did my brother mean my job was just to be a husband? Of course, I am.*

Upon their arrival at the hotel, Gretchen and Lily took their positions with others at the registration table.

Gretchen nudged Lily and lifted her dress. "See these strappy silver heels? I can run like the wind in them. My lovely black gloves are on. I'm not sure I should be wearing them for a summer evening event, but maybe I'll set a new trend? I have my waterfall ring with the sharp prongs, my brooch, and that hairpin I told you about. My tools of the trade are ready for warfare."

"Shush. These people really work for the charity. I'm sure they don't know anything." Lily looked over at the young man and the three women working the sign in. They knew that Gretchen and Lily were only there to welcome special guests, including Khalid. These special guests were to be given flowers. The women would wear theirs on their wrists, but the men would have boutonnieres. Gretchen would pin them on, every one of them, including and especially Khalid. Gretchen had a plan.

Their covert operation would only be the beginning of Khalid's discomfort for the evening. If all went well, the man who haunted the thoughts of Lily's husband, would be far away from them.

With twenty minutes remaining before the event was to begin, Lily and Gretchen had only one flower needing a person. Khalid had not yet arrived. Lily looked over to the wall of security, of the men looking over them. There were a couple of hotel security guards plus JT and Jackson.

Gretchen winked at JT. He returned the wink. "That man has been modeled after the body of Adonis."

Lily followed her friend's attention. "And you should know. You did date Adonis, didn't you?"

"In those days there was less clothing to remove," Gretchen said, her sarcasm dripping. "The more I look at him, admiring him from afar, he looks very familiar, yes very familiar. His shoulders and chin remind me of this young ensign I knew years ago in Coronado. Was his father in the Navy?"

Lily glanced over at JT. Even though she knew so much about him, she realized as with all of her new-found family of men, she knew so little. "I don't know. Wouldn't that be weird if you did date or do whatever you did with his father?" *Now I can't get that visual out of my head! Thanks, Gretchen.*

"Our mark is here." Gretchen nodded her head in the direction of the throng of security men surrounding only one person.

JT saw the same man. "He did show."

Jackson nodded politely as Khalid smiled in his direction. "Copy that. Gretchen, you're up."

Gretchen heard the voice in her earpiece and used the lingo. "Copy that. Gretchen on the move."

Jackson placed his hand over his mouth in embarrassment. "Ari is going to miss a show. He's going to hate that."

JT pulled out his phone. "I'm going to film it."

Jackson watched Gretchen sashay over to the terrorist. "You are not."

JT had his phone already filming. "Yes, I am."

"Fine," Jackson muttered. "Then I want a copy of this."

Gretchen removed the pin from the flower and was only a foot away when she was stopped by Khalid's personal security. "Your Lordshipness, I have this flower for you in appreciation for all you've done. Please, your Imperial Highness."

Khalid waved his guard away and stood in front of Gretchen. "Of course. How considerate of you, lovely lady."

Gretchen giggled like a schoolgirl. "I had heard how attractive you are, but their description didn't do you justice, your highness."

Khalid acted embarrassed. "How kind, and it is just Khalid. You may pin that flower on my lapel."

He stood tall as Gretchen prepared to take aim. She lined up the flower. She was touching one of the worst men on the planet. He was warm. He smelled good. *Is that an Italian fragrance?* Gretchen took a deep breath and jabbed the pin into his body. While Khalid was screaming, Gretchen placed that pin in her plastic baggie-lined pocket of her dress. "Oh, I'm so sorry. I was so nervous. Let me try one more time."

One of Khalid's devoted guards grabbed her shoulder. Khalid, still wincing, waved him off. "Fine, just be done." He smiled, but his patience was waning. Gretchen pinned the boutonniere on the lapel perfectly in a second.

"There. It is perfect. Oh my, you have something, maybe a little lint in your hair here. Let me get it." Before Khalid could protest, Gretchen dug her ring into his hair and pulled back several long pieces. *There better be a follicle on this!*

Khalid yelled out again in pain. "Dear woman. That is enough. Back away, please." His jaw was clenched. He was losing his calm demeanor and slipping into who he really was. This time he allowed one of his security team to literally pick the intruder up and set her to the side.

Gretchen slipped the ring inside the same pocket. She shrugged her shoulders in disappointment as she joined Lily once more. "I didn't get to use the brooch."

"How were you going to use that?" Lily asked and then thought again. "No, I don't want to know."

"I hope this works, but I'm not sure." Gretchen's lamentation matched Lily's fear.

JT finally pressed stop. He was a trained SEAL. He was a CIA operative. Years of training had prepared him for everything, everything except Gretchen Malloy. He was trying not to laugh, but his face was becoming a very deep shade of red. He looked over at his cohort, and Jackson shielded his face with his hand. They both turned away from each other so they could compose themselves.

"I almost, almost felt sorry for him for a minute," Jackson admitted.

"Me too. Hey, what's Keeting doing with Lily?"

"I'm listening," Jackson admitted.

"Where's your husband?"

Lily remembered the man from the church parking lot, from church when she had shaken his hand in peace during Mass. "He's inside and that's where I'm headed now."

"I need to talk to him. Get him out here." Brad Keating's eyes followed Khalid's back as he entered the ballroom. His entire security detail vanished inside the room with him.

"You can talk to me, Keating." JT stood like a wall in front of Khalid's sidekick. "You need to go down the street and talk to your handlers at the CIA. Maybe if you give them the right answers you won't be tried for treason."

"I haven't seen you in a long time, JT, but this is not the time for a reunion."

"Then you talk to us," Jackson demanded as he arrived next to the two men. "Lily and Gretchen, you should go on in."

Lily was more than happy to get off of her feet and be next to her husband's side. "You boys play nice, especially if it's my life that is hanging in the wind." Lily took Gretchen's hand and led her away from the three formidable men. "You just tell me, Gretchen, anything I need to know immediately."

"You've got it, bestie."

Finally, Gretchen did as Lily commanded.

"Keeting, spill." Jackson didn't have time for loose ends and Keeting was definitely loose, perhaps even loose with the facts.

"I know what Khalid wants to do, and I'm not comfortable with it."

Jackson shook his head. "But you're just fine with all those men killed in Paris? You were fine with those kids at that concert maimed and dead?"

"Why should we believe you?" JT was finding it hard to believe that all of a sudden Keeting had acquired a conscience.

"Don't then, I don't care, but this is sick. I wasn't that comfortable with those kids dying. We don't have time to go over everything I've done. Hell, I wanted to kill your brother in Paris, but Khalid wanted to wait. You all are fair targets, as is your brother, but his wife isn't."

"You showed up at Danny's church."

"Yah, to show him that Khalid could do anything. I was casing it for a fire to accidentally happen. Heck, right now, I think he has teams out to set time-sensitive bombs at your homes."

"He hurt Paul's wife, and there was poison sent to Lily." Jackson's voice was low and threatening.

"Fine, the truth is, he cut me out. He has his own men here now that he has diplomatic immunity. They do too. He has plans that make 9/11 look like a trial run. He paid me off and said I was no longer useful. He didn't appreciate the misgivings I had for what he wanted to do to your sister-in-law."

JT reached over and grabbed the front of Keeting's shirt. "Tell us now what he wants to do to Lily. Now, Keeting, and maybe I'll let you live."

Jackson and JT listened intently. They both breathed a sigh of relief as they released Keeting into the streets of Washington. Of course, he would be followed. The CIA would have the final say as to Keeting's future.

"We don't need to trust him," Jackson admitted as JT entered the ballroom. "We already know, thanks to Ari, that he is telling the truth. Now, we know for sure. I'll see you all later. Watch over my brother. I have one of my FBI buddies looking over Dad. We will all meet back at Dad's house at the end of all of this."

JT watched as Jackson left the hotel. He only hoped Ari was right. Khalid was in for another surprise this evening, and if he thought Gretchen packed a punch, just wait for the second round.

Gretchen went to their assigned table. She met Dev's friend Paul and his wife. Despite her wheelchair, Jill wanted to prove that the terrorist had not conquered her. She stared at the seat next to the podium. Khalid sat there.

Lily walked by the many photos of the girls the charity had supposedly helped over the years. She expected that many girls were helped, in the beginning, before Khalid got his grubby hands on its mission.

She could feel Dev behind her before he began to speak. "You know they used to have the Boy and Girl Scouts of Afghanistan in the 1960's before the wars came. Before Russia invaded, before the Taliban, before us and all the other insurrectionist groups."

"And the poor kids have suffered," Lily mumbled, her thoughts with the smiling girl's photo in front of her. The little one held a book proudly, *Goodnight, Moon.* "I'll read that book to our child."

She felt Dev's warm hand on her shoulder. Despite everything that had happened and that could happen here tonight, she felt at peace and very secure just being with him. She smiled at Gretchen's attack. She would tell Dev later and try to replicate all of her actions. "Yes, you will. You'll read that book and any other book you want to read. He won't take our freedom away."

They both knew who "he" was. Lily knew her husband would fight until his last breath to ensure that freedom and her safety, and that's what frightened her to her core. It was Khalid and his attacks. It was that Dev would never stop protecting her, their family and their friends. That was the only reason why she agreed with Jackson on how to complete this mission.

The crowd noise behind them increased. They turned to see the Vice President's wife entering the large ballroom. There was no Vice President. "That's interesting," Dev whispered into Lily's ear. "I'm surprised they allowed her to come."

"Maybe they couldn't stop her. This charity used to be wonderful, and maybe it still is, but a lot of money is being funneled by Khalid." Dev nodded to JT as he strolled by. *JT is still walking the perimeter of the room. Old habits are hard to break.*

Lily and Dev joined Jill and Paul at the table. Lily noticed Gretchen holding her ear. *Is she okay? What is wrong with her? Oh, she's listening to Jackson. He should be nearing the airport by now.* Lily patted Dev's hand. "We are going to be fine," she whispered. Dev said nothing. He only kissed her lightly on her cheek. *Dev needed to be Dev. Jackson; you better be right about all of this.*

"Do you think this is just a decoy, all of this?" Paul spotted the priest walking toward them. "Here's Dan."

"I spotted Jackson in the lobby earlier. I also noticed at least ten other agents or secret service." Dan sat down next to Gretchen. "I was wondering, do you think that's enough men?"

"There's never enough men or weapons when it comes to Khalid." Dev's voice trailed off. "What the hell is my dad doing here?"

"That's easy," the priest responded. "Your brother brought him."

Dev's eyes darkened. "Why?"

"Did you really want him home alone? Think, Devlin." Dan took a drink of water. "Do you know if this is safe to drink?"

"We will in a little bit, won't we?" Lily watched the priest swallow the water. *Should they be drinking the water, or eating the food? Had the FBI thought about that contingency? Of course they did, didn't they?* Lily's confidence was wavering. She took Dev's hand and held it tightly. *I need to do something.*

"How are you feeling, Dan?"

Dan had an understanding of all things Lily by now. He knew what she was attempting to do. "I'm feeling fine. I guess I was just thirsty." Dan winked at her just to see her smile, to relax the nerves that were escalating at this table. Dev's father and JT filled out their group. The priest could see Dev searching for his brother. This is the appropriate reaction they all wanted from Devlin Pierce. Dan had been informed of the operation. At first, he had disagreed with Jackson's freeze-out of Dev, but then as the brother explained, they needed Dev's honest and raw emotion. He would be the one that Khalid would watch and have watched. Dan had informed Paul of parts of the operation, but not everything.

The FBI considered this a major sting if they could take down Khalid on United States soil. They had teams at all their homes. A SWAT team had been sent to Dan's parish. The State Department was looking the other way for now. They had all their bases covered. But had they done enough? At this very moment, some of Khalid's accounts were being frozen. Thanks to Bernard Notte, INTERPOL knew where his funds were in Belgium and Italy. Also, thanks to the drug trafficker and art smuggler the Italian police had one of Khalid's villas surrounded.

JT drank down his own glass of water. "You know, why and how can Khalid go on all these years? I mean, we even get tired of fighting, but not him. Besides, he has to know we have enough firepower in this room to blow the place up. What could he possibly do to us in the open, in a crowded ballroom?"

"He always has to make a statement. He loves the show, the misdirection. Agents and police are watching all of our homes just in case he has designs on bombing us when we open the front door." Dev winced as he made the statement. They would go in through the garage only after he knew the house was cleared.

As if reading Dev's mind, JT described his own idea. "I'm going through a window, a back window. I'll check for trip wires, of course."

Dev glanced at him. "Of course, you will. Always safety first."

"By the way, I haven't had my safety on since I dressed tonight. It was pretty cool to get passed through security when I was carrying three guns on me."

"Geez, JT, we aren't going to war tonight."

JT shook his head. "Aren't we, Boy Scout?"

An announcement was made for the guests to take their seats.

Lily pushed her chair back a bit. "I have got to go to the bathroom, again."

Jill bobbed her head knowingly. "Gosh, when I was in the last trimester with both girls, I didn't dare leave the house unless there was a bathroom ten minutes away."

Dev began to stand up, but Lily placed her hand on his shoulder. "Sit. Khalid is up there so he won't be doing anything. Gretchen, you'll go with me, won't you?"

"Of course, bestie. I'll take care of her, Dev."

Dev was the picture of calm on the outside, and inside he was a raging storm. He needed to trust Gretchen. He knew his wife was involved in much more than she should be, but for some reason no one had shared the intel with him. *What do they want me to do? Just sit here?*

Dev followed with his eyes every step Lily made until she vanished behind the door. He turned his head quickly to question JT.

"JT, what the hell is really going on? My brother isn't here, is he? Ari and he have some concocted crazy op going on, and you all have frozen me out."

"Dev, it will be okay."

Dev picked up his butter knife in a defensive position. "That always worries me when you tell me it will be okay. That means it isn't right now. Lily is the target, and you know it. You know what is going on."

"Dev, take a breath," Dan suggested in a soft voice.

Jack Pierce watched his son become someone he didn't know. Dev had the appearance of an offended warrior in a tuxedo.

Dev lifted the knife in Dan's direction. "And you, Daniel, when you say take a breath that means I'm spot on. You all kept me out of this loop."

A spotlight found the attractive man at the podium. "Good evening, ladies and gentlemen." All eyes were focused on a smiling Khalid, his white teeth shining in the lights. "I welcome you and say thank you to our American friends who have brought so much to Afghanistan. You all know me, but this is the first time that I'm allowed the privilege of representing my country in an embassy position. We are blessed to work for the education of girls in Afghanistan. This charity has accomplished so much over the years. Diplomats, such as I, are just instruments used, but all of you are the shining gold pieces that provide all of the good works we do. Perhaps you will never meet these young women who wish to learn. They are half a world away. They are lost without your generosity. Their lives depend on you. Thank you for all that you do. Do enjoy your dinner before we begin our program and have a pleasant evening."

Dev became sick to his stomach. Danny, Paul, and JT looked toward him. They all knew what he was talking about; they knew the threat. The reality of their situation was now. *Shining gold pieces? Little girls are dying?* Dev turned back in his chair to look above the crowd. There was still no sign of Lily. She was with Gretchen. She was still safe in this building. Gretchen was probably talking her ear off about this man or that sailor.

Jack Pierce saw Dev's frantic searching eyes. "She should be back by now, Dev, shouldn't she?"

JT's face contorted. "Keeting warned us."

Dev stood. "JT? We will talk about that later, but we need to move **now**!"

"Yes, sir, we do." JT had just heard from Jackson. "Grant lured her out of the building. Gretchen is with her."

Dev began ordering his friends and father as though they were his soldiers. "Dad and Paul, you all stay here, just in case. We don't all have to be everywhere." Dev looked to the stage in a glance. Khalid was gone. Dev swore under his breath and walked swiftly to reach an empty lobby.

JT pushed his friend forward out through the glass doors and into a busy Washington Saturday night. A black sedan pulled up in front of them, the tires squealing to a stop. "Get in."

Secret Service Agent Monroe Patton drove quickly through the downtown streets of Washington, D.C. "Dev, we have a tracker on Lily, remember? It looks as though they are headed to the airport. We've already put a stop on all private planes. He won't be getting away this time."

"Unless he pulls his diplomat card, and he has support to back him." Dan voiced his thoughts. Integral to this entire plot was everyone playing nice to protect Lily Pierce.

Dev remained silent, his eyes watching the road but not seeing anything but Lily's face. How had it come to this? All of those agents couldn't protect one very pregnant woman. "So, where is my brother?"

"He is already at the airport. We had a tip. That Bernard Notte guy helped with quite a bit of information." Danny answered the question, and because of his knowledge he would probably receive the wrath of the Boy Scout when this was all over. If it was all over.

As the secret service agent moved expertly through the fierce traffic, the mood in the car was dark and silent. JT couldn't stand the lack of conversation. He didn't know if Dev was more mad or worried, or probably both. "Lily does have her secret weapon with her."

Danny raised one brow. "What are you talking about?"

JT smiled. "She has Gretchen. I might actually feel sorry for Khalid if Gretchen goes crazy on him. We have released the Gretchen."

Chapter Twenty-Seven

*J*T heard Jackson's whispers in his earpiece. He could also hear other agents discussing their positions and readiness. A foreign plane had landed and now a black limousine was pulling into the airport.

Jackson Pierce was in position on the side of a maintenance building at the airport. He checked in with every agent. Two snipers were at the ready. He watched the minister assist Lily out of the limousine, and Gretchen exit closely behind. One of the thugs tried to grab Gretchen's arm. Jackson shook his head as Gretchen used her heel as a weapon on the man's foot.

In every operation there was always that unknown quotient. Grant Sharpe was that in spades. No one, not one person had seen Grant's ability to fly under their radar. Either the man was so frightened of being discovered as a drug dealer and philanderer, or he was one of the best actors he had ever come across. JT had worked with God Boy and deemed him completely believable even though he was one of the biggest jerks walking on the face of the earth.

"Grant, I don't accept your apology or your explanation," Lily yelled as she jerked away from his hand. His very touch made her nauseous. *Or am I just ravenous?* "Do not touch me."

"Lily, you all left me no choice."

"It's always everyone's fault and never yours. We talked about this, Grant. You can be a good guy. You can be a great guy. I've seen you that way. I fell in love with that man. You don't have to do whatever you are doing."

Another black sedan with embassy flags pulled up beside them.

Grant held Lily with both hands on her upper arms. She tried to step back from the intimate stance, but he wouldn't allow it. "Lily, honey, he was going to ruin me."

"You, sir, ruined yourself." Lily turned to see Khalid, the man who seemed to be a legend in his own mind.

"Mrs. Pierce, I wish we did not have to engage you, especially in your condition."

"Let us go, now." Gretchen ground out the words as though they were missiles of destruction.

Khalid clapped as he recognized the woman who had caused him bodily harm. "Ah, I thought there was something about you besides incompetency."

Gretchen clutched her heart. "I have never been called incompetent. I require an apology, sir."

"Who is she?" Khalid asked the question of anyone who would answer him. Gretchen decided she would answer for herself.

"I am Gretchen Malloy, the best event coordinator and planner in the nation, and I'm an American citizen. You cannot hold us here against our will."

"Go get them, Gretchen," Jackson whispered. "JT, make sure you all come in dark."

"I'm not holding you, woman. Go on." Khalid flipped his hand, waving her away as though she was an insignificant fly. Gretchen blinked in disbelief. She took Lily's hand and began to walk away from the car and the guards. "Oh no, Lily Pierce remains here. You are of no use to me. You leave alone. Now go."

One of his soldiers pushed her away from the small gathering. Gretchen pushed back. "Take me instead, not Lily. She's going to have a baby, and she's huge."

Lily bit her lip. *Baby, you are never to call her Aunt Gretchen, do you hear me?* Gretchen clawed her way back toward Lily. "Besides, I'm much better suited to a harem than Lily. I know so many ways--"

Lily rolled her eyes. *Gretchen, stop being so Gretchen.*

"I said to get her away from me." Khalid gritted his teeth in a threatening manner.

"Gretchen, go, please. I'll be fine." Lily's pleading brought tears from her eyes and from Gretchen's.

"No, kill me instead." Gretchen thrust out her ample chest as a target for her own demise. She shut her eyes dramatically. Nothing happened. She opened one eye and then the other. "Lily?"

Lily nodded. "Please, go on. I'll be okay." Lily gulped back her fear as she watched Gretchen blow her a kiss before walking away. Lily was now on her own on the tarmac.

"Ari, you better be in position and have all your papers in order." Jackson swallowed hard. He heard nothing. "Ari, you mutt, answer me."

"Your highness is my proper title. I am a prince, after all."

"Fine, your highness, are you in position?" *There will be no living with him now, ever.*

"We are ready. I have everything we need, and everyone. Do we have ears now that Ms. Malloy is on the move?"

"Nope. It isn't necessary, but it would be useful. There would be no doubt if we could get him to admit to kidnapping and extortion."

"We can move an agent closer," Agent Freeman suggested.

Jackson didn't want anyone else moving unless absolutely necessary. "Stand down for now."

"I suppose I'll have to do it. Besides, the suspense is killing me." Ari's response came seconds before he opened the door of the plane. Every gun of every one of Khalid's men was pointed in his direction. "Good evening. It was so nice of you to greet me. Lily? What a surprise!" Not only had Ari surprised the bad guys, the good guys didn't know what to think of the super spy.

Ari walked slowly down the plane's ramp stairs. His eyes darted. He counted. He saw four men moving in the dark behind Khalid. "Jackson," he whispered through clenched teeth, "please have Gretchen keep heading in that direction. Dev is there." Ari then saw Lily who was feigning a brave face. "Lily, are you well?"

"I'm very pregnant. What a surprise to see you here." Her voice quivered just a bit. She bit her lip hard as the baby kicked up into her ribcage. *Holy, Moly, kiddo. Hang in there. Daddy is coming, and Uncle Ari is going to save us, and Uncle Jackson, JT, and Danny.*

Khalid stood closer to Lily. She felt his hand wrap tightly around her arm as they faced the intruder. "Ah, it is the mongrel. This is a surprise. I half expected to have Devlin Pierce appear, not you, but you are of no consequence."

"Maybe a little one? Perhaps a nuisance, not a consequence?" Ari said as he came closer.

"You and Mrs. Pierce have become quite friendly. You were protecting her in Paris and now here. You always were a lap dog for the Americans."

Ari's smile widened. "But I'm so cute and fluffy. I am loyal to a fault. We can discuss that mongrel comment later. Exactly, what are we doing this fine summer night?" He glanced at Grant. "Lily, is this your former whatever?"

Lily nodded affirmatively. She couldn't talk right now. She always knew this would be dangerous, but somehow, now in the presence of these very dangerous men, it all became way too real. Her throat was dry; her stomach was rumbling. Garrett had frightened her, but she fought back. Paris had frightened her, but Ari and Dev had fought back. She was physically unable to move. The baby was weighing her down. Her fear was incapacitating her completely.

All guns were still at Ari's head. He turned to Grant and shook his hand. "I've heard a lot about you. You make some absolutely terrible choices. If I were you I would travel to a very serene place and find God, really find God. I know a spa in Spain that is unbelievable. It's in an old fortress that the Moors used--"

Lily felt Khalid's pressure on her arm. "Enough. We do not need a tour guide or travel agent, Ari. Move out of my way. I'm flying out of here."

"Fine. Go. I'll drive Lily home." Ari's flippancy seemed to irritate Khalid to the extreme.

Lily didn't understand the direction Khalid gave to his men, but two of them moved to the bottom of the plane's stairs. The remainder were poised with guns steady and on their target, Ari.

"You idiot. Lily isn't going home with you or anyone. You can't stop me this time either. I have diplomatic immunity. My men have that privilege as well. What a wonderful country this truly is. Now come on, Mrs. Pierce."

Ari held his ground. "Wait. Where is she going?"

"You won't stop until I tell you, will you?"

Ari smiled. "We idiots are just that way. Humor me, great Khalid."

Khalid pulled Lily a couple of steps, so they were within a foot of Ari. The men faced off. Lily stood to the side, attached to a terrorist.

"I thought long and hard for many months. My plan is perfect. No blood has been shed, well except that nurse. My man did not follow orders. He was just supposed to cut her a bit. He has been disposed of if it is any consolation. The blood will come tonight or tomorrow when they return home, and to that church. They will open the doors, and they will be gone. It is a shame I won't see it."

"Is everyone hearing this?" Jackson asked those who could hear him. "We better check on those other men on the newspaper list."

"I'm on it right now." Agent Freeman texted his support team.

"You wouldn't believe how easy it is to bribe congressmen, Ari. You might try that in the Knesset. You might actually win a war."

Ari retained his composure. "We have won, several. We will win again with God's and Allah's help."

Khalid pushed Ari aside. Now Lily stood in-between the men. "The perfect plan is to allow Lily and her baby to live. They will have a lovely life. Devlin Pierce will never know where they are. He will never see his child. It will haunt him. He will travel the world searching."

Ari frowned. "Lily, wasn't that a John Wayne film?"

"Yes, I think it was, Ari. Actually, the Duke searched for Natalie Wood the entire movie."

Ari winked at her. "Yes. Why was he named the Duke? I never heard why; do you know?"

Lily attempted to pull closer to Ari. "I think he named himself after the dog. I'm not sure though. His real name was Marion."

Ari folded over in laughter. "Marion? The dog had a better name." When Ari raised up, a gun was in his left hand. "Step away from her, Khalid."

"You don't want a bloodbath, Ari. I have every right to have my men murder you. You are impeding a diplomat. Besides, you idiot, I have you surrounded."

Ari's eyes moved from left to right and back again. "Look again. Your men are surrounded and have surrendered."

Finally, Khalid's calm exterior deteriorated. He pulled Lily even closer until her back touched his chest. He would use a woman in a desperate attempt to flee, and that would be the only reason he would touch her.

"Lily and I are getting on that plane. I don't know how you hid there, but it is my plane. I have immunity."

Gun still poised; Ari smiled. "That dog story was appropriately ironic. You see, you no longer have immunity. Your status has been revoked, and you and your men are being recalled. Actually, your men are recalled to stand trial. The Americans will handle the transport. They might send you a bill for the expenses."

"You are demented. I have diplomatic immunity. I am an embassy official and a prince."

Ari lowered his weapon. "Now, that is the part that is fascinating. Eventually, all is revealed. I'm actually the prince, and you are the mongrel, the one with no pedigree."

"You are insane." Khalid pulled Lily along. Even though the terrorist had no weapon, they all had seen him kill using only his hands. No one moved in on him except for one man.

Dev stood as an impediment to his further progress. "Let her go, Khalid."

"Give me my gold, Major, and you can take your wife home." Khalid twisted Lily's arm hard. She winced.

Dev pointed his gun directly at Khalid's head. "I said let her go, and you know damn well I don't have your bloody gold."

"You cannot stop me. Diplomatic immunity," Khalid yelled loudly.

"But I can with these documents."

All the focus turned to a man in robes at the top of the stairs of the plane. His slender form filled the open door. He was an elderly man with a grey beard. Lily saw the similarity in looks to Ari. *He has the nose, the eyes, and Ari's lips.* He held papers in his right hand. "Khalid, remove your hand from that woman. She is not your wife."

As if he was in a trance, Khalid released Lily. Ari was there to steer her away from the madman. "Uncle? What is your business here? I was flying out tonight." Khalid walked slowly to the bottom of the stairs and looked up to face his oldest uncle.

"We know all about your plans, Khalid. You are finished. These papers revoke your immunity."

"No, that's not possible."

"Khalid, it is. You are no longer a prince of our kingdom. This is surely an injustice to you, but you cannot use your lineage to hide from your crimes. Your crimes, Khalid."

"I don't understand. Why are you doing this to me?" Khalid looked around at the crowd of armed men. He searched for some explanation. Ari was happy to furnish it. He stepped away from Lily, handing her into her husband's arms. Dev still pointed his weapon at the terrorist. He had a clear shot and would be more than happy to take it.

"Khalid, my uncle is telling you that you are not part of the family. In America, they are proud to be mutts. They actually go to shelters, and people prefer mutts as their pets. They love their ancestry just as much as we do. Their history is only a few hundreds of years old, and ours is thousands of years, but it is still blood. It is still family. On the battlefield, when you were captured, the Americans obtained your DNA and fingerprints, anything to put together a database. I took your DNA and compared it to mine."

Khalid began to laugh. "You, you will never be my better nor my equal."

"My father is of the kingdom. The man you thought was your father was his brother."

"We all know this. What does it matter? I'm getting on that plane, now."

Khalid pushed away from Ari and ran up the steps. He looked more like a frightened boy than a murderer. The man he knew as his revered uncle blocked his way. "Khalid, the family knows the truth. I do not know if you are aware, but your mother was not faithful to your father. Your blood does not match our line. Your blood does not match Ari's. You have no ties to any of us."

"No, that can't be, Uncle. Why are you listening to that crazy Jew?" He pointed down to the tarmac where Ari still stood.

"Khalid, that is my nephew. You are not. Now, you may come." The robed man extended a hand of invitation. Two Israeli soldiers grabbed him as he entered the private jet.

Lily shut her eyes, burrowing her head into Dev's chest as they all heard Khalid's shouts for help and understanding. The robed man slowly made his way down the stairs. Ari greeted him to American soil.

"Ari, I have no words." He hugged his nephew. "And we must never speak of this encounter."

"I know, Uncle."

Dev kissed the top of his wife's head. "You knew more than you told me. You and I are going to have a talk."

Lily looked up into his eyes. One of the lights caught them just right, and they sparkled. "It better not be as long as some of Dan's homilies lately." Dev kissed her soundly. She came up for air. "Or, in the words of a great man, we should never speak of this encounter."

Ari tapped on Lily's shoulder. "This is my Uncle Fayed. This is the woman I told you about."

The man's smile warmed her heart. "Ah, this is Lily, or should I call you Sweet Pea? I loved watching Popeye when my children were small."

"Popeye? Have you ever watched Dudley Do-Right?" Lily's question was one that you usually wouldn't ask a high-ranking diplomat. Ari and Dev shrugged. They knew they couldn't ever get away with that kind of a conversation in their lines of work.

Ari's uncle clasped her hands. "Boris and Natasha were my favorites."

As the two highly unlikely fellow cartoon lovers continued to compare, agents and soldiers cuffed and removed Khalid's soldiers. They would be returned to their home. Ari's uncle would take over the diplomatic duties until another suitable candidate could arrive.

Jackson, JT, and Dan stood back with Gretchen. JT placed a protective arm around her. "You did great, Gretchen. You pushed a little bit. That was dangerous."

Gretchen had never been so tired. She laid her head on JT's solid shoulder. "You know, I'm not sure they have harems. That may have been a little over the top. Oh my gosh!" The usually overconfident Gretchen placed her hand over her mouth. "I think I called Lily huge."

"You did," Jackson answered. "You can just tell her you were playing your part. You should hear the terrible things I call Ari."

Dan patted Jackson's back. "Calling Ari names is completely understandable."

Gretchen pulled off her earpiece and removed the baggie in her pocket. "They never searched us." Enclosed was a blood-stained boutonniere pin and several dark black hairs. She handed both items to Jackson. "I think I'm out of my league at the international espionage level, but give me a Kansas City drug dealer, and I'm your girl. Have I ever told you all about my detective business?"

No one answered, instead all three men began to walk to Lily. JT finally turned back to see Gretchen standing alone, surrounded by swarming soldiers. "Come on, Malloy."

She could run in the silver strappy stilettos. She placed her arm in through JT's and joined the happy group.

Jackson reached over his brother to hug his sister-in-law. "You were a trooper. Do you need water? Do you need to sit down? How about something to eat?" His body was suddenly pried from her, spinning around to face his brother.

"What did you think you were doing using her?"

Jackson pointed back at Ari. "It was his idea. Kill him."

Ari nudged Lily. "Is this a good cop, bad cop thing with these two?"

"Nope, it's a brother thing." She nudged her friend. "It's your turn now."

"And you! You risked my wife's life," Dev yelled as he pointed at Lily's friend.

Ari shrugged sheepishly. "Devlin, it worked, didn't it?"

"But you didn't share the part about my wife's kidnapping."

Ari shut his eyes and answered honestly. "We needed you to act like you, the loving husband desperately searching for his wife, besides, we didn't know the minister would lure Lily. We didn't realize how desperate he was. By the way, where is he?"

Danny pointed to two heavily armed FBI agents and the handcuffed man in the middle. "In his desperation he lost his soul and his mind."

"Nice clergy answer, Danny," Lily said quietly. "I don't know what happened to him, but even when we were dating, he did some of the most stupid things."

JT came over to kiss Lily. "He lost his way without you. He admitted it to me when I was working with him. He knew he was way over his head. He couldn't trust anybody. He did help us with some intel. We'll work with him and maybe get him a reduced sentence."

"I won't press charges against him," Lily admitted. "It was all at Khalid's bidding."

Dev took his wife's hand in his. "Bernard Notte even helped. He gave us valuable information about some of Khalid's assets that we didn't know existed. INTERPOL is raiding a villa in Italy at this very moment, and they've been able to get into a few of his Cayman bank accounts. The DEA has already seized accounts from some of Khalid's drug cartel associates. It's a great night, but--"

Lily lifted one eyebrow. "But?"

"You need to get off those feet." He pointed down at her swollen ankles. "I need to get you home." He kissed the top of her nose.

Jackson neared Ari and his uncle but turned to his brother. "Actually, head to Dad's. We will all meet up there to share the information on the bomb retrieval. Paul is taking Jill home. Their house is clean, no bomb there. He'll call you tomorrow for all of tonight's shenanigans."

Dev saluted him. "Sir, yes, sir. Do we have a ride?"

Agent Patton held his hand up. "I'm your chauffeur."

"I'll ride with Jackson," JT offered. The group decided Dev, Lily, Gretchen, and Dan would fit now that JT's broad shoulders wouldn't occupy the backseat. They headed for Jack Pierce's home.

Ari kissed his uncle on each cheek. "I thank you for all you have done. We have a car for you over there. The FBI will make sure you arrive safely at the hotel and tomorrow, your embassy security team will be in place. Uncle Fayed, you need to rest. That was a long trip for you. The FBI will make sure you are safe tonight. Please, take care of yourself."

The elder looked into his nephew's eyes. He saw a good man, a strong man, and a suffering man. "Will you leave tonight for Israel?"

Ari nodded. He swallowed hard at the thought of returning home to try Khalid for the murder of his wife and little girl. It had been so many years.

His uncle wrapped him in a warm embrace, his robes covering his back. "Shalom, Ari. I hope you finally have peace. Now, please promise me that you will not be a stranger. I could meet you in Geneva, or Paris if you do not want to come back to my home."

As they broke away, Ari's eyes were filled with tears. He embraced his uncle one more time. "*As-salamu alaykum.* Fall in Paris would be lovely, not too cool or too hot. We could take in an opera or go to the symphony."

His uncle smiled. "Maybe we go to a fashion show and buy something for Lily and your sister? I wouldn't mind seeing a celebrity, maybe Lady Gaga or a Kardasian? Their father was Armenian."

Jackson shook his hand before the man walked toward the waiting car. He turned to Ari who was wiping away tears, tears from so many years of absence. "What did it cost you to have him hand over Khalid?"

"Well, dear, I've missed you too. It only cost me a few hours with an old man whom I didn't realize how much I missed. I was also escorted by royal guards from the airport to the palace, then from the palace back to the airport. A Mossad agent is not allowed to just roam around, even if he is part Arab."

Jackson focused on the plane. "You want company on the flight to Tel Aviv?"

"What about JT? He needs a ride home, and you're supposed to meet at your dad's. You also have a very lengthy report to write." Ari checked his gun, finally holstering it.

"I'll get JT a ride, and Agent Freeman is more than capable of writing a report. Besides, I want to make sure that Khalid makes it to Israel. I still don't trust you to keep him alive during the flight."

Ari's eyes sparkled with his smile. "My friend, I am wounded to the core of my being that you do not trust me. We were making such progress, Jackson. I thought we had gotten over our trust issues."

Jackson pointed at the plane. "Do you have alcohol on that thing?"

"Actually, yes. It's well stocked."

Jackson looked up and down, sizing up Ari, literally. "Can I borrow some clothes?"

"I have a couple of shirts on the plane. You'll have to shop after we land."

Jackson glanced at Dev and Lily. His brother's frown warned him of the impending punishment for being a bad sibling. "Besides, I'm not sure what my brother has planned for me. I might be safer in Israel. Let's take a road trip." Jackson patted him on the back.

As they walked toward the plane, they both breathed in air of contentment, each for differing reasons. "You know, Jackson, I believe I like you much better than your brother. You are so much more understanding. You are a man of the world. I believe I can take you anywhere and not be embarrassed by something you might do."

Ari bounded up the stairs, Jackson followed slowly.

"I'm not sure I like all those off-handed compliments. This is going to be a long trip, isn't it?"

"If you aren't careful, it'll be a longer friendship," Ari answered.

Ari entered the plane. Jackson turned around on the last step and glanced at the Washington Monument lit in the darkness. Tomorrow would be Independence Day. Almost one million people would fill the city to watch fireworks. Devlin didn't even know that they had intel from Keeting, that Khalid had a plan to leave several IEDs around the Mall at two of the Smithsonian Museums. Homeland Security arrested the three embassy flunkies while Khalid was fleeing the charity dinner. Two congressmen were under investigation as well. He'd be more than happy to share that information with Khalid during the flight.

He heard Ari yelling. "Come on, Jackson. We have schedules in Israel."

"I'm coming, mother. By the way, don't do any of that kissing stuff on me. It's a handshake and that's all."

"I'm not a loose man." Ari handed him a glass of fine bourbon as he entered the cabin. "Besides, I don't kiss on the first date."

Jackson grabbed the glass and toasted. "To life."

Ari bowed his head. "Yes," he murmured. He straightened and drank down the liquid. Lily's baby would be born in a matter of weeks. *Joanna and Chaya, I'm coming home.*

Chapter Twenty-Eight

1. Put all of this chaos behind us
2. Need more diapers
3. Must stop eating ice cream
4. Make some meals to freeze
5. Make sure Dev goes to final pregnancy class
6. Place post-it notes all over fridge and baby's room
7. Am I ready for this? That little head is coming out of where?
8. I'm not ready for this

"Jack, they really are perfect for each other." Gretchen was assisting Dev's father in the kitchen. None of them had eaten any dinner, and now it was almost midnight.

Jack Pierce finished preparing the last sandwich. Dan arrived to grab a plate of fresh-cut fruit. "They are. I noticed that the first time I met Lily. They didn't need any marriage preparation class."

"I agree, Daniel." Jack picked up two other platters and headed into the family room. Dev and Lily sat on the couch, their legs stretched out upon the coffee table. Dev's arm spread over Lily's shoulders. Her head shot up from its laying position on his chest when the others entered the room.

"Oh, thank you so much, Jack. I don't know if I'm more tired or hungry." The baby kicked suddenly, and her face contorted.

Dev gazed down upon her. "Everything all right?"

"The baby is just hungry." She smiled, but she was concerned with the painful movement. If the baby came early, Dev would blame the entire secret operation and all its stress on her decision to participate. He'd blame Jackson. He wouldn't necessarily say out loud that he blamed her, but every time she wanted to do something a little outrageous, he would scold her. *Baby, just hang in there. I promise to feed you. I'll sleep in tomorrow and not even go to church. Sorry God. I'll have my feet up all day, and I'll eat healthy. Just give me a few more weeks.*

"Hey, is this where the party is?" JT's booming voice filled the room. Dev pulled Lily up from the couch. She headed over to her favorite SEAL.

As they embraced, she held on for several seconds, neither one of them pulling away. "Thank you, Popeye," she whispered.

"Right back at you, Sweet Pea."

Lily looked up to JT. "Where's Jackson?"

"He's on one of the longest road trips I've ever heard of, to Israel."

Dev looked up from the sandwich he had just picked up. "My brother is with Ari?" *Jackson can't avoid me forever. He has a lot of explaining to do.*

Lily led JT to the table of food. "Yep. Those two are getting tight. I'm not sure that is safe for the world." JT grabbed a pickle spear and ate it whole. "I don't trust either one of them."

Jack Pierce booed at JT, but Dev nodded. "I'm with you, JT. I don't trust either one of them, and I'm not sure they trust each other."

Lily playfully swiped at her husband. "They trust each other as much as you trust them."

"But, darling, the truth is I don't trust either one of them." Dev's eyes were twinkling, but his tone chilled Lily. *He really doesn't trust them, does he?*

Dan was the first to finish eating and to announce his departure. "I am saying Mass in," he looked down at his watch, "less than six hours. I've got to get a little sleep." Before he left, he leaned down and kissed Lily on the cheek. "It is debatable whether or not I have this power, but I'm giving you dispensation from church tomorrow. You rest and give that baby and your husband a rest. Got it?"

Lily returned his kiss with a slight glance of her lips on his cheek. "Copy that, Father. I'll make up for missing Mass another time."

Dan winked. "Goodnight, or good morning. See you all."

"Tomorrow, well today, later." Dev stood up to walk his friend to his car. "Let's get together for dinner. I'll grill. I feel like celebrating."

Jack Pierce watched as his daughter-in-law leaned her head back against the back of the soft couch. "Lily, do you and Dev want to spend the night here? We can get you to bed in a matter of minutes."

Lily yawned. "No, I want to sleep in my own bed. Gretchen, we should get going."

Gretchen was huddled with JT. Her head bounced up at the mention of her name. "Lily, you aren't going to believe this. JT and I were talking, and I believe I knew his father years ago."

Lily's hands moved to her temples. "Oh no. I think I have a headache."

"And Lily, I'm so sorry I called you huge earlier when we were abducted by that insane man. I meant you were pregnant. I was trying to protect you. But isn't this amazing? JT's father is a retired Navy commander. We were both so young and beautiful then, well he was handsome, I was beautiful. I used to have legs that went on from San Francisco to San Diego, if you know what I mean?" Gretchen leaned into JT playfully. "I knew you looked like someone I knew; someone I knew so intimately."

Dev tenderly grasped Lily's elbow. "Come on, I'm going to be sick if I hear anymore. JT will you bring Gretchen back to the house? I've got to get my wife home."

JT stood up quickly. "Oh no, we are done reminiscing. You take Gretchen."

Gretchen giggled. "I feel like a teenager being fought over by the football quarterback and the captain of the basketball team."

Lily stomped one of her swollen feet. "Gretchen, that's enough. Let's go. Get in the car." Her statement was taken as a demand as Gretchen shot out of her chair and walked past Dev and Lily.

"Goodnight, Jack. I guess we are leaving." Gretchen continued out the door and into the early morning darkness.

Lily shook her head. "Yet, I believe she is a good person, and I think we are best friends. I'm still dealing with that one. Goodnight, guys. See you for dinner."

Dev said his goodbyes and led Lily off to the car and the waiting Gretchen.

Jack brought another beer over to JT. "Son, why don't you just spend the night? I feel like drinking."

JT was completely confused. He took a large drink from the bottle and saluted Jack. "I think I will. My father and Gretchen were intimate? How much beer do you have?"

"If that's the vision you have in your head, JT, there might not be enough beer in Virginia." Jack knew he had a twelve-pack in the garage refrigerator. Jack began to visualize the same scenario. "JT, be grateful she isn't your long-lost mother."

JT finished his beer in one more drink. "I'm calling my dad tomorrow. He has a lot of explaining to do."

Jack patted the boy he had known for many years now. Of course, these boys were men, but to him, they were like his own. He had Dev and Jackson, and he adopted Dan, JT, and even Paul at times. But his thoughts were with his only daughter. Lily was extremely pale, and she did look huge, big enough to give birth at any minute. It looked as though the baby was shifting. His grandchild would be here in a few weeks, if not sooner.

He walked slowly to the garage and grabbed four more bottles. Dan hadn't offered him dispensation, but it had been a very stress-filled evening. God would have to understand just this once. He placed the beers on the coffee table and yelled for JT to join him. The former SEAL did as he was told.

"JT, you have to remember your dad was a young man once. He was just like you and probably enjoyed the same things you did when you were younger."

"Jack, I just can't get this out of my head. What was he thinking all those years ago?"

Jack laughed. "He was probably thinking the same things you were thinking at that age. Remember?"

JT looked at his beer bottle. "I remember, but I still deserve an explanation."

Jack remembered another young man telling his father that he deserved an explanation. Dev never could understand why his mother never shared how very ill she truly was. She made her own husband promise to not worry their son while he was over there fighting. Thankfully, Bernadette had left her son a letter explaining her decision to hide the complete truth from him. For over two months after Dev received her written apology, Jack hadn't heard from him.

Jack looked at JT's somber face. "JT, sometimes explanations don't need to be given, nor are they enough. When love is involved, dads are just men too."

JT took Jack's statement to heart. *Gretchen? Really,*

Dad? "Fine, but you better have more than just these four beers. You want to order a pizza?"

Jack smiled. "No. Did you know I taught Dev how to make that omelet you like?"

"I did not, sir. Can you add Italian sausage to it?"

"Sure thing. I can tell you some dumb stuff I did when I was dating."

JT followed Jack into the kitchen. "Jack, if you don't mind, I don't need any more visuals tonight."

"Have a seat while I make us the trash can omelet." Jack Pierce began to remove his needed food items from the refrigerator. This recipe really wasn't his own. He still had a photo of Bernie on the side of the refrigerator. *Love you, honey. I miss you more every day, and don't worry, I wasn't going to tell JT that you were the first and the last girl of my life. I was going to make something up.*

"Hey, Jack, have you ever heard the story about Paul, me, and the longest running volleyball game in Afghanistan? I'm sure we could've had a world record, especially for the longest volleyball match in a war zone. It was terribly hot when we started that day--"

Jack kept adding ingredients. He had never heard this tale, but he was pretty sure he'd never been up this late since that Christmas when Jackson had attempted to make the dog disappear. *What did JT just say? He dressed a goat as what?*

Chapter Twenty-Nine

1. Check in with doctor tomorrow
2. Make sure Abby and Jeremy come tonight
3. Pack bag for hospital
4. Drink water today
5. Rest and rest some more
6. Baby don't come early
7. Find out when Gretchen, Abby and Mort are leaving
8. Get back to boring normal

"Are you making lists in your head?"

"No, Dev," Lily lied. The sun had been up for some time, but Lily and Dev were still lounging in bed on a Sunday morning. Lily thought she'd heard Gretchen in the guest room, and then again as the woman headed down the stairs. In fact, Lily thought she could smell coffee. *Holy Moly, I could use caffeinated coffee right about now.*

Dev's arm looked like the Great Wall of China as it laid over Lily's large mountain of baby. "You looked like you were making lists. By now, I do know when you are doing that."

"Because you are some sort of a special agent?"

Dev nuzzled her neck. "Nope. I'm very observant. I'm also the most wonderful husband ever."

"Really? You think so?" Lily glanced to the side and was eye to eye with those luscious lashes. *How can he look so good in the morning? I need to encourage him to wear a tuxedo more often.*

"You keep saying that I'm the best."

"But I didn't say at what, did I?" She watched as his one eyebrow raised.

"Ah, so you want to play this morning?" Dev leaned up on one elbow. Usually, he would tickle her in all the right spots, but after last night's adventure, and the fact they were only a few weeks away from their child making an appearance, he stopped short. "How are you feeling, really?"

Lily sighed deeply. "I'm hurting. I won't even lie to you. Yes, I was making lists. I need to pack that bag for the hospital."

"You haven't packed the go bag yet?" Dev didn't understand that concept since he always had a bag packed. For many years, he had lived in rapid response mode. His own sat at the bottom of the closet.

"No, I've been kind of busy being an international target." Lily said it with a straight face but began to laugh at Dev's crossed eyes.

"Intrigue is messy stuff, isn't it? We will talk about all of that, but it will be later, maybe when the baby is a year old?"

Lily caressed his unshaven face. "Thanks, honey. That would be perfect. Am I hallucinating? Do you smell coffee?"

They both uttered their houseguest's name.

"When are they leaving?" Dev's question was one Lily was already thinking.

"Soon, I hope. Abby has to get back to the shop, and I would assume that Gretchen needs some sort of income now and then."

Dev fell back onto his pillow. His laughter filled the room. "JT was scared to death last night. He was having a real problem."

"That should make dinner tonight very interesting. Maybe he'll bring his dad. We could watch the star-crossed lovers' reunion." Lily snorted in delight.

"We are not watching that. By the way, happy Fourth of July."

Lily counted days in her head. "Oh my gosh! It is Independence Day."

There was a not-so-subtle knocking at their bedroom door. "Devlin, Lily, are you awake."

"It's Independence Day for some people, but not us. We are awake now," Dev muttered. He raised his voice. "Yes, we are. What do you need, Gretchen?"

"I've made coffee, and I have a breakfast casserole in the oven. Lily, dear, you need to eat something healthy this morning."

Lily swung her arm out and lightly hit her husband. "You know, Taco Heaven sounds good to me."

"The restaurant around the corner is not called Taco Heaven."

Gretchen was calling one more time. "It would be heaven to me, Dev. My very dear friends need to go home. **Now.**"

"I'll put Dad up to ask when they are leaving. He can do it at dinner." Dev slowly got up and sat on the edge of the bed. "I need to go to the store if we are feeding everybody tonight."

Her arm stretched out. "Please, sir, take me with you."

He turned from his position and kissed her slowly. Dev ran his hand softly through her hair. "You need to rest. I'll go. I need to call Paul and Jill to invite them."

"Check the refrigerator before you go. I'm not sure what Jackson, your dad, and Ari still have in there."

"Ari." Dev rolled his eyes. "He and I have quite a bit of unfinished business. I also think my brother went with him to avoid me."

Lily placed her finger on his lips to quiet her husband. "Stop. Besides, we will have a *simcha* for the baby when he returns."

Dev's eyes flashed in displeasure. "English, please, wife."

"*Simcha* is Yiddish for an occasion, a joyous party, that sort of thing. He wants to celebrate the baby's birth. I think it's lovely," Lily cooed.

Dev wanted to strangle Ari right now, for many reasons. "He has you fooled, but you do tend to see the good in just about everyone. The proof of that has made coffee and a casserole in our kitchen."

Lily frowned; her lips formed a pout. "I have acquired some real characters as friends since I've met you. Maybe you are the reason for all the eccentrics in my life?" She raised a hand to mess up his hair.

"So now I'm the reason your life is crazy? I'm shocked, and I'm hurt."

Lily lowered her hand to his cheek. "No, you're the reason why my life is full. You've brought color to my black and white television show."

Dev grimaced. "I'm not sure I'm happy about that one. I'll have to think about it while I'm grocery shopping. Look at me, Lily. I go grocery shopping now. I do laundry, and I make the bed. You've made a housekeeper out of me."

Lily's eyes darkened. She patted her stomach. "And you've made me very pregnant. You are a very special housekeeper." She strained to kiss him quickly, but Dev lowered his head to finish the kiss properly.

"I'm rather proud of that job." He kissed her neck and whispered softly into her ear. "I love you, even with all of your crazy friends."

"Except for Gretchen, Jeremy, and Abby they are all your friends, including the dog. They just happen to like me. Oh, you need to make sure Jeremy and Abby are coming. Could you call or text them?"

Dev saluted and rose from the bed. "Make me a list for the store. I need a quick shower and some of that coffee and casserole."

Lily giggled. "I can make a list, no problem!"

Later that day, the sound of firecrackers could be heard outside as all their guests, including the dog, filled the kitchen area and the back patio. Lily had made her list, but the remainder of the day she rested. Gretchen was waiting on her as though she was a queen. *I need to film this so I can use it as blackmail someday.* She watched Gretchen stand in as hostess. *The woman can schmooze!*

Paul and Jill brought both of their daughters. JT was at ease with Gretchen despite his headache. Apparently, he had put out of his mind the visions of his father and Gretchen doing anything. Coincidentally, Lily's father-in-law was also suffering from the same malady. *How much did they drink last night?* The priest was dressed in cargo shorts and an Army shirt and assisting Dev with the grilling of the hamburgers and hotdogs. Jeremy and Abby were visiting with the cooks as Dev threw a ball into the yard for Mort.

Lily was stretched out in Dev's large leather chair, her legs and feet comfortable on the hassock. She felt the cool leather and remembered the first time she'd sat in it. He had brought her to Virginia to introduce the guys to her during the Army-Navy football game. That initiation into the team had served as the first step in her job interview for the role of Mrs. Devlin Pierce. Dev had been called away on some operation that weekend, but before he left, they both knew where they were headed.

"Abby and I want to show you the completed room. We need to leave tomorrow." With a glass of red wine in her hand, Gretchen stood in front of her. Lily's eyes focused on the liquid. *As soon as I can, baby, I'm having a glass of wine.*

Lily acted disappointed. "You have to leave? Oh no. Sure, we can look at the room, but Gretchen I wish you would've listened to me and not done all that work."

"Pish, posh. I don't want to hear anything you have to say. As the godmother for this baby, it is my pleasure to provide the very best for this little princess."

"I need to get up." Lily began to struggle in her movements. Gretchen put down her glass and helped her friend. "I suppose we could do it now, or we can wait until everyone leaves."

Gretchen supported Lily's back. "Now would be perfect. Everyone will want to see it. I'll get Dev."

"Gretchen, we really need to talk about that whole princess thing." Lily's words fell on the air as Gretchen clicked on the wood floor in her heels. "Why does she always wear those blasted heels? That noise makes me nauseous." *Everything is making me nauseous today.*

Danny took over the grill at Gretchen's insistence. Dev helped the slower than usual Lily make it up the steps to the bedroom at the top of the steps. Gretchen followed behind.

"Here, Lily. I thought you might need this." She handed the pregnant woman a small cup of ice cream.

Lily's eyes brightened instantly. "Gretchen has been

getting me this chocolate and peanut butter concoction through this entire decorating adventure. I tried to tell her so many times."

Dev watched as his wife became a zombie feasting on the cold dessert. "You didn't tell her we weren't using this room? You didn't tell her not to do pink because we don't like pink?" Dev stopped asking the questions, mesmerized by Lily's passion. She loved that ice cream. She couldn't say no to that ice cream.

Dev understood completely. Gretchen was opening the door to her masterpiece. "They fed you, didn't they?" Dev asked so only Lily could hear. Lily nodded. "They fed you, and you couldn't tell them?" She nodded again. "Oh, honey. Why do you have to be so nice?"

Lily continued to eat. She raised her shoulders in an uncertain shrug. Gretchen invited them in with a sweeping arm guiding them.

Dev took a step in. It was beautiful, and it was very Gretchen. There was tulling gathered almost like mosquito netting over the ivory and gold crib. In one corner of the room was a massive rocker in pale pink with a matching ottoman. The changing table had a soft ivory blanket hanging off the side. Shades of pink filled the room from the walls to the ivory rug that featured small rose buds. There was eyelet bedding and lace pillows. The curtains were tulle and lace, held back with ties with the same rose pattern.

Dev looked around and saw the installed wall shelves. They were filled with teacups, a china vase, books, and a multitude of stuffed animals, all perfect for a little girl to hug. He looked down at Lily's face. She was smiling widely, touching the fabrics, and surprised at all the knick-knacks. "Oh, Gretchen, it is so beautiful. It's so you, but it is so amazing." Lily hugged her friend. She held her hands. "The room is just like you, beautiful and amazing. Thank you."

"Well, you should thank Abby too. She did help implement my vision."

Lily placed her arm around Gretchen's waist. *This room is certainly a surprise, just like Gretchen.*

"Do you like it?" Their attention moved to Abby who had just entered the room.

Dev and Lily smiled, uttered their gratitude, and continued to examine all of the work of their two friends. Gretchen explained that Abby did most of the manual labor, and she provided the funding, the color palette, the design, the layout, well just about everything else. All of her details were described in full Gretchen fashion.

"Gretchen, why are you so certain it is going to be a little girl?" Dev's question silenced all three women. Abby looked at Gretchen and then at Lily. Lily looked at Dev in an unpleasant way. Gretchen looked at Lily and Dev.

Gretchen's nervous laugh filled the room. "Don't be silly, Devlin. Of course, it's going to be a girl. I won't have it any other way. I'm going to dress her in the prettiest things, and when she gets old enough, I'm going to take her doll shopping, and to *The Nutcracker* at Christmas. You can't do that with a boy."

Lily said more with her eyes than words ever could.

She was pleading with her husband. *Please, Dev, don't say anything. Just do what I do when it comes to Gretchen, smile and ignore.*

Dev didn't ignore Lily's unspoken plea. He moved over to Gretchen, placed a hand on each of her shoulders, and kissed her softly on the cheek. "We will have a little girl just for you, Gretchen. You can be her fairy godmother. She will be so lucky to have you love her. Lily and I thank you, and we love you."

Gretchen's eyes blinked twice. She waved her hands in front of her eyes, preventing her mascara from running. "Oh, thank you, Devlin. It doesn't matter if you don't have a girl. I can dress a little boy in sailor suits."

Dev's brows almost touched in displeasure. "Fine, maybe not sailor suits. Little teddy bears would be the perfect design. I could visit and take him to the Smithsonian. We can get ice cream and maybe see a baseball game. I do like baseball players."

"Of course, you do, Gretchen." Lily held her friend's hand. "No matter what, this baby is coming in just a few weeks." She grasped Abby's hand in hers too. "I am, we are so blessed to have two wonderful friends like you both. This baby will be surrounded by love."

Dev stood back as the three friends hugged and cried. He looked around the beautiful room, completely fit for a little princess. *Is that a pink camel? I never saw pink camels when I was over there.* He picked up a small white fluffy lamb. *We have to have a girl.*

Devlin Pierce's world was very different now, complete with a house filled with old friends, and new ones. He shared his bathroom with a woman who placed post-it notes on his mirror almost every night. When he woke to go to the office, he stumbled into the bathroom, closed the door so he didn't stir his wife, and turned on the light. The first thing he saw was that post-it note with only two words written on it, "love you". Admittedly, he enjoyed placing a note that said the same, only on her stomach.

When he walked into that Kansas City flower shop just a few years ago, he never thought he would be worried about a school rating for his child or concerned about proper placement of a childcare seat. Dev looked up from the fluffy lamb to see Gretchen showing off a few of the small garments she had purchased for the baby. *How much did Gretchen spend?* Abby held up a very small dress.

"Are they really this little?" Abby compared the dress to her arm.

"They can be smaller. That's for an infant, not a newborn." Gretchen pulled out a smaller outfit.

Dev shook his head. He walked behind Lily, his hand sliding along her back. "I'll leave you three alone. I need to get back downstairs, honey." He kissed her on the cheek.

Lily grasped his hand, pulling him back for a short kiss of her own. "Thank you." Her whisper against his lips was intoxicating and understood.

"I totally get it. They fed you. You just couldn't say anything when you began to see all of this coming in."

Dev looked toward Abby and Gretchen. "Abs, I know you worked hard for this mad woman with a plan, and Gretchen, you have completely outdone yourself. I don't know how we will ever thank you for all of this."

Abby smiled, but Gretchen took a deep bow. "I'm sure I'll think of something, Mr. Delicious."

Lily rolled her eyes. "You just had to ruin it, Gretchen."

"Oh, Dev loves it. You know he does." Gretchen playfully blew him a kiss.

Dev shrugged. "I'm standing right here. I can hear you." He slowly pulled away from his wife and headed down the stairs to a more comfortable and familiar setting.

As Gretchen and Abby oohed over the smallest pair of tights ever made, Lily's lower back began to hurt. A perfectly good rocker would be the perfect thing. It was a nice height. She leaned on one of the upholstered arms and lowered her body into it. She sighed.

If I just had a little more ice cream in that bowl over there, this would be perfect. Lily took the room in. All of its pinkness should be too much, but it was absolutely lovely, and perfect for a baby girl. What would Gretchen think of her? *Gretchen will be over a thousand miles away when she finds out.*

I tried to tell them. Every time I was going to say something, Gretchen waved me off or Abby fed me french fries with a chocolate shake. I couldn't tell them we already had the other room set up as the nursery.

"I should've told you both we are having a boy," Lily muttered. She placed her hand over her mouth. "Holy Moly, did I just say that out loud?"

Abby and Gretchen's conversation suddenly stopped. Both women turned their heads in her direction.

"What did you just say?" Abby placed the little shoes in her hand down in the crib.

"We are having a boy. I'm so sorry. I didn't want to hurt your feelings, and when the crib came in, then the chair, the furniture, well, it's hard to stop you two. When I started to see all the pink blankets, I didn't know what to do. I did try to tell you."

Gretchen, for the first time in her life, was indeed speechless. Her long, fake lashes blinked several times. She cleared her throat. "The boy will have to like pink."

Lily's face wrinkled in embarrassment. She pointed down the hall. "We already have the other room ready for him."

"Fine." Gretchen's arms crossed over her ample chest. "This will be for your second child. You'll be ready."

"I have to have this one first, Gretchen."

"Fine. Have this boy, then have the girl."

Lily snapped her fingers. "Just like that."

Abby began to back away from her two friends. "I think I'll go downstairs. It'll be safer down there with all the dangerous people."

"Lily, yes, just like that," Gretchen answered. "Dev said he didn't know how to thank me, so now you do. Have a girl next time."

Lord, how do I make Gretchen happy? Lily was the recipient of her bestie's glare. She was expecting an answer, a definitive solution to the problem. If she gave into her, Lily would offer a ridiculous answer. If she didn't give in, Gretchen would be hurt. *But she does know how this baby thing works, right? We are having a boy. I'm not having twins, and I can't get pregnant with a girl until I give birth to the boy. What if I get pregnant again, and I don't have a girl? What if I have another boy? He'll have to like a lot of pink and enjoy white tights with bows on the heels. Right! Dev won't stand for that.*

"Gretchen, I'm so sorry. I was just caught up in everything. I didn't even realize you were using all this pink on the wall, the curtains, the rug. I had all this terrorist stuff going on."

Gretchen tapped her shoes in impatience. "Sure, sure, blame it on an international terrorist. I do understand, but the next baby better be a girl, or there will be problems, and I'll make that Khalid fellow look like a fluffy bunny."

Lily saluted. "Yes, ma'am. I completely understand, and as you said, the room will be ready."

"Make sure you schedule it, please." Gretchen still wasn't smiling.

Lily struggled, slowly raising her bulging body up from the chair. She crossed the short span between them, hugging her friend until Gretchen's arms held her too. "Thank you, bestie."

"You are welcome, bestie. Lily, you better put that girl at the top of your priority list."

Lily's head rested on Gretchen's shoulder. "I'll put post-it notes all over the bedroom. Will that make you happy?"

Finally, Gretchen broke. "Yes, because it is all about making me happy. Dev is going to be thrilled, I'm sure."

"We need to get back down to the party. Come on," Lily directed. She took Gretchen by the hand and headed to the top of the stairs. "Hey, Mr. Delicious," Lily yelled, "you aren't going to believe what we have to do to thank Gretchen! You're going to love every minute of it."

Notes From the Author

*O*bviously, our little florist is branching out and flowering! You could almost say she is blossoming in her new role as wife, future mother, and a friend to international spies. Enough with the flower puns, but her life has certainly changed and is ever-expanding. It is also a "no judgement" zone when it comes to eating ice cream.

In this novel, Kansas City is the background for one visit. Knowing Lily, I know she won't be able to stay away from her hometown for very long. Besides, now it is the home of NFL Champions, the Kansas City Chiefs. We are all very proud of that accomplishment, after fifty years waiting from our first Super Bowl win. Lily won't lose her friendships with Abby or Gretchen either, and those two may get in their own trouble along the way.

Most of the action this time, takes us to Northern Virginia and Washington, D.C. I love this area and have family who still live in Virginia and Maryland. I have so many memories from time spent there including visits to Nora Roberts' bed and breakfast in Boonsboro, Hershey Park (they have chocolate there!), Gettysburg, walking from the Smithsonian Museums to the Lincoln Memorial (my favorite is Jefferson's), and taking in a musical at The Kennedy Center. It is a magical, historical area.

I also love the vineyards of Virginia. If you can't visit each one of them, Mount Vernon (President George

Washington's home) hosts a wine and jazz event twice a year. You can taste wine after wine by moving from table to table, and you can lounge on George's lawn overlooking the Potomac. You can't have a better night than that.

On the east coast, I also enjoy all those small towns with their buckling brick sidewalks and their abundance of history. The battlefields of Antietam, Manassas, Gettysburg, and Fredericksburg all have towns nearby where you can still see the facades of the civil war. I've strolled through those towns shopping for antiques and eating some of the best food. The past is embraced to this day, preserving so much of who we are, and who we were.

Which brings us to Lily...she runs right into her former boyfriend. What would you do if this happened to you? If it has happened to you, what did you do? I don't know one of us who hasn't wanted to tell that former special someone exactly what is on our minds. Usually, we don't have that opportunity. Lily's former love has always left her wondering about the end of their relationship. Dev believes Lily's ex has also left her a shattered self-image. Don't we all want someone like Dev cheering for us and threatening to take out the hurtful person who made us feel less?

And doesn't Lily have an ever-growing abundance of fans? Of course, her in-laws love her from Aunt Maggie, Maureen, her twin (we may see more of her in the future), her father-in-law Jack, to her brother-in-law Jackson. She is also now a member of the team with her very own nickname. Paul, Jill and Lily seem to be the adults of the bunch. The priest and the SEAL are uniquely her best friends. To add to all those characters, Ari Gurin has nudged his way into her heart. Well, he did feed her! All of the men, including her husband, seem to have their secrets. She's willing to stick around just to get their back stories. I hope you continue with her on future adventures.

When given the opportunity, travel to see the smaller towns in our nation. If you don't want to go too far, visit within fifty miles of your own hometown. There are more secrets to discover.

C.L. BAUER

C.L. Bauer grew up and lives in Kansas City, Missouri. Her first novel The Poppy Drop, A Lily List Mystery was well received by the top 100 Books of Independent Publishers when it launched in 2018.

The Lily List Mystery Series features the highly organized, post-it note, and list making florist Lily Schmidt. Readers have enjoyed the adventures of the mystery loving woman and the wedding stories that are highlighted in these novels. Ms. Bauer draws on true events from her family's wedding and event flower business. With over one hundred years of serving families on their special days, Clara's Flowers has received numerous awards in the wedding world, including "best of" and "legacy winner" for service and design.

C.L. Bauer's first love of writing provided an early career in journalism. During high school, she began as a sports reporter, became an editor in college, and continued professionally in every writing medium including advertising and creative direction.

The author enjoys her family, travel, a good book on a rainy day, bulk post-it notes, and meeting her readers. She can always be swayed to feast on Mexican food, watch a hockey game, and drink the occasional fruity libation. If you've read her novels, you already know she loves Kansas City during the holidays.

You can reach C.L. Bauer on all forms of social media including her author pages on Facebook, Instagram, Twitter, Amazon, and Goodreads. Please review this and any of C.L. Bauer's published works. They are widely available for purchase in print and e-book forms. She's available for book club discussions virtually or in-person.

As always, happy reading!

Sign up at www.clbauer.com for this author's newsletter, promotions, pre-order information, free chapters, and upcoming publications. Contact C.L. Bauer directly at clbauerkc@gmail.com.

Coming in 2021...A Lily List Mystery Exclusive! Can't get enough of your favorite characters? The Exclusive novels feature more adventures with Lily's friends. Mysteries, murders, and more romance are coming your way!